Instant Attraction

Jill Shalvis

BRAVA

KENSINGTON PUBLISHING CORP.
http://www.kensingtonbooks.com

BRAVA BOOKS are published by

Kensington Publishing Corp.
850 Third Avenue
New York, NY 10022

All Kensington titles, imprints, and distributed lines are available at special quantity discounts for bulk purchases for sales promotion, premiums, fund-raising, educational, or institutional use.

Special book excerpts or customized printings can also be created to fit specific needs. For details, write or phone the office of the Kensington Special Sales Manager: Kensington Publishing Corp., 850 Third Avenue, New York, NY 10022. Attn: Special Sales Department. Phone: 1-800-221-2647.

Brava and the B logo Reg. U.S. Pat. & TM Off.

ISBN-13: 978-0-7582-3123-9
ISBN-10: 0-7582-3123-7

First Printing: February 2009
10 9 8 7 6 5 4 3 2 1

Printed in the United States of America

Instant Attraction

Chapter 1

"Live life balls out," Katie Kramer told herself every night, and even though she didn't own a pair, she hoped the mantra would keep the nightmares away.

It didn't.

Death and destruction and horror still dogged her dreams. Until tonight, that is. Tonight she'd miraculously been nightmare free. So when she opened her eyes sometime just before one, she felt . . . confused. She wasn't screaming about the bridge collapsing, about being trapped in her car, hanging upside down by her seatbelt fifty feet over the side of a cliff with flames licking at her. . . .

Which meant something else had woken her. And whatever it was, she wanted to kill it for interrupting the first solid sleep she'd had in four months.

There was a fatal flaw with this logic, of course. Because most likely it hadn't been an *it*, but a someone.

She wasn't alone.

Not prone to hysterics or drama, she shook her head in the dark. She'd locked the cabin door. She was safe. Plus, she wasn't in Los Angeles anymore. After the accident, she'd gotten into her brand-new used car and left town to fulfill her "balls out" motto. She didn't know what adventures were ahead of her exactly, but the not knowing was part of the plan. She'd gone north because Highway 5 had been the only freeway moving faster than fifteen miles per hour and she'd needed to move fast, needed to get as far from her old, staid, boring, careful life as a tank of gas could get her.

Eight hours later, she'd found herself in the Sierras, where it was *real* winter. None of LA's lightweight weather where flip-flops were risky for a few weeks in January, but the real deal complete with snow piled high in berms on either side of the roads and frost on her windows.

When she stopped for dinner in a tiny old west town named Wishful, she'd nearly froze her fingers and toes right off. And yet, after all her nightmares of heat and flames, she loved it. Loved the huge wide-open sky, loved the way her breath crystallized in front of her face, loved the way the trees smelled like Christmas.

Then she'd seen the want ad.

LOCAL OUTDOOR ADVENTURE AND EXPEDITION COMPANY SEEKING TEM-PORARY OFFICE MANAGER, ADVENTUR-OUS SPIRIT REQUIRED. CALL WILDER ADVENTURES FOR MORE INFO.

That had been it for her; she was sold. She'd been working for Wilder Adventures for a week now, the best week in recent memory. Up until right this second when a shadowy outline of a man appeared in her room. Like the newly brave woman she was, she threw the covers over her head and hoped he hadn't seen her.

"Hey," he said, blowing that hope all to hell.

His voice was low and husky, sounding just as surprised as

she. With a deep breath, she lurched upright to a seated position on the bed and reached out for her handy-dandy baseball bat before remembering she hadn't brought it with her. Instead, her hands connected with her glasses and they went flying.

Which might just have been a blessing in disguise, because now she wouldn't be able to witness her own death.

But then the tall shadow bent and scooped up her glasses and . . .

Handed them to her.

A considerate bad guy?

She jammed the frames on her face and focused in the dim light coming from the living-room lamp. He stood at the foot of the bed frowning right back at her, hands on his hips.

Huh.

He didn't look like an ax murderer, which was good, very good, but at over six feet of impressive, rangy, solid-looking muscle, he didn't exactly look like a harmless tooth fairy either.

"Why are you in my bed?" he asked warily, as if maybe he'd put her there but couldn't quite remember.

He had a black duffel bag slung over a shoulder. Light brown hair stuck out from the edges of his knit ski cap to curl around his neck. Sharp green eyes were leveled on hers, steady and calm but irritated as he opened his denim jacket.

If he was an ax murderer, he was quite possibly the most attractive one she'd ever seen, which didn't do a thing for her frustration level. She'd been finally sleeping.

Sleeping!

He could have no idea what a welcome miracle that had been, dammit.

"Earth to Goldilocks." He waved a gloved hand until she dragged her gaze back up to his face. "Yeah, hi. My bed. Want to tell me why you're in it?"

"I've been sleeping here for a week." Granted, she'd had a hard time of it lately, but she definitely would have noticed *him* in bed with her.

"Who told you to sleep here?"

"My boss, Stone Wilder. Well, technically, Annie the chef, but—" She broke off when he reached toward her, clutching the comforter to her chin as if the down feathers could protect her, really wishing for that handy-dandy bat.

But instead of killing her, he hit the switch to the lamp on the nightstand and more fully illuminated the room as he dropped his duffel bag.

While Katie tried to slow her heart rate, he pulled off his jacket and gloves, and tossed them territorially to the chest at the foot of the bed.

His clothes seemed normal enough. Beneath the jacket he wore a fleece-lined sweatshirt opened over a long-sleeved brown Henley, half untucked over faded Levi's. The jeans were loose and low on his hips, baggy over unlaced Sorels, the entire ensemble revealing that he was in prime condition.

"My name is Katie Kramer," she told him, hoping he'd return the favor. "Wilder Adventures's new office temp." She paused, but he didn't even attempt to fill the awkward silence. "So that leaves you . . ."

"What happened to Riley?"

"Who?"

"The current office manager."

"I think she's on maternity leave."

"That must be news to his wife."

She met his cool gaze. "Okay, obviously I'm new. I don't know all the details since I've only been here a week."

"Here, being my cabin, of course."

"Stone told me that the person who used to live here had left."

"Ah." His eyes were the deepest, most solid green she'd

ever seen as they regarded her. "I did leave. I also just came back."

She winced, clutching the covers a little tighter to her chest. "So this cabin . . . Does it belong to an ax murderer?"

That tugged a rusty-sounding laugh from him. "Haven't sunk that low. Yet." Pulling off his cap, he shoved his fingers through his hair. With those sleepy-lidded eyes, disheveled hair, and at least two days' growth on his jaw, he looked big and bad and edgy—and quite disturbingly sexy with it. "I need sleep." He dropped his long, tough self to the chair by the bed, as if so weary he could no longer stand. He set first one and then the other booted foot on the mattress, grimacing as if he were hurting, though she didn't see any reason for that on his body as he settled back, lightly linking his hands together low on his flat abs. Then he let out a long, shuddering sigh.

She stared at more than six feet of raw power and testosterone in disbelief. "You still haven't said who you are."

"Too Exhausted To Go Away."

She did some more staring at him, but he didn't appear to care. "Hello?" she said after a full moment of stunned silence. "You can't just—"

"Can. And am." And with that, he closed his eyes. "Night, Goldilocks."

Cameron Wilder tried to go to sleep, but his knee was killing him, and his bed buddy was sputtering, working her way up to a conversation he didn't want to have.

"You can't just . . . I mean, surely you don't mean to . . ."

With a deep breath, he opened his eyes and took in the woman sitting on his bed. She wasn't a hardship to look at, even though he'd much rather be alone. She had light brown hair, which was currently in bed-head mode, flying in crazy waves around her jaw and shoulders. Her creamy skin was pale, with twin spots of color high on each cheek signifying either arousal or distress, of which he'd bet on the latter since he hadn't exactly been Prince Charming.

And then there were those slay-me eyes, magnified behind her glasses. They were the color of her hair, and also the exact color of the whiskey he wished he had straight up right now.

Clearly, she needed him to reassure her, but he didn't have any reassurance in him. She'd asked who he was, and the fact remained—he had no fucking clue anymore. None. He'd spent some time trying to figure it out, in Europe, South America, Africa . . . but there were no answers to be found. He hadn't felt anything in months, and yet there she sat staring at him, wanting, *needing* him to feel something.

They were both shit out of luck.

"I can't stay in the same cabin with someone who . . ." She waved a hand at him, at a loss for words.

He had the feeling that didn't happen to her very often. "Could be an ax murderer?" he offered helpfully.

"Exactly."

"I told you I wasn't."

"But you didn't tell me who you *are*. Whoever that turns out to be, you should know, I'm a black belt in karate. I can kung fu your ass."

Uh-huh. And if that were true, then he really *was* an ax murderer. He didn't challenge her, though. He couldn't summon the energy, not for a fight. Which was a sad commentary on his life all in itself. Not that he started fights as a rule, but he'd sure as hell never walked away from one.

She pushed up her glasses and stared at him with cautious curiosity. And he couldn't help but wonder if she liked her sex cautious too. He liked his—when he could get it—a little hot and sweaty, and a lot shameless. And definitely, decidedly, *not* cautious. "You can relax. I'm a Wilder. Cameron Wilder."

She said nothing, his favorite thing ever, so he leaned back and closed his eyes again, so damn exhausted he could sleep for a week.

And then, finally, the reaction. "Cameron *Wilder*?"

Yeah, there it was. Once upon a time, at the height of his career, he'd been a fairly common household name. He'd made a lot of people excited. Mostly women. They'd gotten excited and wanted an autograph, a picture, even just to look at him, anything. Any piece of him that they could get.

But those days were long gone. He was damaged goods. Now, apparently, he was reduced to scaring the hell out of women instead of turning them on, and if he hadn't been so tired, he might have laughed at the irony.

"You're related to Stone."

It was a sad day in hell when his brother was better known than he, but he should be used to the bitter taste of humble pie by now. "I'm his brother."

"And you . . . you live here? In this cabin?"

"Used to anyway."

"So you're the boss as well."

He hated the idea of being in charge of someone else, had always hated it. Hell, he could hardly be in charge of himself. But fact was fact. At the moment, he was nothing more than part owner of Wilder Adventures. A regular Joe Blow. "For better or worse, I suppose."

"I threatened to kung fu you. Oh my God."

"Don't worry. I didn't believe you."

"And I'm still in your bed! *Crap*." This was accompanied by a flurry of movement. "Maybe we can just forget about all this and start over."

He'd have said he was too tired to care what the hell she was doing, but curiosity got the better of him and he cracked open an eye.

She was hopping out of his bed, small but curvy in a pair of plaid boxers and a dark blue tank top—no bra, which he noticed because one, hello, he was male, and two, he'd gone one full year without sex.

"So can we?"

He blinked and brought his bleary vision back up to her face, which was fixed in an expression that clearly said they were going to be talking for quite a while. Oh, yay. "Can we what?"

"Forget about the kung-fu thing? And the bed thing?"

"Absolutely, if we can also stop talking." Leaning back again, he snuggled into the chair, enjoying the blissful silence—until she cleared her throat politely.

He ignored her.

"Excuse me. Mr. Wilder?"

Jesus. Mr. Wilder? That had been his father. Not him. Never him. He didn't need to throw his weight and authority around, demanding respect but getting none. "Look, Goldilocks—"

"Katie."

"Fine. Katie. You should know that I don't care if *you're* an ax murderer. I need sleep. Kill me while I'm at it if you must, but do it quietly."

"So you're just going to sleep right there? Really?"

"Yeah. And I'll give you a raise to be quiet, very, very quiet."

"You don't even know what your brother is paying me."

No, he didn't. He didn't because he hadn't talked to his brother. "I'll double whatever it is."

"Well, that's just crazy. It's only a temporary position, a month, until your regular office manager comes back, and—"

"I'll *triple* it," he vowed rashly. "Just please, *please* stop talking."

She fell into what he hoped was a lasting silence, and he let out a sigh.

"You're too big to sleep in that chair," she murmured.

"Are you offering to share my bed?"

"No!"

Yeah, he didn't think so. "Hence the chair."

"I'm sorry, but you really need to leave now."

"Or you'll what, kung fu me?"

"You said we could forget that," she said with disappointed censure.

Wow, that was new, disappointing someone. "If you stopped talking. Which you didn't."

Indignant was a good look on her. Her eyes were flashing, arms all akimbo. And he was really enjoying that tank top, especially since she'd gotten a bit chilly in the past few minutes.

"I can't sleep in your bed while you're right there staring at me."

Yeah, pissy too, and actually sort of hot with it.

"I'm sorry about the mix-up," she said stiffly. "But—"

"You. You're the mix-up. You're in my cabin."

"Fine. I'll just go to another cabin."

"Perfect." He stayed where he was, happy to have her do just that and leave him alone with his own misery. Oh, he'd accepted his new limitations . . . well, almost. But the not knowing what to do with himself, *that* got to him.

Move on.

If he had a penny for every time some well-meaning asshole had told him that, he'd buy each and every one of them a fucking clue. He wanted what he'd lost, and short of that, he planned to continue to wallow in peace.

But she didn't leave. He knew this because he could feel her whiskey eyes boring holes in his face. "What now, Goldilocks?"

"It's dark out there." She was peering out the window into the admittedly dark, cold night. The sharp wind whistled through the trees and rattled the glass. "It's so secluded." She turned to him. "A gentleman would offer to walk me."

He didn't know how to break it to her, but he was no gentleman.

"Cameron?"

"Shh, he's sleeping."

She let out a sound that defined annoyance. "You are the singularly most unhelpful man I've ever met."

Yeah, He already knew that.

She was shifting around again and bumped into his legs. "Please move so I can get by."

He didn't. Interesting that he usually shied away from touch—with the exception of sex, that is—and yet he remained utterly still now, absorbing the fact that her legs were knocking into his.

The sensation was shockingly pleasant.

Unlike her talking. That was distinctly not pleasant. He wanted silence. Needed silence. Needed that more than his next breath.

"Excuse me."

Without opening his eyes, he dropped his legs down so she could pass him, then settled in again, his hands linked low on his belly, head back, eyes still closed.

The front door opened, then shut.

Ah, yeah. Perfect. Finally alone, where he could contemplate how he'd tell his brothers and Annie that he was back—

"Dammit."

He shook his head and opened his eyes. Yep, there she was, still with him, leaning against the door, chewing on a thumbnail, her hair wild around her face, her eyes filled with misgivings, her body—

Well, wasn't that a shame. She'd dressed.

She'd put on white jeans and a pink soft fuzzy sweater that zipped from chin to waist, with two tassels hanging down stopping just short of her breasts, pointing to them as if in emphasis of how long it'd been since he'd last seen a woman's breasts.

"It's really dark out there."

"Yes," he agreed, looking to where the stars littered the

black velvet sky like a sea of diamonds. There was no sky on earth like a Sierra night sky. He waited to be moved by it, as a sort of test, a gauge of his emotional depth. He waited for the mystic wonder to hit him like it used to.

Waited.

And waited . . .

Nothing. Not even a twinge. "Which means it's also too dark for any ax murderers to find you," he pointed out.

"That may be, but there's something else out there, something that always lurks in the bushes and makes this sort of rustling noise. It's done it all week."

He met her gaze. Those pale, clear depths could really haunt him, could make him yearn. Except he no longer did things like get haunted or yearn. "Nothing's stalking you. Unless . . ."

"Unless what?"

"Well, there's been some sightings of Big Foot over the years."

She looked horrified but spoke bravely, "There's no such thing."

"Tell that to the people who reported seeing him. Or to the bushes next time they . . . rustle?"

She nodded in confirmation. "There must be an explanation."

"Sure there is. It's Old Pete. He runs the gas station in town. He grew up on a commune and hasn't shaved since the seventies."

Her gaze narrowed. "Is this amusing to you?" Her hands went to her hips. "Making fun of my fears?"

What was amusing was his own reaction to baiting her. Why it was so much fun, he had no idea, but he was enjoying the spark in her eyes, the attitude all over her, and for some stupid reason, loved her crazy bed-head hair. "I'm sorry."

"You are not."

Okay, he wasn't. "Look, I'm tired. It's like three in the morning. I'm feeling punchy."

"It's one. One in the morning."

"Well, it feels like three. I've been up for thirty-six hours straight and I'm dead on my feet."

"Does that mean you're not moving?"

"Not a single inch." He closed his eyes again.

"Maybe Annie—"

"Go for it. But fair warning, she's cranky when she doesn't get her sleep."

A sound of frustration left her, but Cam was already drifting off, dreaming about his knee *not* aching, dreaming what Annie would be cooking for breakfast in the morning up in the main lodge, dreaming about his feisty Goldilocks sleeping in his bed and whether he could coax her to share the bed tomorrow night . . .

Huh.

Seemed as if maybe he was feeling plenty of things, after all.

Chapter 2

Cam woke up to the sun slanting through the window into his face.

And something else was right in his face.

The temp, the one with a healthy fear of ax murderers and the dark. The one with the quick wit and shiny hair and the sweet soulful eyes that stared into his as if he were a loaded shotgun. Odd how he found that sexy. "Hey . . ." He'd already forgotten her given name.

"Katie," she supplied helpfully, in the tone of "Bite me, asshole."

Aw, she thought he was sexy too.

"You fell asleep," she said tightly. "*Dead* asleep, as if it was no big deal for us, two perfect strangers, to sleep together."

She had a point, and in the light of day, which was currently blinding him, he felt just a little bit guilty that he hadn't gotten up and left her his cabin. "I was really tired—"

Abruptly, she turned and left the bedroom.

Yeah, that charm of his was working wonders.

She'd made his bed. She'd changed her clothes, fixed up her hair, and apparently also built up a pretty big attitude. With a sigh, he got up, his knee giving him a hot, fiery stab of pain just for shits and giggles. Wincing, he thought belovedly of the Vicodin he'd given up because he'd liked it too much, and followed her into his living room, noticing that her hair smelled good, damn good. "I really am sorry."

"You are forgiven," she said formally, even politely, as she handed him back his key and picked up her bags, turning toward the door.

In his experience, women weren't much into forgiving, so her words left him a little confused. "I'm forgiven?"

"Absolutely." She struggled to hold her stuff and open the front door, so he reached around her to help. Their hands tangled on the knob. Her hair smelled good. And then there was her booty, a very fine booty, which bumped into the front of his thigh, and he abruptly, unexpectedly, noticed her as a woman.

Okay, so he'd noticed her as a woman last night, in her tank top sans bra. He'd have to have been dead not to; but it magnified now, much like those eyes behind her glasses, and if he'd been all the way awake instead of groggy and hurting, it might have shocked him. He wasn't used to being back among the living, feeling things like hot and bothered.

"I've got it, thanks." She pulled open the door, shivering as the early icy air sliced through them. "Don't worry, I'll be sure to tell Stone you tripled my salary. It's very generous of you."

"Hey, wait. *What?*"

But she was out the door, shutting it in his face. He yanked it open in time to see her swinging her very cute little ass down the front steps to the path. "Goldilocks."

"Sorry. Can't stop." She was peeking beneath each bush that she passed. "I don't want to wake up Big Foot."

"Aren't you funny."

"Oh, I'm a riot." She flashed him a quick look over her shoulder as she paused to push up her glasses, looking quite pleased with herself. "I've got to run. I have a meeting with Stone, and I'm never late."

"I did not offer to triple your salary."

"Oh, yes, you most definitely did. You said, and I quote, 'I'll triple your salary if you stop talking.' "

Oh, Christ. He *had* said that. He quickly switched mental gears from figuring out how to get her back into his bed to getting her to forget the raise because Stone was going to kill him. "But you didn't," he said, just a little desperately. "You never stopped talking."

She only smiled, flashing a little dimple on the right side.

Hell of a time to remember that once upon a time, before he'd fucked up his life, he'd had a serious softness for dimples.

"How would you know if I did?" she asked. "You were snoring."

And smart-asses. He had a soft spot for smart-asses too. Had he thought her a sweet little thing? Try feisty as hell.

Another personal favorite.

What was happening to him? He'd been having a great time feeling sorry for himself, wallowing. Plus, he'd spent his entire life being wary of people since all they'd ever wanted was a piece of him—past tense—and here he was, already forgetting to put up his guard. "I don't snore."

"Oh, yes, you do. Loudly. Like this—" Turning back to face him, she snorted air through her mouth, sounding like an elephant in heat as she backed down the path toward the main lodge.

"You're making that up. I don't snore, and you weren't quiet. There was no way you could have held your tongue." He pointed at her. "You, Goldilocks, are not a tongue holder."

She laughed again, and he felt something tug deep in his gut as she sauntered off. And for a long moment he just stood there in the doorway of the icy morning, watching her go. Eventually, the cold got to him.

In no hurry to face his family, he headed back inside the cabin to the shower. As far as delaying tactics went, it felt like a good one. He hadn't seen his brothers or Annie in close to a year. Hadn't seen anyone who'd once mattered to him in all that time. But he'd hardly stepped out of the shower before he heard his front door open and Stone call out his name.

Showtime.

Cam opened the bathroom door and faced the music.

Stone stood there with Annie. She'd been only eighteen when she'd taken in an eight-year-old Cam as her own, but she owned the age-old maternal expression on her face, the one that said she didn't know whether to hug him or kill him. Stone too. The both of them stood there staring at Cam as if they'd seen a ghost.

And to be fair, he certainly must look like one after all these months without a word. They had the same green eyes, which could be warm and laughing, or icy and slicing. Annie, short but mighty, stepped forward, hers definitely doing the latter. "Hey, Annie—"

Which was all he got out before Annie put two hands to his chest and pushed. "Don't you hey me."

Ever the middle child, and therefore the peacemaker, Stone pulled her back before she could push him again.

"Let me go. I'm not done with him yet."

"Yes, you are." Stone eyed Cam evenly. Eleven months older than Cam, he'd made it his life's goal to be superior, bossy, and nosy as hell. He took one good long look at Cam and then just let out a breath. "You're really back."

"In the flesh." Far more pummeled by looking into his brother's face than from his aunt's shove, Cam just soaked the sight of them in because damn, it was good to see these guys, the only people in his entire life who'd ever accepted him for who he was outside the celebrity.

And just like that, a whole bunch of messy, shitty emotions slapped into him, emotions he hadn't wanted to face, emotions that gripped his throat like a vise. Still wearing only a towel, he carefully let out a breath. "For better or worse."

Nothing in Stone's face gave away his thoughts except his eyes, which seemed suspiciously bright, so maybe, possibly, he was every bit as moved as Cam. As the Wilders were all good at hiding their feelings, it was all but impossible to tell.

"Where's T.J.?" Cam asked Stone, thinking their older brother would be the easiest to face simply because he'd always been the calm, level-headed one.

"Alaska. Halfway through a six-week ice climb." Stone kept staring at him. "You might have called once or twice."

They'd never been a demonstrative family, thanks to their father. Nope, William Wilder, a bronco champion, had had a long ego and a short fuse. At least he had up until his unceremonious death from a hoof to the back of his head from his prized bronco. Before that, he'd treated his youngest son—a bastard thanks to his wife's inability to resist any ski bum—to pretty much the same treatment whenever he could.

That is, until Annie had taken Cam, even though she'd barely been legal herself. She'd done her best to parent him, though there'd been times when he'd needed more of a parole officer than a parent. For better or worse, they'd raised each other, and though he'd been an adult a good long time now, she still thought of him as hers.

"You could have contacted us," Stone said. "A text, a fax. Sent a fucking letter . . ."

"But then I wouldn't have been able to terrify your new employee in the dead of night. And undoubtedly piss off Annie for the inconvenience of having to ready another cabin."

Annie didn't jump to the bait. "Katie's your employee, too, you idiot."

Idiot. Good to know he could count on his family to keep his feet on the ground.

"And you own this place as much as T.J. and Stone."

An old argument. A questionable argument. Sure, he'd put up the money for Wilder Adventures, but that had been easy.

It'd been Stone and T.J. to make this place; it was *their* sweat and blood, and he well knew it. He'd never had the heart for it. Hell, he didn't have the heart for anything, not anymore.

And Jesus, wasn't he ever so damn tired of himself.

"We've already moved Katie to another cabin," Stone told him quietly, studying him. "And she wasn't terrified. I'm happy to say she seems to be made of sterner stuff than that. As for Annie, she's *always* pissed off. So don't go flattering yourself about causing that."

Annie hissed in a breath but didn't respond. Hard to dispute the truth apparently.

"So why the new hire?" Cam asked.

"Riley's wife is having a baby." Stone shrugged. "He wanted paternity leave. I hired a temp replacement for the next month."

"Katie's different than Riley."

"If by that you mean she doesn't have a penis," Annie said, "then yes. Great to see you haven't misplaced your amazing observation skills on your trek around the planet. And let me just make it clear: You stay away from that girl, you hear me? She's sweet and kind, and not one of your rabid floozy ski bunnies."

Cam looked out the window. It was an old habit and a defense mechanism, tuning Annie out. He could have told her he hadn't had a "type" in an entire year and wasn't interested. And yet even as he thought it, he watched Katie head toward the last cabin. He needed sunglasses to look at that pink sweater against all that virgin white snow, but he couldn't take his gaze off her.

He had no idea why he felt so transfixed, but it didn't matter. Little did except putting one foot in front of the other. Forcing himself to turn from the window, he opened his duffle bag for some clean clothes. Unlike Katie, his bag had been haphazardly thrown together. Once upon a time he'd had people around him, an entire entourage, and his bag had always been organized for him.

But he was alone now. Loser has-beens didn't have much use for entourages.

Stone stepped closer, getting in his way. He was as big as Cam, broader actually, and beefier. But his move wasn't aggression. "Not to send you scampering off into the sunset again, but there's something you should know."

"What?"

"We're glad you're back."

Cam looked at him, but because that hurt he turned to Annie, who was standing there arms folded, attitude all over her. A general in waiting.

But she rolled her eyes, dropped her arms and her attitude, and sighed. As big of an admittance as he was going to get. Yeah, they really were glad he was back, but that would probably change very quickly. "I didn't scamper."

Stone's mouth quirked a little.

"I've *never* scampered."

"What do you call running off like a little girl just because the going got a little tough?"

"A little tough." Cam choked out a laugh. "Jesus, Stone."

"Look," Annie broke in, getting in the middle as usual. "I'll give you this. It was brave of you to go. Really. Brave of you to try to find yourself, but—"

"Not brave." Try the opposite. Try cowardly. Yeah, that's what Cam called his leaving rather than facing his own reflection in the mirror, rather than face what he'd lost, or the fact that he didn't know how to deal with it—*cowardly*.

"Things happen," she said softly, reminding him she knew of what she spoke. "People get hurt."

He'd been taken out of a bad situation when he'd been a kid—by her. But she'd had no one to take her out. She'd grown up on her own—no parental support, no money, and diabetic to boot. Not easy. "Yeah, people get hurt," he agreed. "And I needed to go somewhere to forget that, and just be."

"Did you find that place?"

"No." The restlessness had followed him, relentlessly. Everywhere. He'd lost his dream, which he could deal with if only he could find a new one. He'd come back here as a last resort, a part of him believing that doing so would be so overwhelming he'd just die on impact; but oddly enough, here he was, still breathing. "I nearly stayed away, nearly kept looking."

Annie made a noise and Cam braced himself, but she threw herself at him, hugging him tight.

"Damn fool," she breathed, sniffing noisily in his ear. "A stupid damn fool that I'm so very, *very* happy to see." She burrowed closer, squeezing the hell out of him. "Don't you ever do that again." Her voice broke, nearly breaking him as well. "Ever. Your place is here. Goddammit, Cam, it's *here*. With us."

Unbearably moved at her tears, he pulled her in tight and buried his face in her hair. "I'm sorry. Please, Annie, don't cry. Not over me."

"I'm not crying, I've just got something in my damn eye." Shoving free, she turned her back, lifting the hem of her shirt to serendipitously wipe her eyes while Cam looked helplessly at Stone.

But Stone stepped in closer, his voice rough with emotion.

He hugged Cam hard. "She's not the only one glad to see you, asshole."

Yeah. Yeah, he really was an asshole. "So you're okay with me being back."

"Go figure."

And with those two simple words, uttered sarcastically, both with edge and temper, yet filled with relief and unmistakable love, Cam nearly lost it. Annie's continued sniffing didn't help. "Annie," he murmured, devastated.

"It's just allergies!" Eyes red, she pointed at Cam. "Get dressed. We've got work. Unless your knee is bothering you?"

It was, it always was, but he'd learned to live with that. "I'm fine. What work?"

"You remember those ads that T.J. placed for Wilder Adventures in all the outdoor magazines?"

"Yeah."

"Business exploded," Stone told him, smiling. "Continuous groups coming and going. T.J.'s guiding a bunch of trust funders. There's a group arriving today to go to Cascade Falls, so I'm out of here for two days."

"We've been trying to hire another expedition leader," Annie said. "But apparently egotistical, cocky sons-of-bitches are hard to come by. Good thing you stopped by, as you know these mountains like the back of your hand." She jabbed a finger into his chest. "You're hired."

"Maybe I'm not done feeling sorry for myself."

Stone snorted. "You're back here, you're done."

He wasn't so sure. "I'll think about it."

"You'll think about it?" Stone repeated. "Bro, you're in. If you don't want to do it for your own entertainment, then do it for us. We're overworked, and we need you."

They needed him. So even if his world felt more than a little rocky and he had no idea of his place in it, he was needed here. In some small way, that was a relief. Them against the world, as always.

Again, he glanced out the window at the majestic mountains that had once upon a time been his whole world, at the wide-open space they'd taken for their own, and there, among the snow-covered trees and white winter wonderland was another world wonder.

Katie.

She was walking away from her newly assigned cabin now. She'd changed into dressier clothes and silly boots not really meant for their weather. A classic city-girl mistake. She was heading past the row of eight staff cabins toward the main lodge to go to work, and just like that, yet another unwanted emotion hit him.

Okay, two.

Curiosity and intrigue—two things he hadn't felt in a damn long time. "I'll think about it," he said again.

"Fine," Stone said. "You do that. But think fast."

Chapter 3

Katie saw Stone briefly, and by briefly, she meant when she'd literally run into him just outside the big lodge as she'd been coming in and he'd been going out.

He was as good-looking as Cam, slightly bigger, but a kinder, gentler version in that at least he could hold a conversation without dragging his knuckles.

"I'm sorry," he said, pulling his iPod earpieces away from his ears and dropping them around his neck. Rock blared out from the speakers. "I know we have a meeting to go over everything you need to do while I'm gone, but something's come up. Can you handle closing out the month on the books, writing a few checks, and possibly renting out some equipment? Annie can give you the rundown."

Sure," she said as he moved off with his long stride. "No problem." Hopefully. She turned to enter the large two-story log-cabin structure that made up the lodge.

The foyer was lit by the long windows on either side of the huge front door, and also by two moose lamps mounted on the log walls. There was a beautiful wooden bench and a long row of hooks for jackets. Still not used to the 6,300-foot altitude, she hugged her jacket closer, not yet ready to take it off as she stepped into a huge open great room that always made her think of a mid-nineteenth-century saloon. Hardwood floors, open-beamed ceilings, and a Wild West decor gave a warm glow to the place. There were big, comfy couches spread throughout, and in the far corner, an old-fashioned salon-style bar. Next to it was the biggest fireplace she'd ever seen, glowing with embers from the rip-roaring fire of the night before.

Annie came skidding into the living room. The Wilder Adventures chef wore baggy jeans and a large, long-sleeved T-shirt, making it impossible to see her figure. Ageless as well, she wore no makeup and might have been sixteen or forty. Her green eyes said, *Don't mess with me.* Her apron wasn't much friendlier. It read: MY KITCHEN DOESN'T RUN ON THANKS. Her sable hair was thick and long down her back. "Did my medical delivery come—" She picked up a white bag from the foyer bench. "Crap, I missed him."

"Who?"

"The hot delivery guy, who else?" Seeming very distracted and more tightly wound than usual, Annie opened the bag, looking through it. "Getting my insulin isn't nearly as fun without the flirting."

"Stone said there's some things he needs done while he's gone, and that I should get the full lowdown from you."

"Dammit." Annie pulled out her phone, checked the time on the display, then blew out a breath. "Okay, lowdown . . ." She began piling her long, thick hair on top of her head in a haphazard fashion, sticking pins in it from her pocket. "If you have to rent anyone any snow equipment, it's not difficult. You know the two large storage garages where it's all kept?" At Katie's nod, she went on, "The helicopter's keys are in the first one, but you shouldn't have to worry about that unless someone wants to go heli-skiing."

Katie's jaw hit the floor. "Uh—"

"Kidding." Annie flashed a grin. "Sorry. But if someone wants to rent a snowmobile, you can handle that, right?"

"Sure," she said much more confidently than she felt. Rent a snowmobile, maybe. Drive one? She was barely back to driving a car . . .

Baby steps. This was just one baby step in a series of many, all heading toward the goal of risking, living. *Balls out, baby.* "No problem."

"Okay, so the lodge." Annie pointed to a wide hallway off to the right of the living room. "You've seen it all by now. The wing of eight guest rooms, the crew that comes in from Wishful to clean . . . they'll probably come by your desk for a check today. Pay them or they won't come back." Annie pointed to the opposite hallway off to the left, where there was a movie room, the dining room, and a huge kitchen. "Sometimes I hire additional help from town, like today. They'll want to be paid as well."

"Got it."

Annie pointed to the portion of the living room done up like an old western bar, where if there were overnight guests, it could get really hopping. "And whoever comes in to bartend tonight will want to be paid as well. Okay, gotta go."

"Wait. Month end?"

"I have no idea, but if Stone does it, it can't be that hard. Oh, and you're not on our bank account yet, so he probably left you a few checks signed."

"He left signed checks?" she asked, a little horrified.

Annie patted her hand. "Honey, this ain't LA."

"But someone could steal a check and wipe out your account."

"Girl, you're in the mountains now. If anyone came in here and tried to steal a check, someone would just shoot him." She shook her head and laughed at the idea.

Katie didn't, because holy crap, she didn't actually think Annie was kidding. Her next words proved it.

"The shotgun's in the closet upstairs, if you need it."

"Ohmigod."

"Just remember, Stone loves to read reports and stuff, so make sure to print everything out as you go—"

She broke off as a tall, lanky man in well-worn jeans and a tool belt walked into the room. It was Nick Alder, Wilder Adventures's heli-pilot and mechanic. He was good-looking in a "been a ski bum for twenty years" sort of way. He had a mop of brown curls exploding on his head and matching brown eyes to go with the tanned face and easygoing stride, which came to an abrupt halt at the sight of Annie.

"Nick," she said in a chilly voice that had Katie taking another look at the two of them. In the week she'd been here, she'd not seen them together before. The tension level was . . . interesting.

"Annie." Nick, normally approachable and laid-back, looked extremely uncomfortable as he shoved his hands into his pockets. "I thought you'd be . . ."

"Out of your hair?" The chef's mouth curved, but her eyes were flashing . . . hurt? "No such luck. Stone needs you. Uh . . ." She took a quick glance at Katie, then turned back to Nick. "Something came up."

"I already know," Nick said.

"You *know*?" This clearly pissed her off.

Katie thought about warning poor Nick that there was a loaded shotgun just upstairs, but Annie spoke first. "You might have told me, Nick."

He opened his mouth, then shut it again. "You told me not to tell you anything. You told me not to talk to you, remember?"

The sound Annie made spoke volumes on how she felt about *that*.

"Look, I'm sorry."

"Yes, you are," she agreed. "You're one sorry son-of-a—"

"If this is about the divorce papers—"

"It's not. Or it wouldn't be, if you'd just *sign them*!"

Nick rocked back on his heels and said nothing to that.

Katie tried to disappear into the floorboards.

And Annie just shook her head. "Oh, forget it. You'll have to sign them eventually." She turned to Katie. "I'm sorry, but I can't give you any more time right now."

In other words, *go away*. Message received. Leaving the two of them at their stalemate, Katie went up the stairs and into an open reception area. Her desk was huge and gorgeous, made from an old oak door tipped on its side. It was piled high with paperwork, and also held a computer and the usual office supplies.

Katie was a numbers girl. Before her accident, she'd been content working at an accounting firm. In that world, things needed to add up in order to make sense. Things fell in line and had a purpose.

But no longer. After the accident, life hadn't balanced, no matter how hard she'd tried to get it to do so.

She pulled off her jacket, and as she did every morning, she looked at the wall. It was covered with awards for various world-class winter events: Winter X Games, Burton European Open, Olympics, and many more. There were shelves, too, filled with trophies, some stacked three thick.

All of them for one person—Cameron Wilder.

How she'd not placed that until now, she had no idea. The phone on her desk rang, and still staring in amazement at the wall that now made sense, she picked it up. "Wilder Adventures."

"Katie, it's Stone. I need you to grab the set of keys in your top right drawer, go out to the equipment garage, climb into the Sno-Cat, and start it. One of our neighbors is coming to borrow it, and it takes forever to warm that sucker up."

"Okay." She pulled out the keys and looked out the window at the garage. "One question. What's a Sno-Cat?"

That got her a laugh. "It's the big orange machine right inside the garage door that looks like a giant's Tonka toy. Climb into it, put the key in the ignition, push in the choke, and turn the key while pumping the gas twice. Leave the garage door open so you don't die of carbon monoxide poisoning. Sam'll bring the Cat back later and drop the keys off with you."

Okay . . . Katie pulled her jacket back on, ran down the steps and outside, sucking in a breath as the cold slapped her in the face. So different from the hot, sticky, non-winter of Los Angeles, for which she was eternally grateful.

She made her way on the trail around the lodge, the snow crunching beneath her feet, the breath soughing in and out of her lungs because apparently a week was not long enough to adjust to the high altitude. Luckily for her, the keys were labeled. At the equipment garage side door she eyed the huge sign that read KNOCK FIRST, and then did, hoping someone would be here to help her out.

No one answered, so she let herself in and flipped on the light.

A huge, orange machine stared at her, indeed looking like some giant's Tonka toy.

She stared back, feeling some of her courage dissolve. Feeling other things dissolve, too, like oh, the bones in her legs as a flash came to her, one that usually hit only in the deep dark of the night. The Sno-Cat wasn't anything like the crane that had been required to rescue her when the Santa Monica bridge collapsed, but apparently it was close enough.

It'd been a simmering hot day. The asphalt had been steaming by 8:45 A.M. She'd been late for work and knew her boss would be peeved, so she'd gotten on the bridge and sped up, only to be cut off by a semitruck. Stymied, she'd been stuck behind him, which in hindsight had saved her life, because when the bridge had collapsed, the truck had fallen into the void and she'd slid off the side instead of sinking. She'd flipped too many times to count, rolled down the embankment, coming to a horrific halt upside down, caught on a tree as her car burst into flames . . .

Sweating and shaking now, she blinked the Sno-Cat back into focus. "No." Hell no. Not having a nightmare in the middle of the damn day. "Don't be ridiculous," she said out loud. Her doctor had taught her that trick, speaking out loud to snap her out of it. "You're fine."

Proving it, she lifted her chin and eyed the beast. "I'm doing this." She climbed up and pulled herself in, landing on the big driver's seat. Stomach quivering, still sweating, she wiped her brow and looked out the windshield. She was high up, sure, but she wasn't upside down in her little car. There was no danger here. Repeating that to herself, she put the key in and turned it, already wincing—

But nothing happened.

"The choke." She repeated Stone's words back to herself, "Push the choke in." She searched for and found the thing, then pushed it in and turned the ignition over while pumping the gas twice.

The Sno-Cat roared to life, the engine rumbling and shuddering and vibrating beneath her, around her. With that came a burst of heat from the vents, a blast that blew her hair back and burned her eyes, and with a shocked cry, she cringed, stomach revolting, violently, and without warning. Not rational and knowing it, but unable to care or stop herself, she flung her body out of the Sno-Cat, landing hard on her knees. Crawling out of the equipment garage and into the snow, the blessedly cold snow, she gulped for air, managing by the grace of God not to lose her breakfast.

"Goldilocks?"

Dammit. Not him, not now. She fisted her hands in the snow,

letting it sink into skin, cold and wet, reminding her where she was.

The Sierras, taking that baby step on the way to the rest of her life.

Risking.

Adventures.

All of it, everything she'd never given herself pre-bridge collapse.

"Katie." Cam crouched at her side putting his hand on her back. "Hey, are you okay?"

"Yes." *Please go away.*

Instead, she felt his hand skim over her spine, as cool and soothing as the snow beneath her. "Are you sick?"

"I'm okay."

"You're green is what you are."

"I just need a moment." She pushed to her feet and headed back to the lodge, figuring he'd take the hint and leave her alone. After all, he seemed to like being alone.

But she could hear his boots crunching in the snow behind her. "I'm *fine*," she told him over her shoulder. "Really." To prove it, she sped up, and then what the hell, ran, wishing she could outrun her demons as easily. Inside the lodge, she raced up the stairs, and then at the top, ran out of gas, sagging against the accolades-laden wall.

Whew, this altitude was killing her.

That, or it was the panic attack, which sucked. While she concentrated on getting air into her overtaxed lungs, she tipped her head back and read Cam's plaques for the hell of it. Slope-style champion. Overall champion. Gold medalist. Half-pipe champion. Winter X Games champion . . . It went on and on.

It was amazing to her, the guy who'd appeared at her bed-side last night, the same guy who'd been at turns irritating, surprisingly kind, then irritating again, seemed to have won just about every single winter event there was over the past twelve years.

There was nothing for this entire year, though, which struck her as odd.

Since thinking about Cam was infinitely more appealing than facing the fact she'd just had a doozy of a panic attack, was still having if her near-hyperventilating breathing was any indication, she kept at it. She had to wonder why, after the incredible career outlined in front of her, had he suddenly stopped placing in events. Had he retired? "I could get behind retiring," she muttered, "if I wasn't so fond of eating."

"Do you always talk to yourself on the job?"

As she turned to face the champion himself, her damn glasses, clearly not aware of the panic attack in progress, fogged.

Chapter 4

Okay, so apparently he was always going to appear when she was somehow embarrassing herself or out of her element. She turned to face him. With her glasses fogged, she could see only the outline of him, the tall, dark, and attitude-ridden Cameron Wilder. He was encroaching in her space, so she put her hand out to hold him off, setting it against his chest. He was solid, so unexpectedly, thoroughly solid, with the heat of that strength radiating through his sweatshirt, that she ended up holding on instead, fisting her fingers into the soft material just below the Burton blazed across his chest.

"What happened back there?" he asked quietly, calmly, and as the cool snow had, his voice soothed her frazzled nerves. He brought his hands up, running them down her arms once in reassurance.

"Oh, nothing. Just a little panic attack." Okay, a major one. "No worries, it passed."

"Okay." She could feel him looking at her very carefully, he of the sun-kissed unruly brown hair, razor-sharp green eyes, and scruffy face. He removed her fogged glasses, cleaning them on the hem of his sweatshirt while she squinted and focused the best she could, surprised to find what she'd said was true—her panic attack had passed.

"Why do they fog?" he asked, which wasn't the question she'd expected.

But then again, nothing about him was expected. "Um . . . they do that sometimes." Apparently, if a hot guy got too close, which almost never happened.

He set her glasses back on her nose. She could have told him not to bother, that if he kept doing stuff like breathing, they were probably going to keep fogging, which was odd, because this close up she could see that he wasn't classically handsome. Nope, his nose was slightly crooked, and then there was the scar bisecting his left eyebrow. He had fine lines fanning out from his eyes, reflecting he'd lived his life, a *real* life out here in the mountains, and also apparently all over the planet with a board strapped to his feet, which fascinated her.

She bet he never had to remind himself to live balls out.

Now that she was okay, his eyes were filling with a general mischief, wicked bad-boy glint, but she also sensed a hint of something much deeper inside him, something . . . haunting, and though she had no idea what it was exactly, it was that that drew her in.

"So why the panic attack?"

"Oh." She shrugged. "It's just a residual thing I'm dealing with."

"A residual thing. Such as . . . ?"

"Really? You want to talk? Because last night you paid me not to—"

"I want to know what scared you."

Ah. So he still didn't want to chat, not really, but was asking out of concern. Probably wondering if his brother had hired a crazy woman.

She picked up the phone message pad and turned on her computer, watching as Safari automatically loaded Yahoo news.

And there for her horrified eyes popped up a news video of the Santa Monica bridge, collapsed as if it had just happened, cars sticking out from beneath like from a horror flick.

She didn't see her car. That was because, as she knew all too well, hers had slid off the cliff, catching on two large trees, leaving her hanging, literally.

A few gray spots swam in her vision. *Shit.* She heard something hit the floor and realized it was the pad falling from her fingers.

"Katie?"

She swallowed hard and shut the browser on the screen. Marginally better. "Long story."

"Cliff Notes version," he said, eyes narrowed in on her face.

"Okay." She'd done her best not to talk about it, never to talk about it, but clearly that wasn't working for her. "I had an . . . accident. A bad one. I nearly died. Actually, I sort of defied the odds by *not* dying. It messes with my head sometimes, that's all." She looked at him, saw the sympathy in his eyes, and decided she liked it better when he was irritated by her. Much better. "So what do you say you give me a hand with month end?"

She saw the relief come in to his eyes. He'd probably been worried that she was going to do something horrifying, like cry. Ha! She was tougher than that. Way tougher.

Almost always.

"You do remember me from last night, right?" he said, playing along with her, letting her change the subject. He leaned that tightly muscled body against her desk, hooking his thumbs into his front pockets. "The most unhelpful man you've ever met?"

"Yeah." Much as she was grateful that he'd let the panic attack go, she winced at the memory of him finding her in his bed. "But in my defense, I was a little . . . discombobulated last night."

"Yeah." He offered a little smile that fried more than a few brain cells. "Me too."

"Really?" He'd seemed . . . exhausted, but definitely at ease, especially in his own skin.

"Hell yeah. I came home and found a beautiful woman in my bed that I didn't put there."

She stared up into his face. It didn't say much about her love life that having him call her beautiful made her melt in spite of his extreme unhelpfulness.

Except now that she knew he'd been a professional athlete, she knew something else too. He probably had women throwing themselves at him all the time. Groupies and snow bunnies and the like. "I didn't realize you were a celebrity."

He looked puzzled until she gestured to the walls that were a shrine to him.

"Annie did all that." He looked around and gave a visible wince. "I've taken it all down a hundred times. The last time, she threatened to cut off my food supply, and I take my food supply very seriously."

"It's just so surreal. You're an Olympic champion. An X Games champion. You're—"

"I've read my bio, thanks."

He didn't like to talk about it, which was hard for her because she wanted to talk about it. "Okay, well, we could pretend we're meeting for the first time."

"And that I didn't find you in my bed?"

"Yes, that would be really great, actually."

He gave a slow shake of his head, his gaze filled with a good amount of trouble. "I don't think I can do that."

"Why not?"

"Because every time I close my eyes, I see you there." The glint in them turned positively wicked now. "Naked."

She nearly choked on her shocked laugh as he effectively

did what nothing else had been able to—make her forget. She looked at him and realized that he wasn't just being crude for the fun of it, he really was trying to take her mind off whatever had gotten to her.

And it was that, that right there, which opened her heart to him just a little.

But only a little, because hot or not, he was still quite contrary.

And hot, and oh good Lord, there went her glasses again, completely fogging over. She ripped them from her face. "You know I wasn't naked."

"That part must have been my dream then."

"You dreamed about me being naked?"

He shot her a crooked smile filled with both shameless admittance and a wry humor, and she had to laugh. "That's a guy thing, right?"

"So I take it you didn't dream about me naked."

"No." And yet she knew she would tonight. "But we irritate each other. Don't we?"

"Yes, but see, irritation originates in the brain. That's not the part of me that was dreaming about you."

"I work for you."

Some of his good humor left. "No, you work for Stone."

That was quite a distinction, one that she wasn't sure she understood. "Are you not a part of Wilder Adventures?"

"I am now. Apparently I'll be planning expeditions and doing some of the leading."

"And sign the paychecks?"

He stared at her for a moment, then let out a breath. "Maybe. Probably. Stone handles most of that, though; he loves paperwork. I think he has a screw loose somewhere."

"I used to love paperwork."

"Used to?"

"Not so much anymore." She broke the disconcerting eye contact because it seemed like he could see inside her. "So. Month end."

"Not my area of expertise."

"What is?"

He merely smiled again, naughty to the bone. Her knees wobbled, and it had nothing at all to do with the big, bad, scary Sno-Cat. "Okay," she said on a laugh. "Never mind. How about this. If you could just tell me what reports Stone wants to see . . ."

"I've been gone all year. I have no idea." But instead of escaping, he leaned back, feet and arms casually crossed, still very much at ease. She had a feeling he was pretty much always at ease.

"You've been gone a year?"

"Give or take." He picked up a file from her pile and opened it. "Interesting."

"What?"

"It's the application you filled out, and a copy of your driver's license, and—Huh."

"What?" She stood up, trying to see what he saw.

He tipped the file and revealed the picture on her license. It'd been taken last year, and showed her with her hair neatly up, glasses on.

The old her.

Cam eyed it, then swiveled his gaze to her.

"It's not my best picture," she said a little defensively. "But it does reveal that I'm responsible and—"

"Not an ax murderer?" She caught the quick flash of humor in his eyes as he took in her fuzzy sweater, wool trousers, and high-heeled boots. "I don't think you have to worry, Goldilocks. I don't think cute office managers from LA who wear high-heeled boots can be ax murderers. There's a code or something."

She stretched her legs so they slid beneath the desk, hiding her feet. "Okay, so I'm a little overdressed, but that's just me wanting to make a good impression. It doesn't necessarily say I'm from LA. I mean, maybe I just like high fashion." Or Target sales . . . "You shouldn't assume—"

"Your application says you're from LA."

"Oh, right." Her curiosity won over her embarrassment. "What else are you learning about me?"

He lifted the paperwork out of her view, not hard since he was so tall. "That you went to college at USC for accounting but didn't take your CPA because you weren't sure you'd stick in accounting. You have a good head on your shoulders, though you're a little uptight and cautious."

She blinked. "My file says I'm uptight and cautious?"

"No, that part was me."

When she looked into his green eyes this time, they were definitely smiling, accompanied by a quick quirk of his mouth.

Oh boy. If she'd thought him attractive when he was all edgy and badass, it was nothing compared to how he looked when he smiled.

Note to self: *Don't make him smile again.*

"I'm not uptight and cautious."

"Really?"

"Really."

"*Really?*"

She deflated like a popped balloon. "Okay, so maybe I've been uptight and cautious, but that's in my past."

At that, he out and out chuckled, and every single inch of her reacted.

Amendment of note to self: *And don't even think about making him laugh.*

"Give me that." She tried to snatch the file from him, but he simply used his superior height to his advantage, still reading as he held the papers out of her reach. Not for lack of trying, though. Her hands were back on his chest now. Such a hardship, once again soaking up the heat and strength coming through. And something else. The beat of his heart. It was steady as a rock.

Like the man.

A little surprised at the depth of her reaction, she pulled her hands free and stepped back.

Oblivious, he was still reading. "Your reference said you're conscientious, tidy, and a hard worker."

"That's true." To give herself a minute, she turned away. She'd never combined a panic attack with annoyance and lust before. It left her a little quivery, from the inside out.

"It doesn't say anything about being adventurous."

She turned back.

Tossing the file aside, he leaned back against the desk again, all casual as he gripped the wood at his hips and looked at her. "Do you have a sense of adventure, Katie?"

"I slept with you, didn't I?"

His mouth twitched. "It only counts as adventurous if it was without clothes."

The image of just that left her a little breathless, as if she didn't already have enough problems. And she couldn't have explained her odd reaction to him if she'd tried. In her life, men were aloof, quite preoccupied, and hard to get. Her father. Her last boyfriend, who'd been so laid-back about their relationship he'd had to be checked for a pulse. Of course, as it had turned out, he'd already been married to someone else.

Cam didn't seem aloof or particularly hard to get. And she'd bet her last dollar that there was far more to him than what he revealed. She didn't know what exactly made her so sure of it but knew it had something to do with the hollowness she kept catching glimpses of. "I have plenty of adventure in me." It was a daring statement, but she was feeling pretty damn daring. And she had no idea what made her say what came out of her mouth next. "I was on the Santa Monica bridge."

"Me too," he said. "Though it's been a while."

"No, I mean I was on it when it collapsed."

He went completely still, staring at her over the file. "Jesus. Really?"

"Really."

"How did you—" He shook his head in disbelief. "My God. There was only one survivor, a woman. That was you? How did you make it?"

She let out a shuddery breath. She'd wanted to say it, and she had, but she didn't want to talk about it. She never did. "I don't really know. But afterward, something inside me sort of snapped. I looked around at my boring, staid life and . . ." She shook her head. "It wasn't enough. So I packed up and set out to make it worth something, at least to me. I promised myself adventures, risk. Excitement. So I got in my car and drove."

"And landed here."

"For the next month anyway. After that, I'm not sure, but that's a part of it, the not being sure. Whatever it is, it'll be bigger and even more exciting. So in answer to your question, I'm *trying* to have an adventurous spirit, always. I'm not great at it yet. . . ." The incident in the equipment garage came to mind. She offered a self-deprecatory smile. "And I realize I've just opened myself up for more of your amusement at my expense, but I'm just trying to be honest. I think coming here, as far out of my comfort zone as I can get, proves I've got some adventure in me."

He was quiet for a long moment, studying her as if seeing her for the first time, all signs of amusement gone. "Doing what you did took guts," he said very softly, with more emotion in his voice than she'd yet seen from him.

He knew of what he spoke, she realized, and swallowed

hard. She hadn't realized until that very moment just how badly she'd needed someone to get it, get her. "You think so?" she whispered.

"Yeah." His voice was low, almost hoarse. "I do. And your honesty will get you a lot further than any sense of adventure, always. I'm sorry I teased you."

And with that, he pushed off from the desk and walked out of the office.

Once Stone and Nick left with their guests on their trip, Cam got away by himself. He needed to think. It used to be that he did his thinking while boarding.

But it'd been just over a year since his spectacular crash, and he'd never gone back to it.

Was he afraid?

Not really. Unless he counted the fact that he was afraid he'd suck. But even that wasn't enough to have kept him off the mountain.

It was his own mortality.

But dammit, he needed to think. So like the good old days before he could afford a lift ticket, he climbed Widow's Peak with his board on his back. On a scale of 1 to 10, the climb was a 100; but he'd done it so many times he could have made it blindfolded.

Just not with his bad knee. Holy shit, he was out of shape. By the time he got to the top of the jagged mountain peak, his legs were overcooked noodles and he was breathing like a freight train. He stood looking out at the valley far below, his past life spread out in a blanket of white glory. An icy wind blew over his heated body, slowly cooling him down.

But it wasn't the sweat drying that made him shiver. It was the knowledge that there was no way in hell he was going to take the board off his back. Every time he tried, his fingers shook, and he remembered the crash in vivid Technicolor.

He'd been racing for a world title, lost his concentration, caught an edge, and had woken up in a Swiss hospital. He'd spent a month flat on his back recovering from three surgeries, one of which had nearly killed him. Then he'd spent another eleven months wandering the planet feeling sorry for himself over losing the only thing that had ever been his unconditionally.

The board was a heavy weight on his back. He wanted to be on it. Wanted the rush of the roaring crowd, the feel of the gates as he flew through them, the dizzying speeds as he headed to the finish line . . .

But that wasn't going to happen, not ever again.

You're as good as you're going to get, his last doctor had declared.

But not as good as he'd once been, not even close. He had seventy percent mobility, which meant he could get out there like the average Joe Blow but . . .

But.

He'd never again be a world champ using the skills he'd honed from the age of five out of sheer determination, grit, and desperation to get away from the life he'd hated. Even after he'd gone to live with Annie, the determination and grit had remained.

He'd been the best of the best, and because of it had been lifted out of poverty, had been offered a life where he could travel every single day of the year if he chose, a life where people treated him like he was somebody.

And now that was gone, forever. Fuck. Fuck it. Without taking the board off his back, he started hiking back down the hill, ignoring the aching muscles in his good leg and the pain in his bad one. A couple of hundred yards along, he heard a yell from above him. And then, "Oh shit!"

"Cody, watch out for that effing tree!" someone else yelled in equal panic.

Two guys burst through a set of trees above Cam, avoided the trees by a miracle, and threw themselves to the snow at his feet.

"Jesus, Tuck," Cody gasped, rolling to his back. "Jesus Christ." He slapped his hands down his body. "We're alive."

"Barely." Tuck lifted his head and smiled at Cam. "Dude, we almost killed you."

Not likely, Cam thought, as neither of them could have aimed and hit him if they'd tried. They were fifteen, maybe sixteen. Both with knit caps low over their eyes, baggy boarding gear and goggle tans.

Cody shoved his cap up a bit to see better. "Hey." He peered at Cam's face. "Hey, I know you."

Cam shook his head.

"No, dude. I do. You're Cameron Wilder. *Dude*," he said, smacking Tuck in the chest. "It's him, look."

"*Sweet*. Hey, man, we need some pointers."

"Stay out of the trees until you know what you're doing."

They both laughed and slapped each other around some. "So why are you walking down?" Cody asked Cam.

"Your knee?" Tuck asked. "It's not better?"

"No." Which was infinitely more appealing than the truth— that it was as good as it was going to get, so he'd switched gears and became a Professional Quitter.

"You're not, like, giving lessons, are you? Cuz my mom would totally pay you to teach me how to board without breaking bones." Tuck pulled up the sleeve of his jacket and revealed a casted wrist.

Teach other people how to ruin their lives too? Huh, what a concept. "No."

"We could walk down with you, and you could tell us about the 2006 X Games, where you—"

"Can't. Sorry." Their faces fell, and he felt like an ass. A complete and utter loser ass. "But you could come by the lodge." Where he had closets and closets full of sponsor gear he'd never be able to use in one hundred lifetimes. "I have extra gear if you're interested."

"Dude!"

"Can we bring our friends?" Tuck asked, lit up in sheer joy.

"Yeah." Why the hell not. He already felt like a one-man freak show, might as well become one.

"Maybe you'll be boarding again before the end of the season and we could tag along," Cody said. "You know, like, sometime."

Cam looked into their young, eager faces and felt a hard tug on his gut. He wanted to say leave me the hell alone, but he couldn't do it. He simply couldn't look into their hopeful, whole-life-in-front-of-them faces and crush their dreams just because his were gone. "Yeah, maybe."

"Sweet!"

They hit the mountain slope again, arguing over who to bring with them to Wilder, and Cam followed.

On foot.

Chapter 5

After flying their clients to Cascade Falls, Stone and Nick spent the day leading them down a series of verticals. By late afternoon, they'd tackled four different peaks and sat at the top of Mt. Paiute, looking out over what felt like paradise.

"Never gets old," Nick noted.

"Nope." Stone turned off his iPod. "Cam should have come."

"Said he wasn't sure what he wanted to do, whether he'd stick around or not."

"Yeah." They were both well used to Cam and his special level of bullheadedness. "I'll call him."

"Don't," Nick said.

"Why?"

"Because you'll piss him off."

"Will not."

"You're his brother. It's what you do."

Yeah, but it was worry that propelled him. Partly that was because Stone was the middle child, and that's what he did, *worry*, and partly because their father hadn't ever worried about Cam. In fact, he'd resented the hell out of the baby who had not only *not* been his but sickly too. Cam had eventually gotten healthy—no thanks to their father's harsh discipline—and had ended up with Annie—a fact that Stone was convinced had saved Cam's life.

The old man was long gone now, but Cam still took everything to heart, deeply to heart, and had a habit of just shutting down rather than feeling something, even before the quick rise to celebrity and fame had closed him off. And then the snow-boarding accident, which had taken away the one thing he'd loved above all else.

Without the rush of his sport, Stone knew Cam was flailing, lost, trying to find his place. What Stone didn't know was how long it'd be before Cam figured out there wasn't a physical "place" at all, only a mental one. With Nick shaking his head, he called Cam.

"You lost?" Cam asked dryly.

The relief Stone felt from hearing his brother's voice made him instantly grumpy. It'd always been this way. Stone doing his damnedest to take care of everyone, especially Cam, and Cam doing his damnedest to make Stone not want to. "Nick wants to come back for you so you can ski with us tomorrow."

Nick rolled his eyes.

"We could use the company," Stone went on. "Our clients are a bunch of spoiled, rich punks who don't want to ski as much as find a good view and sit and drink beer."

"Sounds like you a few years back."

"I was never more interested in beer than skiing."

"Right. You were much more interested in women."

Okay, true. "You coming or not?"

"Not."

Stone tried to keep his cool, but as he considered Cam a flight risk, it was difficult. "You getting restless feet again? Because I swear to God, if you even think about leaving, I'll attach cement blocks to your feet."

"Jesus, relax. I'm not going anywhere." Cam hesitated. "I went hiking. My knee's swollen up."

Cam's pain after the accident had nearly killed him, and had nearly killed his brothers to watch him suffer through it. Stone hadn't realized there was still that particular demon to fight. He swiped a hand down his face and fought to keep his voice even. "Have you been keeping up with your PT?"

"Yeah."

"The meds?"

"Quit them at the same time I quit you."

"Have you—"

"Stone." Cam's voice held frustration, and something else. Defeat? Whatever it was, he didn't sound like himself. "It's just a bad day."

Sympathy wouldn't work here, not on Cam, even though that's what Stone felt. "Sorry, didn't get that you were still so fragile. You just stay there and relax." Beside him, Nick sighed, and Stone ignored him. "Take a nap."

"You know what? Fuck you."

There. *There* Cam was, and just like that, the tightness in Stone's chest eased in relief. A bum knee they could deal with. An attitude-ridden Cam they could deal with. It wouldn't be pleasant and there would be fights, but what they couldn't deal with was Cam vanishing again.

"Look, I'm back, okay? I'm here, and I'm . . . trying. I'm trying to help like you asked."

"I'd rather you *want* to want to be back," Stone said.

"Yeah, well, I'm working on that too. I've spent the past two hours booking no less than four upcoming groups, all of which will bring in more money than you did in the last month."

"Is that why you told Katie I'd triple her salary to shut up?"

"Mentioned that, did she?"

"She did."

"She also mention that she survived the Santa Monica bridge collapse?"

"Yeah."

"She's . . . different."

"You mean because she doesn't worship the ground you walk on?"

"That doesn't happen so much anymore," Cam admitted.

And he didn't know how to deal with that either, Stone guessed. "I'm not the chick police, but she's not your type."

"That's never stopped you, *amigo*."

A not-so-subtle reference to two summers back, when Stone had had a thing with the cleaning crew—two Puerto Rican sisters who'd come on to him one night after too many vodkas and a whole bunch of bad karaoke. The sisters had been excellent at their job and *muy caliente*, but unfortunately also *muy* crazy. "I was going through a phase, okay? It's passed now."

"Well, so has mine," Cam said.

"Your pissy phase? Christ, I hope so."

Cam let out a low laugh and hung up. Stone shut his phone and met Nick's gaze.

"Hey," Nick said. "At least he's still with us."

"Yeah, but for how long? He's looking at Katie, which is interesting."

"He said he hasn't gotten laid since Serena dumped him."

"A year," Stone mused. "Unlike him."

"Because he's never had to make the moves before."

"Yeah." Stone shoved his cell into his pocket. "Who let T.J. go out on a month-long trek so he doesn't have to deal with the day-to-day shit of the ranch, including our baby brother?"

"You. You don't like to be gone for long periods of time, and you know it. You like to be in charge, bossing everyone around, making sure we all do your bidding."

"Now you sound like Annie."

Nick fell silent at that. He'd been with them since before

Wilder Adventures, years before. He'd gone to school with Annie, had been in love with her since day one, and had helped her out with a young Cam. It'd taken a long time to convince Annie to marry him, because like all the Wilders, she tended to work hard at pushing people away, including the best person to ever happen to her. "The divorce sucks."

A man of few words, Nick just nodded.

"You'd think it would make her happy since it was her idea, but she's a bigger nightmare than before." Stone slid Nick a glance. "Can't you fix that?"

Nick shook his head. "She has a thing for the UPS guy."

"*What?*"

"She likes his shorts."

"Then get a pair of shorts, man."

"She said I didn't see her." Nick shrugged his narrow shoulders. "Hell, I don't even know what that means."

"Maybe it's girl code. Maybe she thinks you don't love her."

Nick looked completely befuddled. "How can she think that? I sold my Jeep to buy her a ring. I sold my Skycrane heli when she had that bad turn with her diabetes and got so sick. I sold my *life* to make her happy, and she says I didn't see her?"

"So *see* her."

"Yeah. Any thoughts on how exactly?"

"No, but she's cranky as hell, and she's scaring people. If you don't start *seeing* her soon, we're all going to pay."

"So you're saying I have to get my marriage back together for *your* sake?"

"For the greater good of Wilder Adventures," Stone said.

"For *your* sake."

"Yeah."

Nick shook his head. "All of you Wilders are crazy."

"You're just now figuring that out?"

* * *

Recreation in the mountains was decidedly different than in the city, Katie discovered, and much more exciting. She still had trouble sleeping at night, but she managed to get enough hours to refresh her.

Or maybe that was the high-altitude air.

Every morning, she walked from her cabin to the lodge and looked around in awe. It seemed she could breathe deeper here, see farther. The skies were bigger, the landscape was brighter, a landscape that continued to execute mysterious rustles in the bushes, making her nearly jump out of her skin as she hustled to the lodge steps.

Big Foot her ass, but she had a feeling whatever stalked her was hungry. Still, she refused to run off like a scared little bunny. She stood firm and looked at the bush, which went suddenly still. "One of these days," she told it, "you're going to show your face."

Stone came around the side of the lodge, his downhill skis on his shoulder, an amused look on his face. "Are you talking to the manzanita bush?"

"It talked first."

He laughed and shook his head as he walked by her, up the stairs toward the front door.

"Seriously, what lives in these things anyway?"

"Wolf spiders, raccoons, coyotes . . . you name it."

She'd rather not. She turned back and eyed the bush. "Okay, you win this round." But in defiance, she stood there a moment longer soaking up the clear, crisp air. The mountains were still, the early-morning sun sparkling like glitter over the snow. It was so beyond anything in her experience, and so . . . absolutely soul-soothing.

That she had the bridge collapse to thank for this experience was an odd thought, but she had it anyway.

Her life was definitely no longer the same old boring routine.

Annie opened the front door and looked at her. "You going to stand there daydreaming all day, or are you going to get in here and eat the best omelet on the planet?"

"Yours?"

"Who else?"

Katie went inside, ate what was *easily* the best omelet on the planet, and then spent the day organizing trips, running the office, and helping Stone stock and catalog demo gear that many of the big-name sporting companies sent them.

That night, Wilder Adventures hosted overnight guests, and the living room turned into a bar. The fire was set to roaring, Annie put out food, and a local band set up, with Nick strapping on a guitar.

Stone was walking around, mingling with the guests, taking drink orders.

Cam stood behind the bar filling those orders, his long, lean, rangy body moving to the beat of the music as he poured drinks with an ease that told her he'd been bartending a good long time. He had a way with the guests too. There were three women standing in front of the bar, laughing, talking, flirting. When they moved away, other women in the room moved in.

Katie snagged a few hors d'oeuvres, smiled at Nick, who was surprisingly good on the guitar, and got stopped by Stone, who introduced her around, though the whole time her gaze kept drifting back to Cam.

He wore an opened plaid flannel over a blue T-shirt on his broad shoulders, half tucked into his trademark loose jeans, low on his lean hips. She couldn't see his feet, but she'd bet he had his boots on, unlaced. Simple, typical mountain-man clothing, but nothing was simple or typical about the man.

When Cam's audience shifted to the makeshift dance floor,

she made her way over to him, watching as he worked up a pitcher of margaritas while singing along with whatever alt rock song Nick and the band were playing. "You seem like a natural," she said

"At making drinks? I am pretty good, I have to admit."

"Also at the people thing." Her eyes slid meaningfully to the women, some of whom were still watching him with hungry eyes. "They're falling at your feet."

Over the blender, his green eyes met hers and she felt a little zing. "All of them?" he murmured.

"Well, I'm still standing."

He let out a small smile. "Ouch."

"Oh, it's not you. I'm taking a little break from . . . falling."

He poured the margarita mix into salted glasses and handed her one, watching her closely. "Because . . . ?"

She shook her head at the drink. "No, thanks, I'm a lightweight. And to answer your question, I'm taking a break because the last guy I dated turned out to be married."

At that, he winced. "Yeah, we're pretty much all assholes."

"Not all."

"All," he said firmly.

"We'll have to agree to disagree there," she murmured, trying not to be mesmerized by those eyes of his, the eyes that seemed to see a hell of a lot more than she wanted him to. "But just because I'm not good at the whole dating thing doesn't mean I've given up entirely. I'll get back to it."

"No one's good at it."

"Oh, I don't know." She smiled. "I have a feeling you are."

"Not me. I gave all that up." He shifted away to hand out the margaritas and she figured that was it, the extent of their conversation; but when his tray was empty, he came back, smiling at her as he once again moved behind the bar.

And she had to ask. "You gave up sex?"

His mouth curved wryly. "Not on purpose. But as it turns out, it's been a long dry spell."

"Miss it?"

"Now that you mention it." Shoving his shirtsleeves up to his elbows, he leaned on the bar, shifting close, shooting her a look of pure wicked trouble that shouldn't have revved her engines but did. "Why? Are you offering to get me back on the bike?"

Something inside her quivered, but she hadn't been born yesterday. She tore her gaze off his, but that meant soaking in his chest or his forearms, which were ripped with tough strength. His hands were as rugged as the rest of him, big and calloused and scarred. "Does that ever actually work for you?" she murmured. "That line?"

He chuckled softly. "Not in a damn long time, I can tell you that."

Stone made his way behind the bar and looked at his brother. "You working your magic here?"

"Not with this one." Cam's gaze was still locked on Katie. "She's immune to the Wilder charm."

"Smart woman."

Smart to steer clear? Was she really? Or, as she looked at the two brothers with their matching mischievous smiles, matching stun-the-brain good looks, was she being very, very short-sighted?

Several nights later, Annie dragged Katie out to Juniper Lake for ice-skating and a bonfire. It was a full moon, and the sharp, black outlines of the majestic peaks surrounding them in a full circle were enough to render Katie awestruck as they drove out on the narrow, curvy, almost nonexistent road. The high moon shined over the frozen alpine lake, but the best scenery was Nick, Stone, and Cam, skating as if they'd been born to it. "Look at them."

"Yeah, they've been playing hockey for years," Annie said, mistaking her excitement for dismay over their skills. "Don't mind them."

Nick flew past them so fast he was nothing but a blur, and for a moment, Annie stared after him with a look of such naked longing it hurt Katie's heart.

Giving the chef a moment, Katie got her borrowed skates on and tested herself on the ice, eyeing Cam speeding around the lake.

Did he look good doing everything?

She thought maybe he did, then let her mind wander to what else he might look good doing—like her. Unbidden came the picture in her mind of him doing just that, stripping her naked one article of clothing at a time, smiling that wicked, naughty bad-boy smile as he worked his way down her body with his tongue—

And just like that, her feet flew out from beneath her, and with a teeth-chattering thunk, she hit the ice on her most padded spot—her ass—which didn't make it hurt less.

Cam stopped on a dime with an ease that made her want to knock him on *his* ass, fine as it was. "Don't say it," she warned, pointing a finger at him. "Don't say anything except how the hell do I skate like you?"

He flashed a smile and pulled her to her feet, and when said feet would have fallen out from beneath her again, he held her upright.

She'd just been picturing his hands all over her naked body and here he was, touching her. It had her brain's wiring all crossed, and her nipples went hard.

Bad nipples.

With great concentration, she shoved the sensual images aside, because over the past week since his return, she'd begun to get to know him, and one of the things she knew was that he tended to be a hands-off kind of guy. Stone and Nick were forever shoving each other, and Annie as well. But they were also just as likely to hug, or even just casually touch.

Not Cam.

But he was touching her now, literally holding her up. And looking into her eyes. "You didn't say," he murmured. "Were you injured in the bridge collapse?"

"Just a few burns and a broken wrist." It was her standard reply. Short and to the point, and didn't encourage more questions. "Could have been worse."

"Doesn't always help to know that, though."

No. No, it didn't, and a little surprised at his sharp insight, she looked into his face.

He offered a solemn smile. "Ready to learn how to do this?"

She caught the intent in the flicker of his eyes a second before he put his hands on her hips, turning her so that she faced away from him. Before she could process the feeling of being snuggled up to his chest, he'd slipped his arms around her middle, his long legs pressing to the backs of hers. She felt the warmth of his chest; then the muscles in his thighs flexed and they were moving.

Fast. "Oh God."

"Oh God good, or bad?"

"Good." But she hadn't meant the skating. The landscape whipped past them at dizzying speeds, not what was spinning her head. No, that was his hands on her, hard and firm on her belly and ribs as he took her entire weight against him, reminding her how long it'd been since she'd been touched by a man.

Too damn long.

She leaned her head back against his shoulder and looked up into his face. He wasn't wearing a ski cap tonight, and his light brown hair was disheveled as if maybe he'd used his fingers as a comb. He hadn't shaved. His scar slashing his left eyebrow didn't look all that old, and yet the leather band he wore around his wrist did. Her fingers played with it, and at the touch, he looked down.

"From your travels?"

"South America." He continued to steer her around the lake, the muscles in his body flexing against hers, the heat of him keeping her warm.

As if she could get any warmer. "Does this hurt your leg?"

His expression registered surprised at her question.

"I'm sorry. I've seen you limp sometimes." Plus, he never took the physically taxing trips. Stone or Nick did those. But no one mentioned it, or why.

"It's my knee," he said. "But as long as I don't do jumps, it'll be fine."

She couldn't hold herself up and he could do jumps. She wanted to ask about his injury, about that hollow look that sometimes came into his eyes, about why the others never talked about it, or how they deferred to him, protecting him so much. But she didn't. She sensed he was tired of questions, tired of a lot of things, and she didn't want to make him think about it when there was actually a smile on his face. "Then you need to be careful," she said, then remembered that being careful had never worked for her. "But don't forget to live. Live as big as you can with what you've got."

His lips quirked, his hands tightening on her. "Is that what you're doing?"

She wasn't watching where they were going, but his face. His mouth. It was a really great mouth. Wide and firm but not too much so. She bet it'd be heaven on hers—

"Don't," he murmured.

Her gaze flew to his.

"Don't go there unless you mean it, Goldilocks."

"How do you know I don't?"

He shook his head. "It's a bad idea. We're a bad idea."

"Why?"

"I have this thing. This no regrets thing. And while I wouldn't regret a night with you, I'm not sure you'd be able to say the same."

Would she regret a night with him? Hell no. But would she regret having to walk away in a few weeks once the job was done and her heart had engaged? Because her heart *would* engage with him, she already knew it, and that might be a problem.

At her silence, his mouth quirked and he set his chin on her head. "Yeah, that's what I thought."

Chapter 6

Dawn hadn't quite broken when Cam and Stone pulled out their climbing gear and cataloged everything they'd need for a group trip later that day.

"Katie said that they added two to the group." Stone was crouched by the ropes, going through them. "So there'll be seven. Eight, if we bring her with us."

Cam stopped separating belaying equipment. "We? And why would you bring her?"

"We, because stupid me, I assumed that when I told you I need help guiding, it meant that you would actually help. And we'd bring her because she wants to learn."

"I never promised to do this."

"No, you didn't." Sounding disgusted, Stone stood up. "Look, you know where the door is. Don't let it hit you in the ass if that's what you want."

"Jesus, you're touchy. I didn't say I was leaving right now."

"No, because you don't say anything. You just leave us hanging."

Cam stood up, too, brushing off his hands. "Why don't you tell me what you want me to say. Let's start with that, Stone."

"Okay." Stone tossed down the gear in his hands. "I want

you to say that you're not as stupid as you look, that it's been a fucking year and you're getting the fuck over yourself."

Cam felt his gut clench and he took a step back rather than what he'd like to do, which was wrap his fingers around Stone's neck. "And how am I supposed to get over the fact that it's gone?"

"Snowboarding?"

"My life."

Stone let go of a heavy breath and what appeared to be his temper as well. "Jesus, Cam. It's not gone. Your life is still good. You just have to find something else to do with it."

"I have nothing else."

"Then you are as stupid as you look."

Cam let out a mirthless laugh. "Well, hell, just tell me how you really feel." He kicked at the gear at his feet. "Fine. I'm stupid. This is stupid. It's stupid to be here."

"So you're quitting. Everything. You're just walking away. Well, what's new."

"What is that supposed to mean?"

"You always walk. You can't board for gold, so you walk. Your relationship hits a lull and you walk there too. Mentally. Physically. Whatever."

"I never walked from you guys."

When Stone just looked at him, Cam closed his eyes. "Not for long anyway." He opened his eyes, meeting Stone's steady gaze. "I tried, but I couldn't. Look, I know you think I came back because I was bored, or done walking the planet, but that's not it." He gave Stone a shove. "I'm here because I missed your ugly mug."

"Well, it is so much prettier than yours." Stone sighed. "We good now?"

"Good enough."

"Good enough." Stone gave him a little shove back and then hunkered down to continue separating the gear again.

"So since when do you have a problem with a pretty girl wanting to go climbing?"

"She's a temp."

"And you live your life like a temp. I repeat, what's the problem?"

"Nothing."

Stone took his gaze off the gear and eyed Cam. "Nothing has you two sniffing at each other like a pair of horn-dog teenagers?"

"Hey." Cam paused. "Maybe it's true, but hey."

"You two have a certain chemistry going on."

"It's called irritation. We irritate each other."

"Well, if that's what you kids are calling it these days."

"Fine. She doesn't irritate me. I don't know what she does exactly, though it feels something close to bashing my head against the wall repeatedly."

"And you're going to ignore that, too, like everything else?"

Cam shrugged. "That's the plan."

"That's a really dumb plan, Cam."

"No regrets." It didn't escape him that both he and Katie had been through hell, though they'd appeared to come out with opposing mottos. His was better. Easier.

Safer.

Over the next week, Katie did her best to buy into Cam's whole no regrets thing, but the problem was this: She *didn't* buy it.

Not that it mattered. He was gone a lot, during which time she learned a whole new meaning for the word *winter.* The nights were dark and mysterious, and yet oddly enough, not as terrifying for her as they'd been in Los Angeles.

She still had the nightmares, but they came more sporadically. Every other night instead of every single one.

She could get used to that.

The mornings were different from Los Angeles, too, in that the temperatures hovered right at zero, boggling her mind. Temps in the mid-70s seemed a far distant thing of her past. Nick showed her the trick of tucking her pants into her socks before walking from her cabin to the lodge, which while not at all fashionable, at least kept her feet from getting packed with snow on the walk. She'd asked him what other tricks there were to surviving the wild Sierras, and he'd told her it was a lot like the TV show *Survivor*—outwit, outlast, and outplay, only the opponent was Mother Nature.

She didn't mind that.

But Mother Nature could be finicky. There was no predicting the weather accurately, or making definite plans. So when a storm came and dumped four feet overnight—four feet!—she was the only one surprised.

Sitting at her desk, she looked out the window at the endless conifers and pines, the valley lows, the mountain peaks, *all* covered in a soft, thick blanket of white.

Cam was out there clearing the front path. He wore snow gear that fit his long, lean frame, and he worked endlessly, with the wild mountains behind him and the snow all around him.

He belonged.

A nameless yearning built up within her, for that same sense of belonging.

He stopped working to pull off his cap and unzip his jacket, limping to the porch for his bottle of water, and she pressed her nose to the window for a better look, telling herself she was only worried about his leg, that it had nothing at all to do with needing to see more of that body—

"You looking for the UPS guy?" Annie came up the stairs and tossed the day's mail onto Katie's desk. "It's too early."

Katie whipped guiltily around, trying to hide the fact that it wasn't the UPS guy she'd been drooling over, but Annie's beloved nephew. "Gotcha. Too early." When Annie left, she turned back to the window.

Cam was gone.

"You have a problem with the oven?"

Katie looked over her shoulder at Nick's voice, but she was alone in her alcove.

"No," Annie said. "Why?"

Katie looked around again. Why were her walls talking?

"Your muffins this morning needed less time in it," Nick said.

"Yeah?" Annie responded coldly. "Well, my air needs less of you in it."

Katie looked over the railing. There. The soon-to-be-divorced couple stood nose-to-nose on the far end of the great room below, but the acoustics of the high ceilings had their voices carrying as if they stood right next to her.

"You're impossible," Annie told him.

"Ditto." He nearly plowed Stone over as he passed him on his way out.

Stone raised a brow at Annie, who glared at him.

"I didn't do anything," Stone said, lifting his hands.

Annie sagged against the wall. "I know. Nick's driving me crazy, my cookies burned, the UPS guy asked me out, and Cam's looking at her."

Stone blinked. "Her who?"

"Katie who."

Katie went still.

"And she's looking right back, Stone. He's not ready. Who's going to tell him?"

"He's fine."

"That's what you said after I took him away from your father so he couldn't beat the shit out of him anymore."

"I said that because *you* had him," Stone told her. "He had you. He was fine with you."

"Stone—"

"Look, we just need to back the hell off him and let him be."

"But—"

"No, no buts. The accident was a long time ago and he's getting over it. He's been getting into some of the expeditions, looking like he might stick around for a while. Leave him be, Ms. Doom and Gloom. Don't stir it up."

"I'm going to stir you up," she mumbled. "Doom and Gloom my ass."

They moved away, but Katie stood there long after they were gone, unable to go back to work. Her mind wouldn't let her. It was locked on the image of Cam, big and bad and oh-so-tough Cam. Apparently that toughness had been hard earned, starting from early childhood and ending with some mysterious accident.

The sound of a loud engine had her turning back to the window, where Cam now straddled a huge snowmobile, revving the engine.

To her, the snowmobile seemed as terrifying as the Sno-Cat, but Cam turned his head and looked up at her, and she forgot to feel the kick of nerves. Like her, he'd been through hell and survived—many times apparently. She couldn't see his eyes or even his expression, but something about his body language told her he was on edge.

She definitely wasn't the only one fighting demons.

He lifted his hand off the handlebar, then lifted his head.

And just like that, her face heated, her glasses fogged, and her body reacted pretty much in the same way it had when he'd had his hands on her while ice-skating. She had no idea what he was thinking, but she knew what *she* was thinking, that even though he thought they were a bad idea, her body didn't think so at all.

He cocked his head, then crooked his first finger at her in an unmistakable "come here" gesture.

Oh, God.

She looked at the dangerous snowmobile, as dangerous as the guy astride it. She'd come here for a baby step, the first in a series of adventures. Going outside with him right now would be exactly that. Her next adventure, right there in front of her.

On a snowmobile.

Looking at her.

With a surge of adrenaline, she whirled to stare at her desk and the work on it, chewing on her thumbnail. Everyone deserved a quick break, right? Not every minute of every day had to be scheduled and analyzed, and oh my God, now she was standing there micromanaging the fact that she used to micromanage her time while Cam was outside on a snowmobile.

Hello, adventure waiting to happen.

Grabbing her jacket, she went running down the stairs to catch up with it.

Chapter 7

Cam watched Katie come flying out of the lodge, her clothes all neat and tidy, her hair perfectly pinned up on her head, all pretty perfection except for the jacket she'd left open in her hurry.

In the week and a half he'd known her, she seemed to be unwinding a bit. He wanted to unwind her some more.

Unwind and unwrap . . .

She came to a stop in front of him. "Hi."

"Goldilocks."

"You said we were a bad idea," she reminded him.

"We are."

She grinned at him, and he felt his own reluctantly tug at his mouth. Ah, man. He liked her. That simple. He liked her, and in his experience, that never ended well for anyone. "We got lots of snow last night," he said. "It's—"

"Beautiful."

He'd been about to say "a pain in the ass," because without racing in his life, a storm meant snowblowing, shoveling, clearing paths, making sure the clients could drive the three-mile gravel road in—

"I saw you limping."

A bare admission that she'd been watching him. Another woman would have certainly played coy about that, but not this one. She didn't seem to have a coy bone in her body. Nope, whatever she felt was right there on her face and her sleeve, for the whole world to see. He admired that about her even as he recoiled from it. "Just a lingering ache."

"From an accident?"

"Oh, yeah."

"What happened?"

"You really don't know?" He thought everyone in the free world knew. It'd certainly been all over the news: GOLDEN BOY FUCKS UP, NEWS AT 11:00.

"Does it have anything to do with why you stopped racing?"

"You could say that." She could have looked him up on the Internet and read all about it, about the speculation that he'd been drinking, or abusing prescription meds—none of which had been true until after the crash, but that didn't make good copy. And in any case, why else would a prime athlete crash out of nowhere?

Because he'd lost his focus, that's why. Plain and simple.

And painful.

The truth was his girlfriend Serena had been sleeping with someone else, and his mind had wandered at close to a hundred miles per hour on a forty-degree slope—never smart. "I caught an edge." And had come out of surgery to find his face plastered across every station, along with footage of his spectacular crash.

Over and over . . .

"When I was telling you about my accident," she said, "you never mentioned that you'd had a doozy of your own."

No, he hadn't.

"And you didn't mention it because . . ."

He lifted a shoulder. "I'm not as well adapted as you?"

"Is that a guess?"

"A little bit, yeah."

She looked baffled. "You act like you're a stranger to yourself."

"I am. I was." He shrugged. "It's not as bad since . . ."

"Since you came home again?"

His gaze met hers. That. But something else. Her. Meeting her. "Yeah," he finally said.

"Well, it sounds like you were lucky."

That was a new one. Lucky. "How do you figure that?"

"You could have died."

That was actually quite true. He could have died. There'd been many days where he'd wanted to, but those were all in his past now. He'd lived, and he would do with that what he could.

"It's odd, that whole near-death experience," she murmured. "It changes you."

He found his gaze locked in hers. He had a feeling he knew where this was going and he didn't like it. "Yeah."

"So why aren't you trying to get back to what you clearly love?"

"I'm not good enough for competing. Not anymore."

"You skate. You cross-country ski. You hike—"

"Okay, what part of not good enough don't you understand? I can't win."

She just looked at him for a beat. "If it was your entire heart like it seems it was, then there are always other ways to be involved," she said very gently, and far nicer than he deserved. "Instead, you appear to have walked away from it."

"That's the story that's going around." He revved the snowmobile engine. "Look, I'm going for a ride." He took in the way she was staring at the snowmobile as if it might open its engine compartment and bite her. "You want to come?"

"I don't know."

He remembered her aversion to the Sno-Cat and knew where it came from now. "Safer than driving a car," he said quietly. "Safer than boarding." He looked into her eyes and offered the silent challenge—take it or leave it. To tip the scales, he handed her his helmet.

She stared at it, then at him. "Am I going to need protection?"

"Yes," he said. "Protect yourself. Always." From a fall. From me . . .

And then, to protect *himself,* he scooted as far forward on the seat as he could, which didn't matter when she hopped on behind him, slipping her arms around his waist, hugging up against the back of him. Her jacket was still open, and though he shouldn't have been able to feel anything through his own jacket, he imagined he could feel her every breath, her breasts, her nipples hardening . . .

Jesus, he needed to get laid. "Ready?"

"I don't know." Her breathing was uneven in his ear and she was squeezing the hell out of him, seeming to be pretty close to another panic attack.

Something he understood all too well. "What happened to that new adventurous spirit?"

She took a deep breath, let it out, again in his ear, which brought him both goose bumps and an erection. He rolled his eyes at himself as she squeezed him some more.

"It's okay," he said, "I don't need air."

"Oh! Sorry!" She relaxed the fingers digging into him so marginally it didn't matter. "Okay. Ready."

Her bravado grabbed him. Just snagged him by the throat and held on. She wanted things for herself, and wasn't afraid to go out and get them. Well, she *was* afraid, but she didn't let it stop her. He had no idea why that was such a turn-on.

Or maybe he did. He'd let his fears stop him, a fact that both shamed him and pissed him off.

"Go," she said. "Before I lose it."

He hit the gas and they went screaming off into the snow, literally screaming, or maybe that was just her, crying out in hopefully surprised pleasure. "You okay?" he shouted back.

She had her arms wrapped around him like vises. Her hands had slipped beneath his jacket, beneath his shirt, too, and were directly against his flesh, fingers digging into his ribs. "So okay!" She still had a death grip on him and was screaming at the top of her lungs, but she was okay. He rode up the hill behind the lodge, whipped around a grove of trees and back down again, faster so that the wind whipped at them.

"Oh my God! Don't stop!"

At that breathless demand, he shook his head, unexpectedly wishing that she was flat on her back with him buried deep inside her as she screamed those words.

But he'd made sure not to get there, hadn't he, avoiding being alone with her.

And yet here he was.

Alone.

Also, with her wrapped around him like a pretzel, breathing roughly in his ear, panting, using words like *don't stop*, he was having a hard time keeping his mind out of her pants. He hit the gas harder and they flew toward a snow-filled ravine, heading for another sharp downhill that he knew would make her scream even louder.

Apparently, he wasn't just a bastard, he was a sick bastard.

"I'm not afraid!"

He knew those words she shouted were for her. The joy in them was unmistakable, so he didn't slow or hold back, but let her experience the full speed of the run.

Given the decibel level of her voice, she liked it, and he found himself grinning.

Grinning.

When was the last time he'd pushed himself past his own fears? Hell, up until a year ago, he hadn't had any fears at all, and since the accident . . . Well, he sure as hell hadn't pushed himself in any way at all. He couldn't remember the last time he'd felt exhilarated, excited, the last time he'd had fun. These days, riding was nothing but a mode of transportation when the roads weren't plowed, when he had to get from one excursion site to another quickly, or when any one of the others needed assistance.

But with Katie's breathless laughter spurring him on in his ear, things were different. He was smiling. Laughing. And his body . . . Well, his body was sure as hell telling him loud and clear that there was going to be something about this woman.

Something far more than expected.

Instead of going *there*, he took them over the land, making sharp turns so that she squeezed him tighter, hitting the gas so that she squeezed her legs around his, basically doing everything in his power to give her the ride of her life.

But the joke was on him, because she ended up giving him the ride of his life, and he drove for far longer than he'd intended, incredibly aware of her body plastered to his back, of the sweet heat of her arms wrapped so securely around him. When he finally stopped at the top of Widow's Peak, he shifted to give her a look of the valley far below.

The mountains were covered in snow, looking deceptively soft. But anyone who'd ever lived on these rugged peaks knew the truth—it was the opposite. No softness anywhere; only harsh, tough landscape.

It took a tough person to live here. He should know. He'd grown up only miles from here, under the mean, drunk gaze of a father who hadn't given a shit. Cam didn't blame the land.

Actually, he loved the land.

Because it'd been here he'd had the world laid at his feet by his one lone talent, along with all the fame and celebrity that went with it. Yeah, he loved the land. The land had saved his sorry ass.

Katie stared out at the view and sighed. "It's gorgeous. Who owns all that?"

"Once upon a time, a Wilder. The Wild Wilder, they called him. My great, great, great grandfather." He shrugged. "Legend has it that he shot more men than Jesse James. And as the apple never falls far from the tree, most of the Wilder men who came along after that weren't much better, ending up in jail or six feet under."

"Quite the legacy."

"Cam, T.J., and I grew up as wild as our name implies, happily doing our part of living up to it."

"And yet you're not in jail or six feet under."

"Not for lack of trying, believe me."

She'd craned her neck so that she could peek over his shoulder at him. "You're referring to your accident."

"For one, yeah."

"It changed your life." It was a statement, but also, he knew, a question, and she watched him very carefully, telling him how important his answer was to her.

He had a glib answer on his tongue, but he couldn't give it to her. Not with that look on her face. "It changed everything."

"As in it gave you the perspective to make some life changes?"

"As in it gave me the perspective that I'm screwed."

She pulled back slightly, as if so greatly let down by him she couldn't touch him. And though he rarely gave a shit what people thought, he found himself giving a shit now. "It's different for us, Katie. I lost what I was living for and you found it."

"You lived for racing?"

Yeah. Hell yeah. But hearing it from her lips didn't sound so good. "Well, not anymore."

"What do you live for now?"

He let out a breath, not wanting to make this worse, to make her even more disheartened by him, but he had nothing. "It hasn't been that long."

She nodded, letting him have the fantasy that he was doing fine. But he wasn't, and for the very first time, he wondered what it would take to change that.

A new dream. That's what it would take. Too bad he was fresh out. He hit the gas again, and with a gasp, she gripped him tight.

Which worked for him. Because at these speeds, there was no brooding, no pouting, no rehashing bad shit. Plus, he loved listening to her gasp and laugh as he raced them over the land. It made him smile in spite of himself, and he was still doing so when he finally pulled up in front of the lodge. When he turned off the engine, Katie stayed still a long moment, hugging him.

He figured she'd be distant now, but apparently she didn't work that way.

"We didn't flip," she said against his ear.

His eyes drifted shut. "I would never have flipped us."

"I know. But fears aren't always logical. God, Cam, that was good. I don't feel sick at all." She pushed her face over his shoulder. "Am I green?"

He looked into her eyes. "No."

She smiled, pulled off the helmet, and straightened her glasses. "I didn't have even an inkling of a panic attack."

"You do have helmet hair, though."

She laughed. Putting her hand on his shoulder, she looked into his face. "I have to go back to work, but thank you. Seriously, you made my day."

"It was just a ride."

She looked at him for another breath, and he wondered what she saw. "It was more for me. Thank you." Leaning in, she pressed her lips to his jaw. "Thank you . . ." She pulled back only a fraction and shifted her aim so that now her lips touched his once, softly.

Sweetly.

"Thank you so much," she whispered again as an unnamed raw emotion surged up from his chest so fast he got dizzy.

"I really needed that. The ride," she defined. "Not the kiss." She smiled. "Well, I needed both. Both were great, actually."

She had this incredible way of slicing through all the unnecessary bullshit. She had a way of looking at him, as if she didn't care about anything but this very moment—not his past, not his future, or lack of one. Nothing. It felt . . . good. Too good, and he needed another moment of it. Of her.

No regrets . . . "Goldilocks?"

"Yes?"

"I have a thank you too."

"You do? For what?"

Reaching for one of her hands, he tugged her over his shoulder, pulling her onto his lap. Then he kissed her.

Not sweetly.

Not even close.

This time there was tongue, lots of tongue, and he was gone, diving headfirst into the hottest, deepest, wettest, most perfect kiss in recent memory.

Hell, most perfect kiss ever, in all the damn land.

He told himself that was because it'd been so long since he'd been with a woman, but the lingering doubt was enough to have him going still. He opened his eyes to look into hers, his thumbs gently brushing either side of her jaw as she let out a soft, sexy little sigh.

He knew just what she meant, and shoving all his reservations to the back of his brain under Not Important Now, he tugged her closer and kissed her again. He half expected her to stop him because he knew that she'd only meant that first sweet kiss as a quick thank you, but her hands were running over his chest, his shoulders, into his hair, then back to his chest, as if she couldn't get enough either.

And then they slipped down to his belly.

Oh yeah, baby, go there.

Go as low as you want—

She broke off the kiss this time, mouth trembling and still wet from his, breath laboring in and out of her lungs as she stared at him.

He stared back, one hand in her hair, the other palming a sweet, full, warm breast.

"I got a little carried away with that thank you," she whispered, shuddering when his thumb rasped over her erect nipple. Then she seemed to suddenly notice where her hands were—fisted in the waistband of his pants—and she jerked them back, staring down at her front-row view of him straining against the button fly of his Levi's. "Um."

Yeah. Um. Much slower to retrieve his hands than she'd been, he took a deep, steadying breath because she wasn't the only one reeling. "That might have been me who got carried away. Do I need to apologize?"

"No." She lifted her shaking fingers to her mouth. "*No.* Was that . . ." Her face went a little pink. "I'm sorry. I need to know."

He automatically tensed, but she just blushed a little more. "I was wondering, was that *wow* for you, because that was pretty wow for me, and I just—" Her hand fluttered in the air. "It's been so long—I don't know. Was it? For you?"

Her eyes were so clear, so deep he could see all the way into her heart, which was far, far, *far* too pure for him.

"Oh." Her smile faded. "Gotcha." She hopped off of him and quickly turned away. "Okay, well, thanks again for the ride—"

He caught her hand just in time. Tugging her back around to face him, he waited until she looked into his eyes.

Christ, she slayed him. Slayed him dead. "Katie." His voice was a little thick, his heart hammering, and he was still a whole lot hard. "It was pretty damn wow."

She hesitated, clearly not sure whether to believe him.

"A mind-staggering wow," he clarified.

At that, her smile warmed again and absolutely stopped his poor, confused heart.

"I thought so." And with that, she squeezed his hand and walked away, not asking him for anything more.

Or expecting it.

Chapter 8

After surviving the bridge collapse, Katie had divided her life into two compartments: pre-accident and post-accident.

But now she had new criteria in which to separate things: pre-snowmobile ride and post-snowmobile ride, which had been the time of her life. The sense of wild freedom, the speed, the wind in her face . . .

The utter lack of fear.

There'd been an initial terror, of course. Would they crash, hit a tree . . . die. But she'd learned something about herself during that blissful hour while holding on to Cam. It wasn't death she feared at all.

It was pain.

But there'd been no pain. Nothing except a real joy and laughter.

And . . . and more.

Because it wasn't just the ride she was thinking about but what had happened after, the feel of Cam's warm, calloused hands gliding over her body, slipping beneath her jacket, caressing the small of her back, her breast . . .

And how even when they'd pulled back, he'd left his hands on her, almost as if he couldn't stop touching her. She'd looked into his eyes and had known. She was going to get a whole bunch of adventure here at Wilder, and hopefully a lot more.

She just hoped that *that* didn't involve pain either.

"You okay?" Stone asked when he walked by her desk, stopping to look at her oddly, making her realize he'd had to ask her twice. She managed to nod her head. "Fine." *Just day-dreaming about your brother having his tongue down my throat.*

"You okay?" Annie asked her an hour later.

"Fine." *Still daydreaming . . .*

But Annie didn't buy it as easily as Stone had, and stopped to give her the once-over. "You look flushed."

Yep, that's what happened when one got caught thinking about having her boss's hands up her shirt. "I'm good," she said weakly.

"Well, at least you're finally looking warm."

"Yeah." When Annie had moved on, Katie let out a breath. "Try hot. I'm hot. Hot for him. *Dammit.*"

"Hot for whom?"

Katie jumped, then turned to face Nick, who'd come up the stairs. "No one. And if you could not ask me how I'm doing, that would be great."

"Right." His mouth quirked. "Because you're hot."

"I—" Ah, hell. "Well, I—"

He lifted a hand and shook his head. He didn't need to know.

Which was good. Great. Excellent. She really didn't want to explain how it was that she was overheating over a kiss.

At the end of the day, she closed up and made her way downstairs. Generally, Annie had food in the kitchen. People came and went as they pleased, though several times a week they all managed to eat together. Tonight not being one of those nights, she grabbed a bowl of stew on her own. After-ward, she stood in the foyer pulling on all her layers to make the trek to her cabin—hat, gloves, jacket, boots. Just as she finished the whole production, Cam stepped inside, filling up the small area with his size and nearness that kept her warm in spite of the slap of frigid air he brought with him. "Hey."

"Hey yourself." He started to move past her, appeared to war with himself, then turned back.

She liked that he clearly had no idea what the hell to do about her, and rewarded that fact in a smile she couldn't have hidden anyway.

He shook his head but smiled back. He wore loose jeans, a hoodie sweatshirt with Wilder Adventures's logo on a pec, and a thick black scarf. He looked his usual scruffy, solidly muscled mountain-man self, and gorgeous with it, of course. Not to mention his scent. Good Lord, that scent should be bottled and sold under the name IMPENDING ORGASM. Just thinking it, she shivered.

He came close again, pulling off his scarf. Lifting it over her head, he settled it around her neck, still holding on to the ends. "Better?"

"I don't mind the cold," she murmured, turning her head so the scarf stroked her cheek. It held his body heat and smelled like him. Which was to say delicious.

Still holding her gaze, he slowly pulled on the ends of the scarf, tugging her closer.

Her pulse kicked into gear, her head fell back a little. *Another mind-blowing kiss, please . . .*

Looking down at her, he went very still. Only a heartbeat ago, he'd looked so big and bad and wickedly sexy, so sure of himself. And he was still big and bad and sexy, only suddenly he no longer seemed quite so sure. "You shouldn't look at me like that," he said softly.

"Like what?"

"Like you're good with being this close to me, like maybe you want to be even closer."

"You think you can read my mind?"

"You weren't thinking that?"

"Well, yes. But I wasn't going to say it out loud."

"Good. Don't. Not to me."

"So you don't want me to think about you."

"No." Slowly, with great care, he tucked the ends of the scarf inside her jacket, his fingers lingering on her throat, skimming over skin, causing all sorts of reactions within her. "Yes," he corrected, then shook his head. "Katie . . ."

Her eyes drifted shut. He had that effect on her, creating an odd state of bliss. And God, the way he said her name. She really hoped his sentence was going to end with "can I strip you naked and taste every square inch of you?"

"I'm not someone you want to get close to," he said instead.

Damn. That wasn't anywhere close. She opened her eyes. "How do you know what I want?"

"I'm going off the way you kissed me."

"Hey, there were two tongues in that kiss."

"I know. And I started it."

Well, that wasn't technically true. . . . But she didn't plan on mentioning that. "Good night, Cam."

Leaning past her, he opened the lodge door and gestured her out ahead of him. "You just got here," she said.

"I'm walking you to your cabin."

"You don't have to—"

"I'm walking you." When she didn't move, he took her hand in his.

The moon wasn't out yet, so it was a dark night, but she didn't notice any of that, just the man holding her gloved hand along the path. They didn't speak, which was fine with her. It wasn't talking she ached for.

Halfway there, the bushes rustled. Cam didn't even flinch, so she sucked it up and pretended not to notice.

At the front door of her cabin, she turned to face him. In his eyes was the same fierce hunger she was fighting inside of her own body, which was both cheering and sobering because he could fight this much better than she could. "Cam—"

"I mean it," he said quietly. "You don't want me. Trust me, this thing can't go anywhere. I don't have anything to give. Nothing. Do you understand?"

"I do." She looked pointedly at his hand, still holding hers. "But I'm not the someone touching the someone they don't want to get close to."

He immediately let go of her. "It's a good thing one of us is strong then, isn't it?"

"Me?" She laughed. "You think I'm so strong? I'm trying, believe me, but at this point, it's still just an illusion."

"You're here, doing something new. Out of your element and handling it. You *are* strong. You're one of the strongest women I know."

They were standing close, toe-to-toe. She wanted to be closer, she wanted to be touching, like they'd been on the snowmobile, and she let her gaze soak up his face, his mouth . . .

With a low moan, he leaned in and opened his mouth over hers, making her sigh in sheer, unadulterated pleasure.

A rough sound rumbled up from his chest, and he stepped into the kiss, slipping his hand around the back of her neck, gliding his tongue deeper, pulling her in tighter, hard to his body.

At her tremble, he broke off the kiss, though he took his time to do so, leaving his mouth touching hers for a few breaths before pulling all the way back.

"Cam—"

Breathing no steadier than she, he stroked a finger over her temple, then rimmed her ear. "Go inside, Katie."

She looked into his eyes. Yeah, he wanted her. It was there in the dark, swirling depths of his gaze, in the tension in his body, in the erection she could feel pressing into her belly.

He wanted her badly, which did her no good if he didn't

want to want her. So she did as he asked and went inside. Shutting the cabin door, she leaned back against it, heart still racing. He'd been right about one thing.

She was stronger than she'd thought. But so was he.

Several days later, on a "good road" day, Katie took a drive into Wishful to make a deposit for the business account. Stone had asked Cam to do it, but he'd come up with some excuse, making her realize that in the two weeks she'd been here, she'd never seen him go into town.

Because it'd snowed the night before, she drove one of Wilder Adventures trucks and held her breath the whole time. The roads had been declared clear, but that didn't mean anything to her. They were still white with snow, slippery as hell, and gave her more than one bad moment. She just kept telling herself that the cab was large and roomy, and there were no bridges.

But pulling into town always made her smile. Wishful was an authentic Old West mining town, filled with nineteenth-century false-front buildings. Back in the day, that being the 1800s, Wishful had been infamous for its wild saloons and lawless residents. Tamer now, it was still alive thanks to its close proximity to Lake Tahoe.

As she headed down the main street to the bank, she kept her eyes peeled for a source of caffeine. No Starbucks in sight. She got in and out of the bank in three minutes, then a sign caught her eye: WISHFUL DELIGHTS. From within the bakery came a mouthwatering scent that had her stomach quivering hopefully. She practically dove inside, delighted to find the place decorated like an old-time French café, complete with black wrought-iron tables and chairs, and pale-pink-and-white stripes on the walls, which held prints of the French countryside.

Behind the counter stood a tall brunette who was so beautiful she looked like she might be an actress playing the part of baker instead of the real thing. Perfectly put together in black pants, a white blouse, and a black-and-white checkered apron, she smiled pleasantly at Katie. "Hello."

"It smells like heaven in here." Her nose was twitching. "I'll take one of everything you've got in low fat."

The woman laughed softly. "Sorry. No low fat in the house."

Katie sighed. "Yeah, I was afraid of that."

"You're new. Small town," she explained at Katie's look of surprise. "Everyone knows everyone here, and I don't know you." She held out a tray with an assortment of the most spectacular-looking cookies Katie had ever seen. "Sample?"

"Oh, most definitely yes." Katie took a bite of something warm and soft and chocolaty, and it melted in her mouth. "My God. Some of those. Lots of those."

The woman nodded and began to fill a pretty black-and-white paper bag with the cookies, her gaze coming back to Katie, and the red bank bag she held that had WILDER ADVENTURES blazed across the front. "You're the temp at the lodge?"

"Yes. You know the Wilders?"

The woman wrapped a ribbon around the top of the bag to close it. "Everyone does."

"I guess they do," Katie said, still eyeing the samples, wondering if it would be rude to take another. "Cam told me the Wilders are somewhat of a legend around here."

The woman went still, her previously friendly expression switching to surprise. "Cam's back?"

"Yes." Katie pulled out her money and set it on the counter, reaching for the bag of cookies. "Thank you for the—"

But the woman didn't release the bag, her eyes registering shock, hurt, and—Oh, damn. Love.

"He's really back?"

Uh-oh. Had she just stumbled on to the reason Cam was avoiding town? "Yes, he's back." Again, she tried to pull her cookies free, but the woman had strong fingers. Must be all that kneading.

"I haven't seen him since just before his accident," the pastry chef murmured. "Nearly a year ago now." She paused. "Could you tell him something for me?"

"Uh—"

"Tell him to come see Serena?"

Katie nodded, thinking she could tell him all she wanted, but Cam didn't seem the type to do anything except what he felt like doing.

Serena finally released the cookies, and free to go, Katie mindlessly ate half of them on the drive back to the lodge. The snow was piled high in berms on either side of the road, which wasn't a problem except she felt a little claustrophobic. Or maybe that was the sugar rush. The temp had dropped, which made the roads more than a little icy and slippery. The rough going was jerking the truck around pretty good.

But she could handle it.

To ease the pre-panic attack feeling, she spoke out loud. "You're good. Town was nice. The cookies are great and . . . and I wish I knew what was between Serena and Cam . . ."

Whatever it was, it appeared to be over. But forgotten? Not for Serena, in any case. As for Cam, she couldn't say. She didn't know him well enough. Well, other than he made her yearn, made her laugh, and that he looked fantastic on a snowmobile.

And that he was a hell of a kisser.

But she had to admit he was more than that, much more. She'd seen him help run Wilder Adventures, deal with clients, seen him reveal a sharp, quick wit that was as attractive as his rare smile. He'd been hurt, so damn hurt, and yet he still managed to love and trust the small, tight circle he'd surrounded himself with.

Okay, so maybe she knew him better than she'd thought—

Her front tire caught a deep, icy groove in the road, and the truck lurched violently to the left. "Oh shit, oh shit." She fought the wheel, her entire life flashing before her eyes as the truck swerved, then slid toward a snow bank.

Okay, not her entire life, just the longest minute of her life, the one on the Santa Monica bridge. She'd slid then, too, slid right off the bridge—

Oh God. Her vision filled with black spots, not exactly conducive to driving; but just before she totally gave herself over to the panic, the truck's tire caught some traction. In a blink, she was back on the road, heading straight. Heart pounding nearly out of her chest, glasses crooked, she stopped the truck right there in the middle of the road and dropped her head to the steering wheel while she gulped in some air. And then some more, her hand to her chest to hold in her jumping heart.

She took another moment to breathe, but she couldn't just stay in the center of the road all day, even if she wanted to. So after a minute, she cautiously took off again. Going five miles per hour, she was grateful when no other car came up behind her so she didn't have to speed up. When she finally pulled up in front of the lodge, she got out on shaky legs and just barely managed not to be sick.

Cam was outside with a group of teenagers, handing out and signing gear: boards, boots, T-shirts, microfleeces, etc. They were all firing questions at him, laughing and nudging each other, having a great time.

Cam was smiling too. He glanced over at her, already lifting a hand in greeting when he got a closer look at her. He instantly handed over the Sharpie to the closest kid and headed straight for her.

Telling her heart to slow down, that she was fine, fine, fine, she pasted on a smile that he didn't buy.

"What's the matter?"

Not quite trusting her voice, she shook her head. *Nothing. I'm great. Just freaking great.*

He just kept looking at her in that deep, calm way he had, and she knew she could pretend all she wanted, that she wasn't really okay, not yet.

"Katie." He reached for her hand, which was clammy. It was twenty-five degrees and she was sweating.

"I'm fine," she managed, nodding now, doing her best impression of a bobblehead doll. But then he stepped a little closer, big and strong and capable, cupping the back of her neck in a warm hand. God. She wanted to be fine, she wanted that very badly, but it was hard to keep pretending with him looking at her like that, and she went from nodding to shaking it.

With a low sound of empathy, he pulled her in and stroked his hand down her back. "The truck? The roads? A flashback?"

"All of the above." Not going to cry, not going to cry . . . Angrily, she swiped the one tear that escaped and sniffed.

Above her, he set his chin on her head. "It's okay if you want to use my shirt as a tissue."

She choked out a laugh as he'd meant her to. "I'm fine."

"Yeah you are." He pulled back to look into her face. "And green to boot."

"I look good in green." Her voice was shaking. Dammit. She cleared her throat, pretending that she had a frog in it. "Okay, well, I'm going upstairs now."

"Give yourself a second—"

"I don't need any more seconds."

"Next time ask someone else to drive you—"

"No," she said far sharper than she'd intended. "I'm not quitting my life, Cam."

A quick flash of hurt crossed his features, but he was good, very good at masking his feelings, and it was gone when he stepped back from her. "Okay."

She sighed. "That was rude of me. I'm sorry."

"It's the truth, so don't be sorry." When he turned from her without another word, she let out a breath and headed up the stairs to the lodge.

Chapter 9

Annie stood in the foyer waiting for Katie. "Kitchen. *Now.*" Okay. Kitchen worked. There were chairs in the kitchen and she needed to sit down. She followed Annie, noting the chef's very baggy sweat bottoms and oversized T-shirt. Today's apron read: WARNING—COMPLAINTS TO THE CHEF MAY BE HAZARDOUS TO YOUR HEALTH.

In the kitchen, Annie handed over a plate loaded with lasagna, bread, and salad. "Sit. Eat."

Katie's hands were still trembling, but unfortunately no panic attack had ever stifled her appetite. She managed to stuff a bite into her mouth, then moaned in sheer pleasure.

"Yeah?" Annie asked, staring at her.

"Oh, yeah. Seriously, it's great. It's—"

"Yeah, yeah, I cook like an angel. Listen, I have a question."

"Okay."

"Did you see any of the guys today?"

Okay, so Annie had seen Cam hug her. "It's not what you think." Even if Katie wanted it to be exactly what Annie thought. "He was just . . . comforting me."

"You mean Cam. You and Cam?"

"Well . . . yeah. What did you mean?"

Annie was frowning. "He's not your type."

"No," she admitted. Her type was the laid-back LA guy who couldn't be bothered to tell her he already had a wife, or the guy who didn't call for a second date when he said he would. "He's more alpha than I'm used to. And a bit dark and broody. And—"

Annie arched a brow. "And?"

"And nothing." *Shut your mouth, Katie.* "Nothing. Subject dropped, sorry."

Annie stared at her for another beat, then visibly shook it off. "Okay, when I asked about seeing any of the guys today, I meant Nick."

Hey, good going. "I haven't seen Nick today at all. About that Cam thing, I—"

"Forget it." Annie looked like she was going to do her best to do the same. "Nick flew Stone and a group for a heli-ski, but they came back an hour ago. He usually comes into the kitchen to see me."

"But didn't you tell him not to talk to you ever again?"

"Well, I didn't mean it, did I?" Turning away, Annie started rinsing dishes. Her hair, in a loose knot on top of her head, vibrated with tension. "This is so . . . asinine!" She poured enough soap into the sink to wash all the dishes in California. "He stopped seeing me, you know. He stopped looking at me."

"Because you're divorcing him?"

"No, it's *why* I'm divorcing him—if he ever signs the damn papers. I told him to either look at me or find someone else. And he said he saw me just fine. He saw me standing between him and the damn TV. So I said get the hell out." Her face went from anger to hurt bewilderment. "And he did. He moved into his own cabin."

"Oh, Annie. I'm sorry."

"Asinine," she repeated.

"Maybe you could fix it."

"How?" Annie waved her sponge and bubbles rose in the air between them. "The man didn't see me! I've had a thing for him since second grade. I love him more than . . . more than *cooking*."

Katie tread carefully, knowing how proud Annie was, which actually seemed to be a universal Wilder trait. "Maybe he needs your help to see you."

Annie looked at her. "What? How hard is it? I'm standing right here."

"I know, but sometimes guys need to be hit over the head, so to speak. They're visual creatures."

"Oh, Christ on a stick. Don't say I need a damn makeover or some such shit like that."

"How about new clothes?"

Annie looked down at herself. "There's nothing wrong with these."

"No, not if you're a six-foot, two-hundred-pound teenage boy. You have such a great figure, but you hide it."

"I'm chunky."

"You're curvy," Katie corrected. "And if you dress for something other than the rumble in the parking lot, you could show it off a little. And—"

"Ohmigod. There's an 'and'?"

"A very little one. Makeup."

"I'm getting hot flashes these days. I'll just sweat it all off."

"Just a swipe of black mascara. And maybe some gloss. That's it. Maybe pick his favorite flavor."

"Peach." Annie sighed and went back to washing dishes. "His favorite flavor is peach. The damn skinny fool."

"I have some peach gloss, I'll give it to you. But it's not just the clothes and the gloss."

"I'm not doing anything crazy like Botox. I want to be able to look pissed off."

"I was going to say it's all in the attitude. And not a bad attitude." She nudged Annie's shoulders back. "Stand like you're worth something. Walk the walk, talk the talk."

"But I want him to see me *without* all the bullshit. The UPS guy manages to see me just fine."

"Because you smile at him," Katie pointed out. "You flirt. You don't do that with Nick."

Annie took that in a moment. "Well, hell. You just might be right about that." Her eyes narrowed. "Are you using this technique on my nephew?"

"Honestly, I have no idea what I'm doing with your nephew."

Annie's brow crinkled in worry. "You're only here for another two weeks."

"I know."

"Are you going to want to stay, and then eventually either run him over or screw him over?"

"Run him over?"

"Crazy ex. Don't ask."

"Okay," she said slowly. "A big negative to running him over, and also on the screwing over. I have my next adventure to get to."

Annie nodded, but her brow remained crinkled.

"What?"

"I'm just wondering what a guy who's done nothing but take a risk all his life is going to do with a woman who's never taken one until now, except get hurt."

A most excellent question. "No one's going to get hurt," Katie said, wanting to believe it.

That night, Katie finished up her work for the day and headed out of the lodge, where she found herself swallowed up by the night. No streetlights, no city lights, no tall buildings for landmarks, nothing but the glowing snow and the black outline of towering mountains and the even blacker night sky.

As she always did out here, she felt like the only person on the entire planet. Just her and the wild animals.

When the now-familiar rustling sound came from a snow-covered Manzanita bush, she was not too proud to whirl to run. She might have fallen if not for the hands that grabbed her and pulled her up against a hard, warm body.

"Just me."

That voice alone brought body parts to life, parts she'd almost forgotten existed. And let's not forget her handy-dandy trusty fogging glasses. "Cam."

"Expecting someone else?"

"Big Foot."

"Ah. So the bushes are rustling again."

"Probably hungry. I don't want to toot my own horn, but I probably look good enough to eat."

"I can vouch for that." He took her hand and started walking with her, looking tough and yet somehow gentle—an intoxicating mix.

"I forgot to mention something earlier," she said.

"You mean other than you think that I've quit my life?"

"I said I wasn't going to quit *my* life. The thing I forgot to mention was that after going to the bank, I ended up in a bakery. Wishful Delights."

And those eyes of his shuttered right up. It made her stomach drop, because up until that reaction she'd managed to hold out hope that she'd been mistaken about the emotion she'd seen on Serena's face. "Serena wants you to go see her."

He said nothing to that. Shock.

"You two were together," she ventured. "Which I guess had me wondering if you still are. Together."

At that, he looked at her, his eyes unfathomable, as dark as the night. "Do you think I'd have kissed you the way I did if I was with another woman?"

"I kissed you, remember?"

"Oh yeah, I remember." That dark gaze heated and so did all her good spots. "And then I very nearly took off all your clothes right there on the snowmobile and had my merry way with you."

"Yeah," she said, knees knocking. "That was my very favorite part, actually. Look, I'm fishing, okay? You're a puzzle, and I'm missing a lot of pieces, apparently one named Serena."

"Let's play a different game."

"I don't want to play games at all. Did you break her heart, Cam?"

"No."

"She break yours?"

His silence spoke for him.

Dammit. Dammit, Serena had hurt him. "Did it have anything to do with your accident?"

He shot her a look.

"Sorry. I tend to fill silences with chatter."

"Well, that explains a lot about you."

"Funny. What happened with Serena?"

He offered a shrug that was meant to be noncommittal but felt like a lot more. It had her throat tightening for him.

"She left me."

"Because of your mind-blowing conversational skills?"

"Ha. Yeah, that's not how it went."

"How did it go?"

"Guy traveled a lot. Girl got lonely."

"Guy was a famous ski champion," she pointed out. "Travel was par for the course."

"Didn't matter. She got tired of being alone and got herself laid. Then I got all butt hurt, crashed, lost my endorsements and entire future."

Her heart cracked for him. "Oh, Cam."

"Don't. Jesus. Don't pity me. I pitied myself plenty, all year long. And as you've ever so helpfully pointed out, I'm apparently still at it."

"Not all women cheat."

"True. The woman I dated before Serena tried to run me over with her car when I declined a third date."

She gaped at him. Annie hadn't been kidding. "Did she hit you?"

"Just nicked me. Luckily I'm fast."

"My God."

"Yeah, the woman before her took off after MTV's special *The Bad Boys of Winter.* She was in it for the long haul, but after seeing my segment, she decided a Wilder was a bad risk for her investment. I told you, Wilders are bad news, Goldilocks."

"The Wilders were all pretty badass in the past," she agreed. "But how about in this century?"

At her mocking tone, he slid her a glance. "I'm trying to scare you off here."

"Then tell me something scary."

He let out a low breath. "You are the oddest woman I've ever met."

"So I've been told." The dark, dark night continued to cocoon them, giving a sense of intimacy that Katie couldn't tell was real or her own hopeful imagination. The trees swayed in the wind, accompanied by the occasional hoot of something wild that she didn't want to know about. "Serena made a bad error in judgment, Cam, and the women before her were idiots. So your ancestors raped and pillaged the landside. Duly noted. Now tell me how that makes you bad?"

"I disappoint the women in my life."

"Not Annie."

"Serena is a friend of hers, a friend she didn't want me to date in the first place. She's in the middle and hates that. I put her there."

"Okay, maybe, but I don't buy that Annie would choose a friend over you. What about your mother?"

"Not a factor." He said this flatly, subject clearly closed.

When she just looked at him, he shook his head. "She left right after I was born."

He stood there casually, hands in his pockets now, looking like this was all okay, even perfectly normal, but it wasn't, and she felt something inside her crack open up to him.

He'd been so let down. Over and over again. "Putting aside the fact that none of any of that is your fault," she said quietly. "The Cameron Wilder I know so far? I'm pretty damn impressed with. Even if he won't have sex with me."

He choked out a laugh as they came to her front door.

"Yeah." She leaned back against the door. "I know you like that whole no regrets thing, but actually, I kind of feel the opposite. No holding back. Because if you hold back, it's boring. You shouldn't be bored with life, Cam. Not ever."

"I agree with that."

"So why aren't we naked?"

He let out a breath. "My radar's off," he said so sincerely that she laughed; then he laughed, too, and tugged her in for a hug. Turning them so that he was the one leaning back against the door now, he held her against him. "Are you sure, Katie? Are you sure you're not just saying what you think I want to hear?"

"I'm not *that* nice."

"So you're not out here looking for something permanent."

"The job's temporary. My being here is temporary. What could I be looking for?" At his expression, she had to laugh again. "Are you asking if I want a husband and two point five kids? Okay, you caught me. I do, but they're for the future. Don't be scared. In a week and a half, I'm out of here for the Real Adventures of Katie Kramer."

"Where are you going to go?"

"I don't know yet. I've saved every penny from my time here. I was thinking of doing that whole backpack across Europe thing."

"By yourself."

"Or that Alaska trip that T.J. is on sounds cool. Maybe I'll book one of those."

"What does your family think?"

"That I'm crazy. But in their defense, I've been the quite little Goody Two-Shoes all my life, never rocking the boat, never questioning authority . . . never doing any damn thing."

"Okay, I get that. But, Katie, have you ever backpacked before? Or gone mountain climbing?"

"That's sort of the point, big guy."

"And what about after that?"

"A plan, Cam? Really? You want me to have a plan when you don't?"

"Okay," he said. "That's not fair. You and I are different."

"Not as different as you think. Look, I'm not Serena. Or any of those other women. I hardly ever run people over. But things happen. Life's too short. Hearts get stomped on. We both know that better than anyone. It's no big deal."

"It *is* a big deal."

"Only if you dwell."

"Of which I've done my fair share of."

She smiled up at him as she slid her hands up his chest and into his hair. "You about done?"

That dragged another laugh out of him. "I think so, yeah."

She pressed her mouth to his jaw and nibbled. He groaned and turned his head, meeting her mouth with his, his tongue sliding against hers in a movement so delicious, so perfect, her knees wobbled.

That was new, having all her bones just sort of melt right out of her legs, which turned out not to be a problem because he had her. Then he turned them again, pressed her back up against the wood, a motion that freed up his hands, which she was all for. Except . . . She went still. "Did you hear that?"

He was kissing her neck. "I can't hear anything over the roar of the blood in my ears."

God, he was sexy. But she'd heard something. And if it was a hungry bear . . . "I think we should go in. You coming?"

"Hell, yeah, I'm coming. You're going to come too."

"You're talking about—"

"Yeah."

Her legs impersonated a bowl of jelly, and she yanked him against her, just as her door opened behind her, causing the two of them to fall inside.

Above them, still holding the door handle, stood Annie, staring down at them sprawled at her boots. "Oh, for the love of Pete."

"Annie," Katie gasped and sat up. "Hi."

"Oomph," Cam said when her elbow accidentally planted in his belly on his way up.

"I came to show you my new clothes." Annie put a hand on her hips. The other held a plate of brownies as she stared at Katie. "I brought these and Will Smith's latest DVD. Say you're going to pick me, my brownies, and Will over my knucklehead nephew."

Katie looked at Cam, who rolled to his feet. "Thanks," he said to Annie. "Good to know where we stand."

Annie sighed and lost her attitude. "I'm sorry. I think you two are a colossally bad idea, but Stone told me I had to stay out of it. I didn't know you were going to be here. She's the only girl here and I need a girl night. And you . . ." She divided a look between them. "You two need a cooling-off period." She shoved a brownie in Cam's hand, then pushed him over the threshold and shut the door in his face. "There. I thought he'd never leave."

Katie let out a breath and reached for the entire plate of brownies. So close. She'd been so close.

Chapter 10

By the crack of dawn, Annie was back in her kitchen making a boatload of sandwiches for Cam's day trip to Diamond Ridge. She had her hands full of sliced sharp cheddar and fresh honey-baked ham when Nick stormed into the kitchen.

He yanked off his ski cap and slapped it down to the counter. He had the most god-awful hat hair, hadn't shaved in at least two days, and his shirt was wrinkled. He looked ridiculously gruff and frustrated and disheveled, and just laying her eyes on him had butterflies executing summersaults in her belly. "What's your problem?" she asked with as much disinterest as she could mutter.

"You. You're my problem."

Her belly flopped again, unpleasantly this time. He'd been her high-school sweetheart. Her college fling. The man of her dreams. They'd married young, and things had been great. And then they hadn't, but it'd happened so gradually she hadn't noticed until it'd been too late. She'd gotten lazy and had let things drift. And then she'd compounded the error by getting stupid on top of lazy, and she'd quit him.

And now he was quitting her.

All her fault, and she'd deal with that. Was trying to deal with that. "Well, soon enough I won't be your problem at all. As soon as you sign the *damn papers.*"

He swore roughly beneath his breath. "Not what I meant, Annie."

"Then what did you mean?"

"About what you said, about this me not seeing you shit." He hesitated and looked at her the way he used to, with bewildered affection in the mix now. "I was thinking."

"Yeah?"

"Is it something I could fix?"

Her heart actually skipped a beat and she dropped eye contact, busying herself with washing her hands. She'd been waiting and waiting for him to ask that question, and he never had—until now. "You're a pilot and a mechanic. You fix stuff for a living. Theoretically, you'd be a cinch at fixing anything."

"Goddammit, Annie. I need a direct answer."

She went to work making coffee. "Yes," she said after a minute, "I think you can fix it."

"Okay." He nodded. "Does that statement come with directions?"

She met his gaze. "I want you to know how to fix it."

He let out a long breath. "I really hate that answer."

"You know what I hate, Nick?" She set down the coffeepot rather than throw it at his head. "I hate the way you talk to me as if you don't already *know* every single thing about me, the way I know everything about you, down to the fact that you're probably wearing stupid boxers right this minute just because I can't stand them."

"I'm not—" He broke off, pulled out the waistband of his jeans to look, then sighed. "Okay, I am, but only cuz it's laundry day."

She shook her head and pointed to his. "I also hate the way you forget to comb your hair after you wash it and it falls over your eyes." She rolled her eyes when he tried to pat it down. "I hate the way you can read my mind when I don't want you to and not when I *do* want you to." At that, the fight went out of her and she leaned back against the counter. "And I really hate that even with all that, I still don't hate *you*. That I want you to fight for me." Her throat burned, and defeated, she tossed up her hands. "I just want you to see me, Nick."

"Ah, Annie." His voice was soft and slightly gruff as his frustrated demeanor drained. "I see you every single day."

"Then show it." She so desperately needed that. "I need you to show it, Nick."

He scrubbed a hand over his face while she stood there staring at him, yearning, aching. "I'll try," he said.

"That'd be really great." She cleared her tight throat. "In return, I think it's only fair that you give me something to work on. For you. To please you."

She had the pleasure of surprising him; then an unmistakable wicked gleam came into his eyes and she had to laugh. "You'd actually want me that way?" she asked. "In bed? When we're scarcely talking?"

"Hell yeah."

Men. "How about *outside* the bedroom, Nick?"

"Anywhere," he said fervently.

And she had to laugh. "I meant how about me pleasing you while *not having sex*?"

"Oh. Well . . ." He gave the question some thought, which was one thing she'd always loved about him. There was no subterfuge with Nick, no guessing at hidden meaning. If he was mad, she knew it. If he was happy, she knew it. No games.

"Maybe I want you to see me too," he finally said.

She was still staring at him when Cam came into the kitchen. Annie had done her best to leave him out of this thing with her marriage as much as possible because dissension between her and Nick had always bothered him, and after all these years and in spite of the fact that he was a foot taller than her, he was still *hers*, a little, hurting kid who'd been given up by both his parents and needed protecting. Still protecting him, she managed a smile in his direction. "How was the brownie?"

"Amazing." Not fooled, Cam eyed them both. "Do you two need to go to your separate corners?"

"No." Nick had always loved Cam as Annie had, and that had never changed. He clasped a hand on Cam's shoulder. "We're good." Then with one last look at Annie, one that held frustration with a glimmer of an old heat—which sparked a matching one burning inside her—he left.

Cam turned to Annie. "You're good?" he repeated. "Since when?"

Annie handed him a mug of coffee. "We're going to try to *see* each other."

"Okay." He took a sip of the coffee. "And what the hell does that mean?"

Annie sighed. "I really haven't a clue."

"Whose idea was this?"

"Some idiot's."

"Some idiot by the name of Annie?"

Annie slid him a glance. "Dammit. Yes."

Cam burst out laughing, and the sound was so beautiful, so unexpected yet longed for, she just stared at him. "I thought you'd be mad at me."

"I was. You are a nosy, bossy, mean, mean woman."

"I try."

He laughed again, and she could not stop staring at him. "What's coming over you?"

"Nothing. I don't know."

"Huh. Well, whatever it is, I like it."

He just sipped his coffee, and so did she, somehow feeling a little easier at heart for the both of them.

Cam left later for a two-day trip with Stone, taking a group

snow climbing up to the frozen Jackson Lakes, a trip he'd
planned and organized. And as Annie went on with her day,
something different happened. Instead of the usual resent-
ment and anger eating her up during the hours, she had something new stirring in her belly.

Hope.

For all of them.

Cam and Stone climbed mountain peaks all day with a
group from the Bay Area, and it was good. It would have been
great except Cam couldn't think of anything other than getting back to Katie's cabin to continue their whole getting
naked thing.

Actually, he thought of a lot of other things too. Things like
maybe she'd been right to call him on his shit. He *hadn't*
moved on.

He needed to move on . . .

Two days later when they returned to the lodge, Katie was
at her desk, and as he passed by, she smiled at him. He returned it, and her glasses fogged, which was fun.

She'd missed him too.

While she dealt with the ringing phone, he went to his office to change. He'd just stripped out of his shirt when she
knocked on his open door.

"Hey," he said, turning to face her.

She was staring at his chest. Admittedly gratifying. So was
the blush working its way up her throat to her cheeks as her
eyes caught on the narrow tribal band tattooed around his
bicep. "You have a tattoo," she murmured. "It looks . . ." She
bit her lower lip. "Tribal."

"I got it in Africa." He pulled on a black long-sleeved ther-
mal. "How's it been going?"

"Great." She swallowed. "Except I can't seem to find my
tongue."

Oh man. He wanted to strip down again, and then strip her. But first things first. He reluctantly pulled on an outer shell with WILDER blazoned across the front.

"You have a good trip?" she asked.

"Yeah."

"I saw the schedule. You're giving boarding lessons tomorrow."

"Not really. Just meeting a few local kids to go over technique and style, and how to get sponsored. They're on the team at school and their coach doesn't have a lot of experience at that end."

"That's sweet of you."

He looked at her, feeling decidedly unsweet. "Come here."

She swallowed again. "Really? Here?"

He wished. But he gestured her closer and she nearly killed herself to get across the room. He took her hand and opened his closet. It was filled to the brim with outdoor equipment for any kind of adventure one could want.

She looked around. "There's no place to—"

"Pick one."

"Um . . . what?"

"Pick your next adventure."

She blushed, then pushed up her glasses. "OH! Oh, you want me to pick out equipment. I thought—"

"Yeah, I know what you thought," he said, nearly groaning at the look of disappointment on her face. She'd wanted him in the closet. Just the thought made him hard. "That's next. This first."

She stared at him, then tore her gaze from his and touched a pair of skis. Downhill skis. His gut clenched.

He'd figure she'd pick snowshoes, or cross-country skis. Despite his numerous attempts, he still hadn't been on downhill skis or a board since his crash, managing to avoid both like the plague, and everyone had let him.

"These are nice," she said, running her fingers over the edges.

Skiing and sex.

He'd once been great at both. Okay, well it seemed as if Katie wasn't the only one taking a risk today. He pulled out the skis instead of facing the truth.

He was actually procrastinating sex.

God, that was a tough one to swallow.

He had no doubt he could turn on the charm and get her in his bed right this very minute—hell, she would have taken the closet—and it would be great.

But then . . .

Yeah, it was the *but then* tripping him up. It could be any of a hundred things, he had no idea exactly, but he could guarantee it would end badly.

It always did.

And he didn't want this to end.

How ironic was that? He'd always slept with the women he liked. He'd slept with them and then it'd been over. Now this thing was going to be over soon regardless, and he *hadn't* slept with her.

By choice.

He'd lost more than his nerve after his crash—he'd lost his mind.

Katie was still running her hand along the skis. "They look fast."

"You've skied?"

"Not since high school."

"That's okay. It's like getting on a bike."

"I thought having sex was going to be like getting on a bike."

Okay, still hard. "If there is any justice, it'll be even easier. Try these." He tossed her a set of ski pants from the new samples—sleek and black and formfitting.

"These would *maybe* fit if I hadn't been eating Annie's food for two-and-a-half weeks."

He took in her maroon turtleneck sweater, which hugged mouthwatering breasts. Her gray wool pants did the same for her legs and ass, an ass he'd stared at enough times to know exactly what would work on it. "They'll fit."

"Okay, but if I burst out of them, it's all your fault."

And he'd be happy to take that blame. "Don't worry."

"Me worry? I left that behind in Los Angeles." She smiled wryly. "Mostly."

"It's going to be okay, Goldilocks. We'll stay on the easy runs. Now hurry and change, we're burning daylight. I'll wait for you out front."

And then, because she just stood there a little dazed, a little overwhelmed, and a whole lot adorably sexy, he leaned and kissed her.

No idea why.

Okay, maybe he knew exactly why. Because he couldn't get enough. Pulling back, he watched her glasses start to fog. He really loved knowing he did that to her. And after skiing, he was going to do a hell of a lot more to her.

For her.

And then . . . and then if history was any indication, he'd screw it all up somehow.

But that for later. For now, with her still staring up at him in sexy wonder, he left her alone in his office to change.

Chapter 11

Katie looked down at the ski pants in her hand, her heart pounding. They weren't going to have sex in his closet. They were going skiing.

Dazed, she tugged down her pants, then proceeded to get them stuck on her boots. Crouching to fix the problem, she had to laugh at herself—not exactly how she'd imagined getting naked in Cam's office. Giving up on the pants, she unlaced her damn boots, then nearly jumped out of her skin at the low scraping sound beneath the desk.

It was the same sound she heard outside the bushes every time she walked by them. Somehow her animal stalker was in this very office with her, possibly planning on eating her alive. Oh, no. Not going out like this, and she leaped back.

And tripped over the pants around her ankles. Her flailing arms knocked over a huge stack of skis and poles on the way down, all of which fell in a spectacularly noisy cascade to the floor as she landed in a graceless heap on her butt.

Someone came pounding down the hall. "Katie?"

Oh, God. She yelled, "Don't come in—"

But the door whipped open, and Cam stood there staring at her.

She couldn't blame him. She lay on her back, draped over a pile of skis and poles, her pants still around her ankles. She decided to take some comfort in the fact that she wasn't wearing either granny panties or a thong, but a nice pair of cotton bikinis in a demure pale pink.

With a picture of Hello Kitty on the front.

She'd have been far happier in a suit of armor, but what could she do?

Cam crouched by her side. "Are you hurt?"

"No!" She tried to sit up. Not easy with no stomach muscles and her feet weighted down. She straightened her glasses. "And I said don't come in."

He was looking at her panties and smiling. "Hello Kitty."

"As in Don't. Come. In."

"You screamed."

"I did not." Scooting backward, she rolled over and staggered to her feet, pointing to his desk while scrambling to pull up her pants. "And you have a wild animal under there. You—" She stopped when he bent to look and let out a huff of laughter. "What? What's so damn funny?"

"It's just Chuck."

"Chuck." She pictured a rabid coyote. A psycho wild turkey. "Who's Chuck?"

"Take a look for yourself."

She glared at him, then bent a little and peered beneath the desk.

Sitting down there among a few electrical cords and a forgotten pair of athletic shoes was a scrawny, patchy gray cat, nearly all skin and bones.

"He adopted this place a while back apparently, when I was gone. He's feral, and comes and goes as he pleases, though he hasn't been around too much lately. Doesn't like new people."

Chuck was a cat. She bent down and took another peek.

Yep. A cat. Sort of. He had whole chunks of fur missing, and the biggest green eyes she'd ever seen, making him look more like a baby ostrich.

"He's not much of a people person," Cam told her. "But he won't hurt you. I won't hurt you either, Goldilocks."

"Ha."

"Come here, kitty, kitty." Instead of waiting, he stepped toward her, his eyes flashing an assortment of things, most of which made her heart skip more than a few beats.

"Trying to get dressed here."

"I know." Stopping just short of touching her, he dipped his head and took a good look at her from head to toe and back again, lingering at her unzipped pants. "Pale pink is my new favorite color."

She stared into his amused, very heated eyes and felt all her good parts quiver. "You could have seen them up close and personal in the closet. You chose skiing."

"I'm a stupid, stupid man."

Their lips were less than an inch apart. She stared into his eyes, then at his mouth.

"Katie." His voice was low, thrillingly rough as he lifted a hand and ran his thumb over her lower lip. It tingled for another kiss, and she closed her eyes . . .

He gently pulled off her glasses, then not so gently kissed her, long and deep. Her bones went all soft and gushy, but nothing on *him* felt soft and gushy, especially not what was pressing into her stomach.

"One more," he said, his mouth moving down her neck.

"Two would be okay . . ."

With a low laugh, he slid his warm hands up the back of her sweater, making her want to stretch and purr like a kitten. "God, you feel good."

"Yeah. Same goes."

"Skiing," he whispered against her lips, before removing his hands from her and stepping back. He nodded and let out a rough breath. "Skiing. I'll wait out in the hallway."

When he was gone, she let out a rough breath of her own, then stepped out of her pants—removing her boots first this time—and pulled on the ski pants. He'd been right, they did fit.

Like a damn glove.

She moved to the desk and bent down to look at Chuck. "Hey, cutie. What do you think?"

He didn't even blink. Just stared at her with those heart-breaking eyes.

"Right. I'm asking for trouble." She reached out a hand to stroke him, but he put his ears back and let out a low warning rumble. "Okay, have it your way, but I'll charm you yet."

More than a little self-conscious about the pants, she went out into the hallway, where one tall, dark, and oh-so-gorgeous man leaned against the wall waiting for her, eyes hot. "You look great," he said.

Her good parts clamored as he handed her a jacket, hat, and a pair of gloves. He watched her add the extra layers. "I'm an idiot to have given you all that to wear." His sexual frustration was the third person in the room.

Hers was the fourth.

Having no idea where this was going exactly, but suddenly enjoying the ride, Katie straightened. "Let's do this. Let's ski."

Cam had been around the world looking for something to give him a new rush, to kick-start his heart, and he hadn't found it. And yet here he was, his heart kick-started by a woman.

Clearly, he'd lost his mind.

No, Katie had lost her pants, and *then* he'd lost his mind. She'd stood there half naked in his office, wearing a snug sweater and those adorably sexy panties and nothing else, looking more than a little frazzled by Chuck.

And by him.

And he'd gotten turned on. So damn turned on.

So had she.

Okay, so that might be a little self-congratulatory, but it sure as hell hadn't been the cat to make her nipples hard and pouty against the thin material of her sweater.

Now she was covered from head to toe in the best of the best gear available.

Well, hell. He'd come back home to feel something, anything, and it was working. He was definitely feeling something, though not necessarily with his head. At least not the one on top of his shoulders.

He carried his board and her skis, leading her to the equipment garage where he pointed to the Sno-Cat. "That's the fastest way to get there. You up for it?"

"I'm up for all of it. The question is . . ." She waggled a brow. "Are you?"

He laughed. "I've been 'up' since I met you. Get in."

He watched her eye the machine that just last week had struck terror into her heart. With a deep breath, she climbed into it while he enjoyed the way the ski pants fit her ass, picturing those pink panties he knew she wore beneath . . . but also feeling a wave of something other than lust, something deeper.

Because no matter what she said, or how big a smile she flashed him, he knew she was still scared of the Sno-Cat.

And still completely handling herself.

The women in his life had mostly fit into two categories: snowboarder groupies and fortune hunters. Katie didn't fit into either. She certainly wasn't here to stroke his ego or fawn all over him. And she didn't seem to want anything from him.

She could have no idea how attractive that was to a guy like him. He climbed up beside her and hit the gas, not missing how she gripped the sides of her seat.

"We're okay," he assured her.

"I know. One of these days, though, we're going to have to do something I'm good at."

"And what are you good at?"

She flashed him a smile. "Guess."

Once again, he went instantly hard, which both startled and amused him. "*Now* you tell me."

"Hey, this was your idea, big guy. You could be in the closet right now, with me. Naked. And I look damn good naked."

"I bet you do."

"I was hoping to see how good *you* look."

He laughed, laughed while hard, and he knew right then.

He could guard his heart all he wanted, but it was too late. She'd sneaked in past his defenses and leveled him flat on his ass, and now he was down for the count.

Katie stood at the base of the mountain looking up, up, up to where the ski lift vanished just over the peak, and swallowed hard. The ski resort looked like a European Alps village, pretty and quaint, full of old-school charm and character, and if she hadn't been scared to death about making her way down the steep, *steep* mountain looming over it with two skis strapped to her feet, she'd have happily explored the shops and restaurants to her heart's content.

Cam had given her a lift pass, which hung around her neck. She was holding her poles while he held both his board and her skis. With ease, she might add, using all those muscles she was so fond of looking at. At the moment, however, she wasn't looking at him but the terrain, so white against a shocking blue sky. The wind was blowing a white mist of powder snow from the very tip of the mountain into the air. It was gorgeous, and terrifying.

Cam laid out her skis for her. She stepped into the bindings while he locked one of his boots into the bindings on his board.

When he glanced at her, she pasted a smile on her face and let him guide her closer, up the small hill to the lift. The young woman running it wore a ski cap low over her eyes, hair flowing to her waist. She was chewing gum and looking bored, until she saw Cam and her entire face lit up. "Hey there, you!"

"Heidi. How are you doing?"

"Good. Better now." To prove it, she threw herself at him. "I'm so happy to see you!"

Katie would have liked to obsess over the full-body contact Heidi was managing to get with Cam, but she was too busy struggling to stay on the incline without rolling back. There was ice beneath her skis. In serious danger of slipping backward into the line of people behind her, she desperately used her poles to hold herself in place, making her biceps tremble with the strain, threatening to give out while Cam just stood there listening to Heidi babble all over him.

"I'm just so glad you're back," she was saying cheerfully, arms still loped around his neck.

Or at least that's what her mouth was saying. Her eyes were saying, *I want to lap you up like a bowl of ice cream.*

Katie struggled harder not to kill everyone in line behind her, but any second now she was going to slide backward.

And then, it happened. Her poles slipped, and with a gasp she began to go—

Cam's warm hand settled at her back, miraculously holding her in place, easily nudging her forward and off the ice patch.

She gritted her teeth. "You could have done that a lot sooner."

"I was never going to let you fall."

"Now you tell me. My arms are already killing me."

"Do you exercise?"

"It's on my to-do list." At the bottom, but still . . .

"I'd give you the your-body-is-your-temple speech, but your body . . ." He paused to look her over from head to toe and back again, causing certain portions of her anatomy to flicker to life. "Well, I'd worship as is."

Her knees wobbled. "Stop that."

"Really?"

"No."

He out and out grinned, and the rest of her body acted fairly predictably.

"Are you ready?"

She took a look at the lift coming around for them at what seemed like the speed of light and gathered her courage. "Ready," she whispered, and willed it to be true.

Chapter 12

Cam watched the lift come toward them with a heavy dose of his own nerves. His first time back on a board . . . He'd have wallowed in that, but he caught sight of Katie's fierce going-into-battle expression, and he managed to forget about himself. "You okay?"

"I think so." She glanced at him, then frowned. "Are you?"

"Always."

"Because you look—"

"Scoot a little closer," he said as the ski lift came around to scoop them up.

Suitably distracted, Katie gave it her all, but the seat of the lift hit her in the back of the knees, ripping a startled "Oh!" out of her and then a cry of distress as she began to go down.

Cam snagged the back of her jacket as he sat on the lift, holding her up as he did, pulling her onto the seat next to him.

"Ohmigod," she gasped, clutching his arm to her breasts as the lift took off, lifting them up, up, and farther up. *"Ohmigod."*

"I've got you," he promised, but she continued to grip his arm with the force of the jaws of life. "Don't worry, you're not going to fall now."

Neither of them was.

"Okay." She gulped in air, and he felt a little like doing that, too, but then he realized her eyes were closed. "Hey, Goldilocks."

"Yeah?"

"You've got your eyes closed."

She cracked one open. "I forgot something."

"What's that?"

"I don't like heights. Which in hindsight is really, really going to get in the way of my adventures. After this, I'm going with things that don't require height." She closed her eye again.

"Hate to break this to you, but mountain climbing requires heights. And to backpack in Europe, you'd have to fly."

"Good points. I have a backup plan."

"Like?" He planned to keep her talking so that she'd forget they were now fifty feet up, zooming across the terrain to the top of the peak. Yeah, that was all he was thinking about, keeping her comfortable. It had nothing at all to do with him needing his own distraction. Good thing he wasn't nearly as honest as she was.

"Besides learning to risk, I'd like to eventually find a place where I belong."

"Good one? Anything else?"

Eyes still closed, she turned her face toward the late-afternoon sun, and the last of the questionable warmth of the day. The wind played with her hair and pinkened her cheeks. "Actually . . ." She squirmed a little. "Something new has recently come to me."

"Spill."

More squirming, and a visible wince to boot, which piqued his interest. "It's private," she finally said. "Are we there yet?"

"Almost." She was gnawing on her lower lip, which he had the most insane urge to take over for her. "How private?"

"*Very* private."

"Can I guess?"

"No." She opened her eyes. "No guessing." She took a peek around her and squeaked, *"Oh my God."*

Reaching out, he put a finger beneath her chin and turned her gaze back to him, off the view *and* the drop. "A one-night stand?"

She covered her very red cheeks. "I said *no* guessing."

He grinned. "Really? I'm right?"

"Close."

"How close?"

"Great sex, okay? I wanted great sex."

He knew she was waiting for a response, but he had nothing. He had shit-for-brains-nothing because all he could think was . . . *I could give her great sex.*

She blew out a breath and slapped her hands over her eyes, her face even redder. "You know what? I really don't want to discuss this anymore."

"Too late." Charmed by her embarrassment, and also by her sheer, utter honesty, he leaned in and removed her hands from her face. "Great sex isn't all that hard to come by."

"Tell that to the guys in Los Angeles."

"The guys in Los Angeles must be idiots. And you should know, I'm no better than those Los Angeles assholes."

"So you don't get great sex either?"

Christ, she was killing him.

Killing.

Him.

"Listen to me." He took both her hands in his. "I want you. Make no mistake about that. And I know how to make it good, make no mistake about that either. But—"

"Oh my God."

"Yeah, you're right." He winced. "And that sounded like I was bragging. I wasn't, I was just—"

"No, I mean, *Ohmigod, the lift!*" Looking panicked, she turned to him, clutching his arms. "It's ending!"

"You can do it." They both could. "You just glide off and—"

"I should have mentioned . . ." Her eyes were huge. "I'm not good at this part either."

"No problem. When I say now, just stand up and I'll give you a little nudge, and you just ski forward and out of the way. *Now.*"

She glided off, he gave her a little nudge to the small of her back, just as planned. What wasn't planned was the pole she planted, then ran over with one of her skis, which rudely yanked her to the side and then down to the ground.

Screaming the whole time.

Once again Cam fisted his hand in the back of her jacket and hauled her upright, just as the skiers behind them dismounted their chair and nearly ran her over. Moving them both to the side, Cam waited for her to catch her breath. She was gripping the front of his jacket as if her legs weren't quite steady.

He knew the feeling.

Her ski cap had slid down over one eye, her glasses were askance, but she looked up at him and shot him a wry smile.

And absolutely melted his heart.

"I promise, I'm better at the rest," she said, and blew a strand of hair from her face.

There wasn't a woman he knew who could make the best of every situation and keep a positive attitude, including Annie, whom he'd loved since the beginning of time. Quite simply, he'd never met a woman like Katie. Ever. "You okay?"

"Physically, yes. Mentally? The jury's still out." She straightened her cap. "Okay, let's do this. Let's see this run you've got in mind."

"Mt. Easy."

"Mt. Easy?" she repeated.

"It's the bunny slope."

"You don't think I can do this."

"Listen, Mt. Easy is a very nice run, and—"

"You *really* don't think I can do this."

"Okay, let's just say I want to be sure." For both of them. She lifted her chin. "You know what? Bring it on, hotshot. I'm going to show you what I've got." She turned herself and started poling toward the face of the mountain, which happened to be an expert-only run. He should know, the trail was named after him.

"Katie."

"No, I've got this. I'm going to show you what I'm made out of, Cameron Wilder, holder of all the world titles, I—"

"Katie."

"I really can do this, you know, I—" Her breath left her in a *whoosh* when she got close enough to look down at the 2,000-foot steep, moguls-as-high-as-a-house run.

"That's a double diamond," he told her. "It's called Wilder Way."

She stopped so fast her cap slid into her eyes again. "Okay, you know what? Maybe you should lead."

Katie survived skiing in no small part thanks to Cam, who looked like poetry in motion on his board. She could have watched that long, lean, tough body move all damn day, but that wasn't conducive to staying upright on her skis. He encouraged her to make the best of the slopes, correcting her dubious technique when she asked, but he let her have her adrenaline rush, which she did in spades. Hitting the hills with the wind in her face and some questionable speed beneath her skis turned out to be the most exhilarating thing she'd done in a long time.

"So," he said when it was all over and done as they pulled up to the lodge. "Was that good for you?"

Her heart began to hammer because she thought—hoped—she knew what was going to come next—*them*. "It was the best time I've had here yet."

"I'm thinking we can top it." He shut off the Sno-Cat and turned to her, one arm on her head rest, the other sliding over her belly to hold her hip, crowding her a little, which she happened to like.

She crowded him, too, leaning into him. "What did you have in mind?"

With a low laugh, he nuzzled the curve of her neck, which pretty much sizzled her brain cells and melted her bones into mush. He began working his way up to her jaw, coaxing her into a heated bliss as he made his way to her mouth, when he went still.

She opened her eyes.

His were opened too. Not on her but on something behind her. Craning her neck, she locked gazes with Stone outside the Sno-Cat.

"I need to talk to you," Stone said to Cam.

"Busy here."

"Busier than you think. Your group showed up a day early for their cross-country ski into Glory Valley. Crossed wires, I guess."

"Maybe you could take the trip."

"I have something else lined up."

"Yes," Cam said, shooting his brother a meaningful look, "but it's probably not as important as my thing."

Stone just shook his head. "You're up, dude," was all he said, and walked away.

Cam let out a breath. "It's a conspiracy," he muttered.

"What?"

"I'm sorry, I've got to go lead the trip. After I kill my brother."

With sex off the table, Katie headed inside the lodge. Annie was in the kitchen cleaning up after serving their guests chicken enchiladas. One look at her had Katie sighing—baggy jeans, a bulky sweater, and an apron that read: NEVER TRUST A SKINNY CHEF.

Though she'd rather be burning calories right now instead of consuming them, Katie got herself a plate. "Nice apron. What happened to your new clothes?"

Annie grated some more cheese for her. "You ever have a day that's just a complete waste of mascara?"

"You don't wear mascara."

"It's a good thing too. Today would have been a waste of it."

"Annie, you're on a mission, remember? Getting Nick to see you."

"Yeah." Annie stopped with the busy work and leaned back against the counter. "I'm afraid."

"Of what, wearing clothes that fit you?"

"I'm afraid that he still won't see me and then I'll have to kill him. If you think I look bad in these clothes, think of how I'd look in prison garb."

Katie laughed. "Look, I've seen the way Nick looks at you. He's going to see you, I promise. Now remember, you're as fierce as they come. Go show it."

Annie arched a brow. "Aren't you mighty."

"Hey, I'm the Mighty Queen. Besides, you have to dream it to live it."

"You dreamed about running an office out in the middle of nowhere?"

"I dreamed about living my life to its fullest. Balls out."

"You don't have any."

"It's a euphemism."

"Yeah, I don't think I'm as optimistic as you."

"Maybe you ought to try that too." Katie wrapped some extra cheese in a napkin for Chuck and stuffed it into her pocket, determined to win him over yet.

It was snowing. Light, plentiful flakes drifting through the air with a silent beauty, stacking on top of the already snow-ladened landscape.

The bushes didn't rustle.

Back in her cabin, Katie stood at the door and called for the scraggly cat. When he didn't come, she left the cheese out on the doorstep. She put on her pj's and looked at herself in the mirror. Men's boxers and a cami. Not exactly Victoria's Secret material, but it was all she had. She tried to keep her eyes open, listening for Chuck, listening for Cam.

Neither came.

In the morning, she woke up sore and stiff from her foray on the mountain. Walking like an old woman, she opened her door and checked for the cheese.

It was gone, probably courtesy of the fat raccoon waddling off her porch. "Hey, that cheese wasn't for you!"

The big guy actually stopped and craned his neck, giving her a look that had her letting out a startled squeak and slamming the door. She showered and dressed, then tentatively opened the door again.

No raccoon.

No Chuck either . . .

But lots of fresh snow. She made her way through it, which someone had thankfully shoveled from her path all the way to the lodge's front door. She went directly to the kitchen, where Annie shoved a plate of food and a hot mug of coffee into her hands.

"The guys got stuck on the pass last night," Annie said. "Trapped there by the storm."

"Are they okay?"

"They're boys. They love that stuff." Annie looked at her speculatively. "You didn't tell me you skied with Cam."

Katie blinked. "I thought you knew." She paused at the look on Annie's face. "Is that okay?"

"He hasn't been on his snowboard since his accident."

Katie went still, then sank to a chair. "He hasn't?"

"No."

"But . . . I've seen him go off with his board."

"Apparently he never has been able to actually use it. Until yesterday, with you."

"My God." Why hadn't she known that? "I had no idea." Her mind raced back to being in his office. She'd been sidetracked by their chemistry, and then in the Sno-Cat she'd been caught up in her nerves. But just before the lift, she'd sensed something from him, and then she'd been distracted by Heidi, and . . . and dammit. He had seemed just a little off, but then she'd fallen from the lift. "I should have asked."

"He probably wouldn't have said. He's too damn proud for his own good." Annie shook her head. "Right after the accident, he wasn't healthy enough to get back on a board, and then when he was, he left. Just took off. Now he's back, and he's running trips, but never the downhill trips. Stone's done them all."

"Yeah, I noticed that." She thought back to how careful he'd been with her on the mountain, how perfectly kind, never letting on to what must have been a hugely emotional thing for him, and she felt like crap. "I stopped the whole lift. My first time up the hill, I fell off at the end. I was just so nervous, and he . . . he was so sweet. I feel so ridiculous now, given what he must have been feeling."

"And he never let on?"

"No, he was steady as a rock."

"No limp?"

"A little, the usual, but he didn't seem like he was in pain."

"Well, that's good then."

"How exactly is that good, him keeping in his feelings?"

Annie looked taken aback. "Keeping in his feelings? What does that have to do with anything? If he did fine, he's over it."

Katie was beginning to understand not just where Cam had gotten some of his reticence from, but also what Nick was dealing with. "It helps to talk out stuff, Annie. He might have gotten 'over it' a lot sooner than a whole year if he had."

Annie shook her head. "You weren't here, so let me tell you how bad it was. Three surgeries. After the first one he got an infection that nearly took his leg. The doctor told him to get used to a wheelchair. Cam proved him wrong, but it was a month, one long month before he could walk, and then when he could, he still had to give up his entire life."

"I understand. It was awful, *tragic*. But, Annie, why was boarding his entire life?"

"I—" Annie stopped. Blinked. "You know, I never saw a problem with that until just now." She sank to a chair and stared out the window. "All this time I thought I was doing him a favor, babying him, letting him *not* get back out there. Letting him not talk about it . . . I thought it was for the best, not forcing him into anything." Her eyes were shiny when they met Katie's. *"Damn."*

"Well, he got out there yesterday. And looked like he was born to it, I might say. He was amazing."

Annie smiled. "He *was* born to it. Growing up, if he wasn't being worked into the ground by his father, he was on the slopes. Once I got him, he lived on that mountain."

"He was lucky to have you."

"Hell yeah, he was. Did you ski his namesake, Wilder Way?"

Katie let out a little laugh. "Uh, hello, remember me, the woman who stopped the lift? We stayed on the bunny slopes."

Annie choked on that. "The *bunny* slopes?"

"He said that it was good practice for him."

"Honey, that boy used to heli-ski into places that would make your hiney twitch, where even the photogs wouldn't go to catch him on film, and then he'd huck himself off cliffs. For *fun*." She shook her head. "Practice. Good Lord, he must have it bad." She slid her gaze over Katie. "And so do you. Jesus."

"You think he and I would be a mistake?"

"Are you still leaving?"

"Yes."

"Then, yes, it would be a mistake. For both of you."

Chapter 13

Stone and Cam didn't get home that night either. The storm caught a group of skiers off guard near Mt. Bliss, and the guys joined the Search and Rescue team to help locate two missing skiers.

Katie slept in her warm bed and thought about Cam out there on the mountain, out in the elements. Not only surviving but trying to help others do the same.

And she'd been so proud of herself, being so "risky" here at Wilder. She didn't have a clue. She fell asleep determined to reach even deeper for more.

Balls out.

The next morning, she went to the lodge, grabbed some food, then went upstairs to her desk, pulling out a napkin-wrapped piece of bacon from her pocket. She flipped on all the lights, got down on her hands and knees, and searched under each desk. "Here, kitty, kitty . . ."

But there was no sight of the scrawny cat masquerading as an ostrich baby, so she sat at her desk and got to work, only to nearly fall over a few minutes later at the rustling beneath her. Slowly, she bent low and found two huge green eyes staring at her. "Chuck," she breathed, "you came." She unrolled her napkin, holding out the bacon.

His little nose wriggled as if he couldn't quite believe it. His fur was rumpled and clumpy, and there was a bald patch behind an ear. His tail was permanently bent to the right. Clearly, he'd been through hell, and he absolutely broke her heart. "Come on, sweet thing. You know you want it . . ."

Gun-shy, he continued to sniff at the bacon but wouldn't take it out of her hand. Caving, she set it at his feet. "There—"

It vanished so fast she got dizzy. Smiling, she leaned in to pet him, but he let out a low sound from deep in his throat and dashed out from beneath the desk, disappearing as fast as the bacon had.

"Watch your fingers with that one," Stone said as he came up the stairs, looking as big and bad as his brother always did. Bigger, actually, and just as tough and impenetrable. He was the sort of guy who could be dropped anywhere on the planet and manage to survive.

And yet he didn't make her knees knock together like Cam did.

"You good?" he asked.

"That should be my question to you. You find the lost boarders?"

"Cam did, actually. Apparently, wayward boarders think alike." He flipped through the mail, then looked at her. "And before you die of curiosity, he's still in town, talking to the police for the report."

"Is everyone all right?"

"Uh-huh, he's all in one piece and fine. Since that's what you were really asking." Looking amused, he tossed the mail back down. "So I hear you got him out on the mountain."

She sighed. "You talked to Annie."

"Yeah, but I already knew. Small town," he said with a

shrug. "I call it Mayberry with Attitude. Everyone knows everyone's business and are all up in it."

"Are you going to warn me off him too?"

"Nah, he'd try to kick my ass, and then I'd have to kick his, and then Annie would want in on it. It'd be a whole ass-kicking thing. . . ." He set an envelope on her desk.

"What's this?"

"We had a group come in late last night. Five brothers. I'm taking them up Sky Peak today and tomorrow. They want to hike up, then ski down the backside. That's their deposit."

She looked inside and saw all the zeros on the check. "Nice."

"The roads are rough. If you go to the bank today, you'll need the snowmobile to get there."

She stared down at the envelope. Bad roads. Snowmobile. On the one hand, it sounded like a great adventure. On the other, it sounded like an unusual obituary. But she was going deeper . . . so she stuck the check in the bank bag and pulled on all her snow gear. She went outside and stared at the snowmobile sitting so innocuously out front.

The key was in the ignition, the helmet on top of the seat. She pulled it on and straddled the beast, as she'd seen Cam do a bunch of times. "No problem." Yeah, saying it out loud really helped. She turned the key and the engine jumped to life, along with her heart rate. Instinctively, she grabbed the handlebars and squeezed, and that's when the beast betrayed her, leaping forward like a kicked bronco.

With a small, strangled scream, Katie let go of the handlebars. The snowmobile went one way and she went the other, flying through the air.

She landed facedown in the soft, newly fallen powder, which gave way beneath her, so that she sank in like a post. She was stuck so good that moving was all but impossible. She tried to keep it together, but it was dark inside the snow berm and she couldn't get free, and the old panic gripped her. She gasped for air and inhaled snow. *Not trapped in your car,* she tried to tell herself. *No flames licking at you* . . . It didn't work. Choking, coughing, she struggled, feeling like she was suffocating—

A set of hands gripped her hips and hauled her up to her knees, tugging off her helmet so she could see.

And what she saw was Cam, eyes and mouth grim as he hunkered down before her, peering into her face.

"You're back," she gasped, swiping at the snow in her eyes.

"Are you okay?" he demanded.

"I don't know." Heart pounding, knees wobbling, she sank to her butt in the snow. "I couldn't breathe, I—"

He ran his hands down her limbs, then rescued her glasses from the snow and handed them to her. "What the hell were you doing?"

"I . . ." She shook her head. "Need another second."

He blew out a breath, then craned his head to take in the snowmobile, which had hit a tree.

She put on her glasses and gasped. "Oh, God." Nope, she wasn't okay. Spots swam in front of her eyes, as did memories of what her car had looked like after her crash, and the next thing she knew, Cam had pushed her head between her knees and was saying, "Deep breaths, that's it. Come on, keep at it."

"*Crap.*"

"Does that mean you're back with me?"

"I did not faint." She lifted her head and forced herself to look at the snowmobile. "Oh, God. I did, I really killed it."

"Yeah, well, better it than you. So let's get to the part where you tell me what you were doing."

"Attempting to get to the bank. Stone said I could. Hi, by the way."

"Hi. And Stone's an idiot. Did it ever occur to you to ask for help?"

"Sure. But I didn't want to look like the stupid city girl."

He stroked her damp hair from her face. "You're that most disconcerting shade of green again."

"Yeah, I'm sort of having a bad moment."

"I can see that." His calm voice was going a long way toward making her calm. Or at least calmer. "Flashback?"

"My car—" She took a quick peek at the snowmobile on its side near the tree. "It looked like a toy afterward."

"Ah, hell," With a rough sound of regret, he pulled her in close. "I'm sorry."

"I'm okay," she said softly.

"So am I. Let's just be okay together a minute."

She burrowed in, pressing her cold nose to his throat. "I'm sorry I killed your snowmobile. I'll pay for the damages."

"No, you won't. Trust me, we've put it through far worse." He slanted her a look. "On purpose."

"Because you're all tough badass Wilders, and when you ride crazy and crash into things, it's on purpose, right?"

"Not every time."

She closed her eyes, then opened them and cupped his face, feeling the stubble beneath her fingers. "Why didn't you tell me you hadn't been on the mountain since your accident?"

"You were nervous enough, you didn't need to worry about me chickening out."

"Were you close to doing that?"

He flashed a grim smile. "More than you know." He started to get up, but she held him back.

"And how are you now?" she asked.

"How are *you* now?"

"I'm pretty damn fine. Now you."

He laughed roughly. "Always with the talking."

"Talking's good for you."

"Are you sure? I'd think your tongue would get tired."

"It's good for you *here*." She spread her hand over his heart.

His smile faded, but his eyes remained warm as he covered her hand with his. "I'm pretty damn fine too. Skiing with you the other day was . . . good. You thanked me for taking you, but I should have thanked you." He got up and strode to the snowmobile. Grabbing the handlebars, he picked up the front end, muscling the nose away from the tree. Then he turned the key, and once again the engine roared to life.

"Come here," he said, holding the beast.

"Oh." She swallowed hard. "Well, I—"

"Get on."

She looked at the machine, at the man waiting on her all calm and patient. *Balls out.* Heading over there, she slowed her steps when she got close. "Yeah, see I'm not sure about the whole driving thing. I don't think I'm cut out for it."

He held out the helmet. "Let's go."

"You know," she said. "When it comes to your idiosyncrasies, I'm much more gentle than you."

He waggled the helmet.

With a sigh, she put it on, then stood still in shocked surprise when he gently tucked a strand of her hair aside, out of her way, leaving his fingers on her for far longer than necessary. "Okay," she murmured, "that works too."

He smiled, then leaned in and kissed her, not so gently.

"Even better," she managed when he pulled back.

"Let's do this, Goldilocks."

"Yeah, okay." What could she do but swing a leg over the snowmobile and get on?

But then he surprised her again by getting on behind her, slipping his arms around her, his thighs hugging hers. She felt his mouth brush the crook of her neck below the edge of the helmet as his hands skimmed beneath her jacket and shirt, and spread wide over her belly. "Put your hands on the grips," he directed.

With a shiver, she did.

"Good. Now hold tight, and whatever you do, do not let go." His thumbs stroked her ribs, nearly but not quite touching her breasts. "What did I say?"

"Don't let go," she whispered obediently.

"The brake is here." He showed her where to pull with one hand, the other still stroking her belly.

She drew a shaky breath and dropped her hands to his thighs, feeling the power there, squeezing—

He directed her hands back to the grips. "You have to hold on, no matter what happens."

She shivered and tried to crane her neck to look at him, but he held her still. "Face forward. Keep your eyes on where you're headed." He slid his hands to her belly again, stroking up and down, until she was nothing but a melted bowl of goo. "Feel the weight of the machine."

"Cam—" She broke off with a gasp when the very tips of his fingers grazed the undersides of her breasts.

"When you turn," he murmured in her ear, "shift your weight, go with it. Got that?"

"Shift my weight." His thumbs made another pass, higher now . . . Oh God. She was covered in goose bumps, from arousal not fear. All panic gone. Apparently all she'd needed was to be turned on.

She should have thought of that a long time ago.

"Movement is important." His hands kept stroking her, down her belly, then back up, brushing her breasts now.

She shuddered in pleasure. "Cam?"

"Yeah." His voice was low and husky, as arousing as his hands.

"I'm having a hard time concentrating."

He shifted against her and she pressed back, feeling the hard ridge between his legs. "And I'm not the only one," she managed.

He laughed softly.

God, she loved his laugh. "I can't drive when you do that," she murmured.

"The talking, or the touch?"

"Both. Where's the gas?"

He pulled his hands from beneath her shirt and showed her, and then wrapped his arms around her. "Ready?"

Yeah, she was ready. For all of it. The air was crisp and icy, but she wasn't cold, not with Cam's rock-solid body pressed up to hers. In fact, thanks to his erotic teasing, she was the opposite of cold, and getting hotter by the second. "Hold on." She smiled. "Hold on and don't let go."

"I won't."

And with a gulp of air, she hit the gas.

She drove far better than Cam expected, recovering from her fears like a pro. At the bank, she slid off the snowmobile and smiled at him as she took off the helmet. "My next adventure is going to have a hard time living up to this one."

Yeah, so was his.

With another smile, she headed up the shoveled path to the bank as if on top of her own world. She had a nice walk and a sweet ass, in or out of those ski pants he'd given her, and he just stood there watching a moment. He'd resisted her for three weeks now, partly because his family kept getting in his way, and partly—mostly—out of self-preservation. She was already more than a one-night stand to him, and as one of those had never worked out before, he'd told himself he'd had good reason to keep back.

But he was over his past kicking him in the teeth.

Over.

It.

As Katie lived her life, he was no longer going to let a little fear stop him. On anything. Still smiling in marvel at that, he looked around at the sound of boots on the snow and came face-to-face with a part of his past, the part that had once kicked him in the teeth the hardest.

Serena.

"Hello, Cam," she said softly. "It's been a while."

Yeah. Since the day he'd found out she'd slept with someone else, the day he'd crashed and burned.

Serena pushed her dark hair over her shoulder, the hair he'd once loved draped over his body, and gestured to her bakery. "How about some coffee? I've got freshly made brownies."

She was gorgeous as always, her shiny hair scented with the perfume that had once driven him crazy. He waited for a blast of pain and was surprised to find it muted. "I've tasted your sweets, thanks."

"Cam." She looked so disappointed.

Yeah, he knew that look as well as her scent.

"I was hoping we could be friends."

"You know, that's not worked out so well for me before."

"I've tried to apologize. I didn't mean to—"

"Cheat?"

"I'm not asking to get back together." Stepping closer still, she put a hand on his arm, gently squeezing his biceps. "I'm asking to be friends. You seem in the mood for new ones." She tossed a meaningful look toward the bank. When he didn't say anything, she sighed. "She's sweet, but no one knows you like I do. Come on, Cam, come inside. We'll talk, we'll . . ." She slid her hand up into his hair, smiling warmly.

He caught her fingers, and she fell quiet, studying him a long beat. "Something's different." She looked him over some more. "You're relaxed. Less edgy."

"Maybe."

"Definitely."

"Look, I have to go get gas for the snowmobile—"

"I'm glad you're finally back," she said quietly. "Please come inside. Those warm brownies have your name all over them." She leaned in to put her mouth to his ear. "Remember what we used to accomplish with just cookie dough? You'd eat it off my—"

"Don't." He'd thought seeing her again would kill him. He hadn't thought he'd ever get to the place where he didn't want her to hurt as much as she'd hurt him. But oddly enough, he didn't feel the urge to see her hurt at all. He didn't feel much of anything really, except maybe the need to get the hell out of there.

Progress. Go figure. "I'm sorry." And he meant it. "But I don't want to go over our past."

"What *do* you want?"

Only a few weeks ago, his response would have been something hurtful, maybe cruel. Instead, he came out with the utter truth. "Nothing."

"Okay, so you want me to pay some more, I get it—"

"No." He stepped back so that her hands fell from him. "I don't want you to pay."

Confused, she was searching his gaze, looking for hidden meaning, or the catch. "You stayed away so long. I thought—I actually worried you'd never come back."

"I didn't stay away to get back at you, or even because of you. I just needed . . . something."

"I can understand. You were restless. Probably bored without racing. It's how I felt when you were gone all the time. It got me into trouble. Don't let it get you into trouble, Cam."

He glanced at the snowmobile, where he'd just ridden across the countryside while holding on to Katie, grinning just about the whole way. For those few moments, he hadn't felt restless at all. Or frustrated, or empty. He'd been hugged up to Katie and he'd felt . . . amazingly alive. "I think I'm going to be okay."

Serena stared up at him for a long moment, then let out a mirthless laugh as her gaze slid to the bank. "Don't fool yourself, Cam. You're not going to be the right man for her. I've met her. She's so . . . open. Open and expressive."

"So."

"So she'll want a man who's open and expressive as well. And that's not you. Hell, I had to strip you naked every night just to get you to express yourself." She shook her head. "You're not her type. Oh, you'll play with her for a while before you realize that, but eventually you'll hurt her."

When his gaze locked on hers, she nodded. "You know I'm right. About all of it. You hurt me, Cam. I'm just sorry I hurt you back."

Yeah, hell. He had hurt her. "I'm sorry, Serena. So damn sorry."

"Are you? Then make it up to me. Call me."

"I can't." He said this as kindly as he could, but he didn't want to give her false hopes. "Serena, I won't call you."

She stared at him, then let out a low, unhappy laugh. "I've been waiting for you to come to your senses, but you're over me. You're really over me."

Cam watched Katie come out of the bank and smile at him, and he thought, Yeah, he really was.

But that didn't mean he got to move on to hurting someone else. Katie was here taking a baby step, doing her best to move on with her life. How he'd ever thought sleeping with her would help her, he had no idea. Probably because he'd been thinking of himself.

"Don't be selfish with her, Cam," Serena said quietly, nailing the point home. "For once in your life."

If he, indeed, was trying to grow up and move on, he had to admit, she was right. He wouldn't be selfish, not with Katie.

Chapter 14

As Cam let Katie drive back to the lodge, Serena's words echoed in his head, all while extremely aware of how warm and sweet and sexy she felt in his arms.

Don't be selfish with her, Cam. For once in your life . . .

And he had been plenty selfish in his life, she was right about that. Katie had been through hell, and yet unlike him, she was making something of herself. Trying to be happy.

Sleeping with her would make him happy, of that he had no doubt. It'd ease a tension he couldn't seem to shake.

But what would it do for Katie? He knew enough about her to know that when she slept with someone, it meant something to her. She wasn't a one-night stand woman. She deserved better from him. Much better.

When she pulled them up to the equipment garage, she sighed in pleasure, staying where she was a moment, her head resting back on his chest. "Thanks for the ride."

"You drove."

"And thanks for that too." She slid out of his arms and off the snowmobile. When she caught sight of his face, her smile slowly slipped away. "What's the matter?"

"Nothing." Except that he was trying to do the right thing for someone else for a change. "I just have to get going."

"Okay." But she stood there a moment longer, clearly hoping he was going to break the sudden awkwardness.

Not going to happen. He was saving her from himself.

"Okay, well, thanks again." She turned, then looked back. "Look, um . . . Did something happen that I missed?"

"No, I've just got things to do."

She kept her eyes on his. "Okay, I get that. But I ask because the last time I let this odd feeling go, it turned out you were back on the mountain for the first time. So I can't help but wonder what's happening now. Inside you."

"Katie . . . this is for the best. Really."

She blinked. "Oh. You mean . . . you withdrawing. Pulling back."

"Yeah."

"Okay. Wow." She shook her head. "I didn't see that coming."

She wanted to say more, he could tell, but though she was direct, she was not pushy, and in the end, she gave him a smile that didn't quite meet her whiskey eyes. "Good-bye, Cam."

He felt like an ass. Like he'd just kicked a puppy. Like he'd once again let down someone he cared about. "Good-bye, Katie."

With a nod, she turned and walked off without another word, leaving him torn between a huge relief and the feeling he'd just done exactly the opposite of his intention—he'd hurt her.

That, and also, possibly, he'd just let the best thing that had happened to him in a damn long time walk away. With a rough exhale, he turned inside the equipment garage and found Stone coming out. "Hey. Thought you had that trip to—"

"Canceled," Stone said. "But there's a group who wants to go up the summit tonight for a moonlight snowshoe hike. I'm giving it to you."

"No, no way. Not in the mood."

"Get in the mood."

"Why? What's wrong with your legs?"

"Got a date."

Cam lifted a brow. "That new server at Moody's?"

"Maybe."

"Doesn't seem fair, me taking the hike, you getting lucky." Especially considering he'd be sleeping alone for the foreseeable future.

Gee, what a change that would be.

"Seems to me, you've been plenty lucky," Stone reminded him. "And given what I interrupted the other day—"

"Yeah, that's . . . not happening."

"Why?"

"Because." Cam stretched the tensed muscles in his neck. "Because I'm an idiot."

Stone studied him a long moment. "You falling for her? Is that why you're backing off?"

"I don't want to talk about it."

"Ah, so this is the Wilder trait kicking in, the fuck-up-your-happiness trait."

"Shut up, Stone."

"Jesus." Stone shook his head. "Really, Cam? You don't think you've punished yourself enough this year? I get that you're not a hotshot snowboarder anymore, with an MTV crew following you around 24/7 and chicks throwing themselves at you. But who is? Get over it."

"I am. I'm trying." He shoved Stone out of his way and stalked into the garage, then whipped back. "I'm still here, aren't I? And before you get all pissy over that"—he stabbed a finger into Stone's chest—"you should know, I'm still here because I want to be."

"Then why the fuck are you yelling?"

"I don't know." Cam turned to the window and eyed the

white mountain peaks that had once been his entire life, and
were now as well, just in a different way. "I don't know what
the hell I'm doing with myself," he said, his anger draining.
"But I know I feel good here."

Stone sighed and slung his arm over Cam's shoulder. "Okay,
I'll take that. So am I going to get lucky tonight or what?"

"I'll take the damn hike. But as to the lucky part, bro, that's
all on you."

Katie was working at her desk, trying not to think too hard
when Annie came up the stairs with the mail. Her apron read:
CAN YOU HEAR ME NOW, with a cartoon chef flipping her
middle finger.

Katie looked past the apron to the scowl on Annie's face.
The scowl was in no way unusual, but something else was.

Annie was wearing brand-new jeans that weren't baggy. Her
shirt was a plain Henley, but the long-sleeved cotton material
was fitted and unbuttoned to her waist, revealing an even
snugger tank top beneath and a lovely figure. Her hair was
loose and shiny, and though she wore no mascara, she did have
on gloss.

Katie smiled. "I bet Nick's eyes pop right out of his head
when he sees you."

"We'll see. The delivery guy stopped by just now and seemed
to like what he saw just fine." She paused. "So have you seen
him? Nick?"

"With Cam," Stone told her, coming out of his office. He
was thumbing a text message to someone on his phone while
simultaneously flipping through a stack of phone messages.
"They're organizing the gear for tonight's snowshoe hike." He
took a glance at the two women, then executed a comical double take at Annie.

Annie tugged on the hem of her fitted shirt and shifted on
her weight self-consciously. "What?"

"What happened to you?"

"What happened to what?"

Annie's tone clearly said, "Warning: Dead Nephew Walking," but Stone didn't seem to catch it. "You shrink your clothes?" he asked.

Annie slapped the mail against his stomach, hard enough to make him wince. "No, you idiot, I didn't shrink my clothes. I bought them this way."

"I think you look pretty," Katie said, hoping to help avoid Stone's death.

Stone finally bought a clue and nodded, "You do. You look pretty."

"I was going for sexy," Annie said.

"Sexy?"

"Yes, for Nick. I want to look sexy so that your good friend would want to do your aunt. There. Do you wish me to be any clearer?"

Stone winced. "What I wish is that I'd stayed in my office."

Annie tugged at her shirt again and turned to the window. "This is so ridiculous. *I'm* so ridiculous."

"No," Stone said. "It's . . . nice. And you really do look—"

"Ridiculous."

"Pretty."

Annie gave him a long look over her shoulder. "You know that would be so sweet if you weren't completely full of shit."

"Maybe we should develop a code of some sort," Stone said to Katie when Annie had stormed back down the stairs. "You know, like hey, *crazy aunt alert.*"

Katie wasn't thinking of him, but of Nick. "What are the chances that Nick's as slow as you?"

Stone considered a moment. "Good to excellent."

"Well, that's a shame." Katie shook her head at all the men in this place. "I really did like that man."

* * *

That night, Cam's group comprised five coworkers attending a conference near South Lake Tahoe. They'd made the trek up to Wishful in a limo, and from there Nick had retrieved them in the Sno-Cat.

Cam stood in the lodge's big main room assigning everyone snowshoes when he felt the prickle of awareness at the back of his neck. Turning, he met Katie's gaze.

"Yeah," Nick said, standing next to him, doling out the snow poles. "Did I forget to tell you? She's joining the group for tonight."

Cam just looked at him.

"Hey, it's after hours and she signed up." Nick shrugged. "She wants an adventure. It's not my fault you went and fucked everything up, and made it all awkward."

Cam shook his head. "How do you know these things?"

"When are you going to learn? I know everything."

Annie came into the room holding a tray filled with sacked snacks. For once she wasn't wearing clothes two sizes too big, and her aprons were nowhere in sight. She looked softer, even pretty. Cam turned to Nick, who was standing there staring at her, mouth agape, struggling to comprehend.

"Everyone take one and tuck it into your backpacks," Annie called out. "You'll all be wanting to kiss me when you get back, I can promise you that."

This was met with some cheers, and one of the guys shifted closer, flirting with her.

Nick continued to look like his brain had been knocked clear across the room.

"You know everything?" Cam whispered to him. "Really? Do you know how to get her back?"

"Fuck you." Nick accompanied this with a little shove.

Eyes sharp, Annie looked over. Cam smiled at her while speaking to Nick out of the corner of his mouth. "You might want to remember, I'm her favorite. Pick on me and she'll kick your ass."

Nick ignored this and walked up to Annie. "Hey."

She slid him one of those indescribable looks that Cam knew from experience always meant trouble in one form or another.

"Why don't you come with us tonight?" Nick asked her.

She cocked her head. "Why? Is there some reason I should?"

"Yeah, it's a full moon. It'll be a great view. We could wait while you change."

"Is there something wrong with these clothes then?"

"No." Nick clearly sensed trouble, but he wasn't the sharpest tool in the shed when it came to the intricate workings of the female mind and how to follow them.

Annie's voice cooled to subzero. "I'll go if you can tell me what's different about me tonight."

Nick gulped. "Your hair. You did your hair."

Annie's mouth tightened and she slapped a hand to his chest to push him out of her way. "Sack snacks," she said again to the group. "Come get your sack snack—"

Nick reached for one.

Annie held them out of his reach. "Sorry, I didn't make one for you."

"You said you had enough for everyone."

"Everyone but you."

"But you have an extra right there—"

"It's Cam's."

Cam caught it an inch from his face. Annie could throw on the best of days, but when she was pissed, she could pitch for the A's.

Nick sighed and went back to giving out poles to go with the snowshoes.

"Thought you knew everything," Cam said to him.

Nick growled, and Cam moved away just in time to avoid bodily harm. He watched Katie accept her poles and the snowshoes with a sweet smile, clearly avoiding getting too close to him. No doubt, she was more than a little confused by his hot-and-cold behavior. He had no defense, no good one anyway. When it came to her and what the hell was the right thing to do, he no longer had a clue.

When everyone was ready, they moved outside. They were going to take the Stone Creek Summit trail from the back of the lodge, which would lead up the High Sierra Pass to a plateau that on a bright, crystal-clear night such as tonight would seem like the top of the world.

His group consisted of one romantically linked couple, three friends, and Katie. Let's not forget Katie. As if he could, she with the biggest, most expressive eyes on the entire planet, not to mention the fact that she was wearing those ski pants he'd given her and right this minute was bending over to tighten her boots, giving him a nice view of the way they fit her sweet ass. Especially since he'd had his hands on said sweet ass and wished he was getting his hands on her again in the near future, without the pants this time. In fact, he wanted to get his hands on her, his mouth on her, his tongue—

She straightened and turned, and caught him staring.

"Odd to find you staring at me like that," she said lightly. "After earlier, when I figured either you changed your mind about wanting me, or . . . you're so scared of me."

Hell of a multiple choice.

She waited for a minute, then smiled a little tightly as she patted his arm. "It's okay, Cam." She moved away to join the others, leaving him staring after her. After his accident, he'd closed himself off. If he were being honest, he'd done that long before too. But that technique didn't seem to be working for him much anymore.

Only he wasn't sure what to do to change it. Christ, he was

tired of thinking, tired of himself. He turned to the group, clearing his head as everyone began to put on their snowshoes. The night was a good one, about thirty degrees. Better than the freeze-your-balls-off cold it'd been all week. "Anyone having problems?"

Only one hand shot up: Katie's. "I'm sorry," she said apologetically when he crouched down at her side. "I don't know which foot is which."

"With these snowshoes it doesn't make a difference."

"Okay, I'm good then." Standing up, she took a step, and walked right out of the snowshoes, nearly falling on her face. "Huh, maybe not so good."

He gestured her back over to him and helped her, which required him kneeling at her side, putting his hands on her legs, "Katie?"

"Yes?"

"About those two choices you gave me." He lifted his head. "I'm not afraid."

She looked at him a long moment. "No worries. I think I get it."

"No, you don't." He tightened her bindings with a little tug. She gasped and put her hands on his head, gripping his hair, using him for balance. "I've climbed Mt. McKinley," he told her. "I've skied the Death Zone in France. I'm not afraid of much." He paused, then told her the stone-cold hard truth, "But I tend to be a quitter."

"Oh, Cam. No—"

"Don't." He said this more harshly than he'd intended, but as the saying went, the truth hurt. He quit. When the going got tough, the tough got going, and he walked.

Always.

"It's just the way it is. Lift your foot."

She complied, and he tightened the other boot as well so that she'd stay in them for the next few hours of climbing. Her fingers were still in his hair, but more so than that was the fact that his head was at her crotch level. If he turned his face, he'd be within two inches of where he'd wanted to be since he first saw her in his bed. A ridiculously immature thought, but he couldn't seem to help it. "Try that."

She walked a few steps and turned back. "I feel like a duck."

"That's natural. You'll get past it." He took her hand and pulled her in close, tipping up her chin to meet her gaze. "And as for the other choice . . . I do want you. So damn much."

"You don't have to say that—"

"I want to kiss you," he said quietly. "Touch you. I want to do things to you, all night long."

She stared at his mouth, hers falling open.

"I want to feel your heart pound for me when I'm inside you. I'm sorry I wasn't clear on that. I've been unclear on a lot of stuff lately, especially with you because I don't want to hurt you."

"Misguided," she murmured, her voice a little thick. "I take care of myself, Cam."

"You do. I know that. You're so strong, but I . . . Look, I wasn't completely honest. You do scare me. Okay? You scare the hell out of me."

She nodded. "I could hold your hand."

He let out a low laugh and drank in the sight of her by moonlight, trying to fit into his world. *Fitting* into his world. "Just so you know, you are truly the most amazing woman I've ever met."

"Thank you." She took the last step between them. "Oh, and one last thing." She kissed him, one quick, hard, very nice kiss on the lips before pulling back. "That's what you're missing out on by being afraid of me. Just so you know."

When she'd walked away, Nick leaned in. "I'm glad to see I'm not the only idiot in residence."

Still reeling, Cam lifted his middle finger and scratched his nose with it in Nick's direction. While Nick laughed, he called out to the group. "Everyone ready?" He struggled to gather his thoughts. "We've got three miles to cover. At the top, we'll stop for pictures. Hopefully the sky will stay clear and you'll get a great shot at the full moon."

"So romantic," the woman with her boyfriend whispered.

And she was right. It *was* incredibly romantic. Cam slid Katie a quick glance, and found her looking at him.

Nick leaned in to Cam again. "It might be scary up there. Need me to hold your hand?"

"Nick?"

"Yeah?"

"Shut up." Cam led the way, with Nick taking up the rear, still chuckling at the both of them.

For Katie, the snow hike started off easy enough but quickly turned challenging. Even so, it was hard not to be completely awed by the night. The moon shined down on the snow, bouncing the reflecting light over the snow-covered trees, the mountains. She'd never paid much attention to the night sky in Los Angeles. Or to the daytime sky, for that matter. Either it was a dingy blue, thanks to the smog, or it was a dingy black, also thanks to the smog.

But here.

God, here.

Here in the Sierras, the sky had a million different looks, from pale purple in the dawn, to an eye-popping blue midday, to the blackest of black at night, and every single one seemed so large, so stunning.

Sort of like the man who was leading her hike right this very moment.

I want to do things to you . . .

Just thinking about his words had her breath coming faster,

and Cam turned his head to check on her. "I'm good." *As long as I don't picture you doing things to me . . .*

But she *did* picture them as they kept going. And going. And going . . . As Cam promised, after a few minutes, she no longer felt like a duck as they all moved up the same hill he'd taken her up once before, in the Sno-Cat.

This time, under her own steam, it was a challenge. Her breath was huffing in her chest, making little white puffs of clouds with each exhale. They walked single file, the trail didn't allow for anything else. Stone had warned her that snow-shoeing up this particular mountain was pretty much a solitary experience, but that had appealed.

The couple in front of her, John and Sally, had a flask filled with something they kept passing back and forth, which made them giggle with increasing frequency.

Cam turned back often, checking on everyone, and each time he locked gazes with her, her heart stuttered.

He wanted to do things . . . and she wanted him to do those things . . . He kept a close eye on Sally and John, too, probably because after an hour, John was completely hammered and kept tripping over his own feet. Twice Nick had leaned past Katie to tell him to be careful.

Cam did the same from the front.

But John—Sally called him "Sweetie Pie"—wasn't listening too well. He wasn't obnoxious or rude or anything. In fact, he was quite happy and jolly. But he was definitely not heeding any advice.

The trail became increasingly narrower, with a sharp rock wall to their right, and then a decent drop to their left. When "Sweetie Pie" began to sing show tunes, Sally merely laughed. When he added in dance moves, coming extremely close to the edge several times, Katie held her breath. "Careful," she begged him, adding what she hoped was a pleasant smile when she wanted to tell him not to be stupid. "Don't fall."

"I won't," he said just as one of his legs buckled. Katie shoved him clear of the edge at the same time he wrapped his arms around her for balance, but both of them wobbled and teetered, and Katie's life instantly flashed before her eyes. *Another time and place, another cliff . . .*

As the panic hit her, her last coherent thought was, she was going to die before Cam could get her naked, and that was just really, *really* unfair.

Chapter 15

Cam whipped around to see John grabbing on to Katie for balance. Heart in his throat, he dove past the others as Nick did the same from the rear, both getting there at the same time, shoving the locked together snowshoers against the rock only a fraction of a second before they would have fallen off the edge.

Cam lifted his head and eyed the drop-off, which was at least thirty feet—good enough to have cracked more than a few bones. *Fucking idiot.*

"I'm okay, I'm okay!" This from Sweetie Pie Drunk Asshole John. Accompanying this declaration was a loud belch that smelled like a bad combination of Scotch and sewer. "Whew, doggie." He let out a goofy smile as he fanned his hand in front of his face. "That's not good."

Sally laughed and helped pull him off of Katie. "You okay, Sweetie Pie?"

Cam put his hands on Katie's hips, holding her still when she would have gotten up. She'd taken John's full weight, and Cam's and Nick's as well. "Take a minute. Are you okay?"

"I think so." But she didn't give him her usual megawattage smile. She sat up, holding her arm close to her chest as she peered over the edge. She didn't quite go green but close enough, and he knew she was probably only a minute away from hyperventilating. "Oh God."

Crouched beside her, Cam blocked her from the view of the cliff, as well as the others, giving her a minute to collect herself.

"I'm fine."

"Just sit another minute. Bad memories, or something more?"

"I think just memories. Dammit."

Not convinced, he reached for the zipper on her jacket to get a look at her arm.

"No, it's fine. Fine," she repeated when Cam started to speak. The others had shifted close to check on her. "Look, if I don't keep going, then I let the idiot take this away from me—No offense," she said to John, who shook his head, suitably sober now.

"None taken. I am an idiot."

Katie looked at Cam. "I'm good to go."

Because she wasn't a quitter. Not even close.

Using her poles, she struggled to get to her feet, never easy in snowshoes so he helped her, then hugged her close to him. "You're still shaking."

"I'm okay." She peered over his shoulder at the drop and swallowed. "I'm okay," she repeated, but he hugged her in tight anyway, letting her have the illusion of telling him when he knew it was herself she was talking to.

"Hey, I'll take the merry couple back," Nick said. "He's not fit to get to the top."

The others decided to go back with their friends, and Cam looked at Katie. "I'm sorry."

"No, I can still get there." Her eyes blazed with determination, tugging on something deep inside him, making him want to give her whatever she wanted.

He knew what was on the top of her list. It was on top of his list too.

"Please."

Ah, hell. Cam looked at Nick.

"I'll take her if you want," Nick offered. "You can take the others back."

"No." Hell no.

Nick sighed. "Some guys get all the luck."

As they climbed, Katie's lungs felt like they were going to burst, but when Cam asked her if she wanted to stop, she said no and managed to keep going, even if she was breathing like a lunatic. When they finally crested the top, she staggered to a halt at the view. "My God."

The land had leveled out, revealing a 360-degree view that quite simply took whatever breath she had left, admittedly not much. The thin, icy air was still barely soughing in and out of her lungs as she shook her head in disbelief. "It's like being on top of the world."

Cam came up beside her, and as if he knew exactly how she felt, how awed, how small and insignificant they were in the whole scheme of things, he didn't say a word, just let her take it all in.

"It's the most gorgeous thing I've ever seen." She turned to look at him. He stood there tall and strong and vital. Tough. Silent. A virtual rock whenever she'd needed one, and definitely not the quitter he thought he was, and she amended her thought. *He* was the most gorgeous thing she'd ever seen. "Well worth the terror of getting here."

He dropped his backpack, then pulled hers off as well, making her sit on a rock outcropping before crouching at her feet to unhook her snowshoes. "Don't try to walk around up here without those," he warned as he tugged off his gloves, shoving them into his pocket. "That whole drunken fiasco never should have happened. I could have killed him." Cam looked into her eyes, his own dark and troubled. "Are you really okay?"

Unable to help herself, she cupped his face and kissed his jaw. "So fierce and protective over the woman you don't quite know what to do with."

"I know you're still fighting the memories."

"It's better. So much better."

"Are you sure?"

"Very." She began to stand up, but he held her back.

"Just sit still a minute."

"Why? You want to have your merry way with me?" she teased as he reached up and unzipped her jacket.

"I'm checking on your arm."

"It's fine—" But she hissed out a breath when he pulled her arm out of the jacket and then pushed up her sleeve, which was stuck to her arm by her own blood. "Oh boy."

"You must have gotten scratched by one of the poles when you fell."

Her head swam a little. "I don't like blood."

"Just a scratch," he repeated calmly. Reaching up, he turned her chin away, back to the amazing view. "Just keep looking at the moon. Look for falling stars."

She tipped her head up and gasped when she actually saw one. "There!"

"Make a wish."

She closed her eyes and did just that, and when she opened them again, he was looking at her.

"What did you wish for?"

"You believe in wishing on falling stars?"

"Yes."

She smiled. "The stoic, pragmatic Cameron Wilder, a dreamer, after all."

He let out a low laugh. "On my way back to Wishful, the

night I met you, I wished on one. And if you tell anyone that, I'll deny it."

"What did you wish for?"

He met her gaze. "To feel something."

She held her breath, caught, lost in his eyes. "Is it working?"

"I think it just might be."

She felt her heart click and lock into place. For him. "I wished for great sex. Tonight. And if you could tell my guide, I'd really appreciate it."

With a rough laugh, he nudged her chin upward again. She blinked the sky into focus, the way it lit up the entire valley floor below with a bluish tinge—"Ouch!"

He'd sprayed her with something from the first-aid kit in his backpack and was now pulling out some gauze and tape. He ripped a piece of tape off with his teeth, then held it there while he wrapped her up, but not before twice again having to nudge her face away. "There." He smoothed down the tape. "Good as new."

"Then why does it just now hurt?"

"Aw, let me see." Shocking her, he leaned in and kissed the bandage. "Better?"

She stared into his eyes. "No, I think it needs some serious TLC."

His gaze heated, and as always it put her own insides on a slow, delicious simmer as he obediently leaned back in and kissed the spot again, then an inch above her bandage.

And an inch above that. "Better?"

"Not yet."

With a soft huff of laughter against her skin, he tried pushing her sleeve up higher on her arm and couldn't, and while she battled disappointment, he proved just how resourceful he could be by reversing his efforts and slowly pushing the sleeve down from above while holding her gaze prisoner.

The shirt gave way, slipped off her shoulder, and only then did he break eye contact and once again lean in, pressing his lips to her bare skin.

She sucked in another breath.

"Cold?" he murmured against her flesh.

Was he kidding? He could have stripped her naked out here in the thirty-degree night and she'd have still been sizzling hot. "No, don't stop making me feel better."

On a half groan, half laugh, his lips trailed up her shoulder, ending up in the crook of her neck, which gave her a set of goose bumps that still had nothing to do with a chill and everything to do with sheer lust. She tugged off her gloves and slipped her fingers inside his jacket.

"Katie—"

"Dream on if you think you're going to back off now in some misguided protective gesture. Yes, this is big and scary and new, for the both of us, but we've tried ignoring it and can't. Let's try something else, Cam."

"I don't—"

"Don't say you're a quitter, because the man I'm looking at has been dealt some pretty rough blows and he's still standing. The quitting thing is bullshit, Cam. And don't try to tell me you don't feel this thing between us either." She looked politely at the bulge behind his zipper.

With a groaning laugh, he pressed his forehead to hers. "I was going to say I don't have any way of protecting us from being seen."

"No one's up here. We're all alone, and I'm a big girl. I'm ready for this. The question is, are you?"

Cam stared at her, his heart thudding hard and fast in his chest again, as it had when she'd nearly fallen. "You really are the most remarkable woman I've ever met."

"And I'm something else too." She shrugged out of her jacket, leaving her only in the long-sleeved silk long underwear shirt that was already hanging off one shoulder. "Want to guess?"

"Katie, it's butt-ass cold out here."

"Then keep me warm." He yanked down the zipper of his jacket and pulled in her shaking body, holding her up against his body to share the heat he had in spades, only to realize she hadn't shivered in cold, but excitement.

Which, in turn, fueled his. As if it needed fueling. He was already so turned on he couldn't see straight. He certainly wasn't thinking straight or he wouldn't have leaned back against the rock, pulling her onto his lap so that she straddled him, and then kissed them both stupid.

So stupid . . .

Her hands were running over him, everywhere she could reach. "You're only wearing a T-shirt." Which she shoved up beneath his jacket. Then she pressed her mouth right over his heart, which gave one hard lurch.

"I get hot on snowshoes. But not nearly as hot as I am right now—*Jesus*," he breathed when she licked his nipple. "Katie, listen. We should—"

"Yeah, we should." Surging up, she covered his mouth with hers, showing him exactly what they "really should," and with another low, rough groan, he slid his hands beneath her shirt to touch warm skin. God, she was sweet, so damn sweet—

"We should do whatever we want," she murmured, her hands already doing whatever *they* wanted. He tried to catch them, but she was fast and nimble and greatly determined. "You can complain about how much you hate all this later," she told him, kissing his jaw, his ear, her hands eating him up wherever they touched. "God, this fresh air is invigorating."

"Actually, that's you. *You're* invigorating." His hands skimmed over her hips to her ass, squeezing, pulling her in closer so that she rubbed against his zipper, letting out a sexy little moan of pleasure.

"Why, Cameron Wilder," she purred. "I do believe you're as excited as I am. Do you offer this service to all your clients?"

His eyes closed in sheer pleasure when she sucked his earlobe into her mouth. "Only the hot ones—" He hissed out a breath when she bit his ear, then soothed the ache by sucking it into her mouth, and just like that, he was a goner.

Or more likely, he'd always been a goner for her. He didn't know how, but in two seconds flat, he'd slipped beneath her silk shirt, unhooked her bra, nudged it aside, and then, oh yeah, filled his palms with her warm, full breasts.

She gasped, and he lifted his head. "Too cold?"

"No. Yes." She laughed breathlessly, arching her hips against his. "Just don't stop."

He didn't, and she repaid him by slipping her hands down his torso to his lower abs, her fingers playing with his waistband, which was loose enough that if she wanted to, she could—

God. Yeah. *That.* She could dip those fingers in. He sort of lost himself, tugging up her shirt, exposing her breasts to the night air and his hungry gaze only long enough for him to cover one with his hand, the other with his mouth, sucking her in to rasp his tongue over her nipple.

A wordless plea for more fell from her lips as she rocked against him, her head falling back. Her ski cap slipped off, and so did his, aided by her fingers.

Above them, around them, no part of the night objected. The only sounds were the soft rustling of the wind, and their own labored breathing. Her face was flushed, and when he switched to her other breast, she hissed out a breath and rocked her hips to his. He cupped her most cuppable ass, showing her what rhythm worked for him, then slipped his hand down the back of her ski pants. But some idiot had given her a size too small and he couldn't get as far as he wanted, so he came around to the front and unbuttoned and unzipped and, finally, *oh yeah* . . . got inside.

Her panties were silk.

And wet.

So damn wet.

No slouch, she followed his lead and had his pants undone as well; but before she could dive in, he stroked her on that wet, creamy center and she went still, panting out his name.

Loving the sound of his name on her lips, he did it again, just a single stroke with a slow, delicate precision

She still didn't move, she'd gone still as a statue, and he looked into her face. "Katie? Okay?"

Her fingers dug into his pecs. "Ohmigod, *yes.*"

Taking that as a good sign, he gently stroked her again with just the pad of his finger, slowly outlining her, which seemed to galvanize her back into motion. Her hips went to town, moving impatiently against him. "Cam—" She sounded a little panicked. "I—*Ohmigod.*"

She was close, he could tell, so close, so he kept at it, adding another finger, increasing the rhythm, the pressure. She had her hands fisted in his waistband for balance, still rocking her hips as she gulped for air. "Remember, it's been a *really* long time." She had to stop and pant some more. "And I'm fairly primed here, so—"

God, she was so sweet. And hot. So fucking hot. He slid a finger into her and ran his tongue over her nipple, loving the way she trembled over him.

"Seriously," she gasped. "I'm going to . . ."

"Yeah." Knowing it made him even hotter, made *him* tremble, made him feel a burst of something he wouldn't have recognized a few weeks back but was beginning to become habit when he was with her—*exhilarated.* "Come. I want to feel you."

But instead she did something that changed the game. She slid her hand all the way into his pants as well, and wrapped her fingers around him, stroking in the same rhythm he was using on her.

And suddenly he wasn't feeling like smiling smugly at what he was doing to her, for her, at how he was holding her on the very edge.

Because suddenly he was the one on that edge. "Katie." He needed her to slow down or stop, but his hands were full. Full of her. Desperate, his hips rocked helplessly against hers. Gasping out her name, along with some unintelligible plea like "Oh God, don't stop," and more that might have been utterly humiliating if he'd been alone in this insanity, but he wasn't.

Alone.

Not even close. She was right there with him, crying out, shuddering as she burst. And then, while he was absolutely, one-hundred-percent lost in the vision of her as she came stealing the very breath from his lungs as she did—he shuddered too. So far gone in her, he hadn't realized that *her* hands had never stopped, that they were still stroking him, pumping, making his entire body tighten—"Katie, wait—"

She didn't, and though he tried to extract his fingers from her pants, it was way too late, and he was coming in her hands the same way she'd come in his.

Only it wasn't exactly the same, and he jerked back, the horrified apology on his lips. She simply moved with him, planting a kiss on his mouth as he shuddered and barely managed to come back to planet Earth. Opening his eyes, he found hers open on his, her mouth nibbling at the corner of his lips. "Katie, I—"

"Don't." She grinned but didn't pull back. "Please don't say anything to ruin this for me."

Don't say anything to ruin this for her? How about *doing* something to ruin it, like come in her hands as if he was fifteen and jacking off in the woods. "Katie—"

She was handing him a napkin from her pocket, one of the napkins from the bar at the lodge, and straightening her clothes while letting out a running commentary that made his head spin.

"I've never made out with someone beneath the stars like that." She stopped to flash him another grin. "I've always wanted to." She tucked her shirt into her ski pants. "I've shaved my legs all week, hoping." She shot him another smile and stuck her hand back into her pocket, coming up with another napkin. "Do you need—"

"No." Jesus. "Katie, I'm sorry. It's been like a year, and . . ." And he ran out of steam. "And nothing. I should have been able to hold back—"

She shut him up with her mouth. "It was perfect," she said against his lips, kissing him again before pulling back to zip up her jacket.

"We didn't finish."

She shot him a saucy look. "I hate to disagree with you, but you most definitely did finish. And so did I." She sighed, a purely feminine sound of pleasure that made him half hard again. "First time in a very long time for me, too, by the way. I feel like I'm glowing. Am I glowing?"

He stared at her and found himself shaking his head. "Seriously, I—"

"Seriously," she mocked, and nudged him in the chest. "I'm not stupid, Cam. Or inexperienced. I know you think it's ridiculous I'm grinning like an idiot and waxing poetic over a simple hot and heavy make-out session. But you have to understand, in my life, I've never really given myself a lot of chances for fun and excitement."

He felt his heart give. "I know."

"For me, it was that wish on that falling star coming true. Can't you accept that?"

He stared into her eyes, realizing that he was still expecting her to turn into someone else at every turn, waiting for her to turn needy, or clinging, or demanding, or something other than what she appeared to be.

"Cam?" she asked, just Katie. Unique Katie.

Still looking into her eyes, he knew he could do no less than agree. "Yes."

With another of her wide, sweet, contagious grins, she gave him one last smacking kiss. "Great. Now let's go. I'm starving."

Chapter 16

On the hike back down, Katie absorbed the gorgeous night, and the equally gorgeous man leading her. They were quiet. Content. And also on cloud nine.

At least she was.

Orgasms tended to do that for her.

It'd been a really long time, even longer since she'd had one so quickly, so easily, without straining for it. And she'd done the same for him. God, the pleasure of that, she could hardly stand it.

Cam glanced at her as they arrived at her cabin. He caught her smile and sighed. "Still?"

With a laugh, she pulled out her key. "I can't help it. I love it here."

He slipped his hands into his pockets and didn't say anything to that.

So they were going to do this again, the thing where he pulled back and she let him. "Are you worried I'm going to want to stay, Cam? That I don't know the difference between sex and love? Because I am leaving, much as I love it here."

"You'd get tired of it eventually anyway."

"Why? You don't."

"No, but I was raised out here."

"So what does that mean, you're heartier than I am?"

"Well . . ."

"Come on, Cam," she said gently. "What you're made of comes from inside. A person can look like a wuss"—she gestured to herself—"and still be made of stern stuff." She playfully flexed her biceps. "On the *inside.*"

He cocked his head and studied her. "I'll agree, one's strength has nothing to do with what someone looks like on the outside."

She reached for his hand. "And let's just say it. If you're made of sterner stuff than I am, it's because of your childhood. Not where it took place, but because of what you went through."

"Yeah, maybe." He leaned back against the porch post, looking out into the night, his eyes reflecting his faraway thoughts. "Listen, I don't know what you think you know, but I don't want you to think—It wasn't so bad."

"Your mom left when you were born and your dad gave you up when you were eight, that sounds pretty bad."

"Yeah, but him giving me up to Annie was a good thing, not a bad thing."

Her entire heart softened at all he didn't say, at how impossibly horrifying it must have been to have neither parent want him and know it, not to mention the abuse she suspected he'd suffered. Not wanting him to hold back, not when he'd spent too much of his life doing just that, she said, "He hurt you."

He shrugged those carry-the-weight-of-the-world shoulders. "He had a short fuse when it came to me. I wasn't his."

"Do you know who your real father is?"

"My mother never said, and she never came back."

Katie's own parents, so reserved, so distant, had never been all that emotionally available, but this . . . this was nearly beyond her comprehension. "I'm so glad you had Annie. She loves you so much."

"Yes, she had to. I was . . . difficult."

"A knack for trouble, huh. Gee, what a surprise."

"Oh, yeah. And for pissing people off. As I've been trying to tell you, it's a particular talent of mine. With women in general."

"Is that right? You don't piss me off too. You frustrate me sometimes . . ." The acceptance of that was on his face, and she nudged him. "You also make me laugh. You make me think, you make me . . ." She waggled a brow.

He laughed but it didn't get all the way to his eyes, making her realize just how little experience he had with people sticking with him. "I'm new at this whole taking risks thing, Cam, but you're not. I'd think you'd be wanting to take a risk on us. After all, it's a short-term one."

"It's not that." He met her gaze. "Just don't fall for me, Katie. I'm not ready for that."

She raised a brow. "I don't believe I said anything about falling. I wished for good sex, and got it. The end. Now I'm thirsty. I'm going in for a drink. Would you like to come with me and piss me off some more?"

He winced. "Okay, first of all, that wasn't sex, and I'm normally much better at it. And, no, I can't come in, I have to go check on the others."

"You are good at it, and tell Sweetie Pie thanks for giving us some time up there alone. Good night." She leaned in and gave him a kiss, which given the low, rough groan that escaped him, he'd dream about later.

Inside, she took a long, hot shower, put on a big old T-shirt, left out some cheese for Chuck—or so she hoped—and then was surprised to hear something outside. "Chuck," she said with excitement, and opened the door.

"Not Chuck."

Nope. Not even close. But she remained excited as her heart executed a slow summersault at the sight of Cam standing there on her doorstep. He had his hands shoved in his pockets, looking unsettled, frustrated, and sexy as hell. He'd changed out of his weather gear and into baggy cargoes and a sweatshirt, hood up, smelling like soap, shampoo, and sexy guy. "Change your mind about that drink?"

"Yeah. No. Christ." He shoved off his hood, tunneling his fingers into his hair. "*Yes.*"

"I don't mean to be bossy or demanding," she teased gently, "but that glower is really putting a damper on my lingering sexual high from the mountain. So if you could at least try to look like you had a nice time until you're out of my sight again, that would help my ego. A lot."

He looked at her a moment, then behind him as if to make sure they were alone. Clearly not trusting even that, he nudged her inside, followed her, then shut the door.

And looked at her some more, which worked for her. "Hot chocolate?" she asked.

"What are you wearing beneath that T-shirt?"

"Not much," she admitted, wishing he wore the same. Though his sweatshirt looked damn good on that torso. He had his hands on his lean hips, his legs looking longer than the legal limit in those cargo pants. His boots were as scarred as his poor heart, the one she wanted to hold in her hands and keep warm and safe.

Which was a little like wishing she could pet a wild mountain cat, really, because no one touched Cam's heart.

He was doing his damnedest to see to that.

His eyes were stark green and filled to the brim with intelligence and heat, though minus his usual wry amusement. His mouth was a little grim and firm, and she had the sudden urge to kiss all that grimness away. "Okay, while you're very pretty all sexy and brooding," she said, "I'm going to have to insist that you loosen up—"

Which was all she got out before he backed her to the door. "I can't loosen up. I can't do anything with you thinking that what happened up there tonight was the best I've got to give you. It wasn't, by the way."

It was hard to concentrate with his rock-hard thighs pressing into her bared ones. The thick cotton of his pants felt soft against her skin, the muscles beneath those cargoes not even close to soft. Nope, they were rock hard.

And that wasn't all that was hard. She had to touch, had to, so she glided her hands down his chest—

"Oh no, you don't." Taking her hands in his, he lifted them up to either side of her head, pressing in so that she could feel his erection. "I'm not going off early again. This time it's about you." Dipping his head, he ran his hot gaze over her.

She knew what he saw. Her shirt had risen up on her thighs, most likely revealing at least some of her sunny yellow bikini panties. The knowledge that she was so exposed made thinking all but impossible. "I told you, I got plenty out of tonight."

He touched his forehead to hers. "I need another chance here."

"So this is an ego visit? To prove your sexual prowess?"

He paused at that, and she waited for a line from him, a charming, arousing line that would melt her panties right off, as if they needed any more melting. He could have done it too. He was the master of charm when he wanted to be, and she already knew she was helpless against it.

But in a move that startled her to the bone, he went with complete and bare honesty. "Yeah."

She stared at him, moved in spite of herself. "You don't have to prove anything to me. You should know that by now."

"I don't want to prove anything at all, I want to show you."

He nudged a thigh between hers, gliding along the bare flesh of her inner thighs, brushing her panties.

Her breath caught audibly.

"I want to make you feel some of what I feel when I'm with you," he told her.

Halfway there, she could have said—if she could have spoken, that is. As far as charming went, and arousing, it didn't get better than this, but what drew her, what made her melt, was that he wasn't just giving her a line at all.

He meant it. "Again, then," she murmured.

"And then afterward, maybe I'll be able to breathe around you."

"You can't breathe around me?"

"No, and I need to be able to breathe, Katie."

"So you think afterward, it'll all go away? This attraction? Is that how it works for you?"

"Yes." Then he kissed her. Completely. Thoroughly. And good God, the man could kiss. He kissed all her thoughts right out of her head; then he kissed the bones right out of her body. He kissed her until she couldn't have even said her name to save her own life.

It went on, long and hot, deep and wet, his tongue stroking hers, his hands letting go of hers to stroke her body as well, for how long she didn't know. And when they came up for air, she could only stare at him.

Not breathing any too steadily himself, he offered a self-deprecating smile that went straight to her heart. His hair was messed up from her fingers. She'd gotten his sweatshirt off, his shirt unbuttoned. Her hand was over his heart. The hair on his chest was soft compared to the hard, hot flesh beneath. His pants were half undone, and the sight of his ripped abs upped her heat several million degrees.

Closing her eyes, she set her cheek to his chest and felt the beat of his heart thumping in tune to hers. "I'm awfully worked up here, Cam."

His hand came up to her head, the other stroking down her back, slipping into her panties. "That makes two of us." He squeezed her butt, then dipped lower, his fingers unerringly finding her and ripping a hungry sound from her throat as she spread her legs for him.

"God, you're sweet." He bent a little, seeking her mouth with his again as he touched her. "So damn sweet."

"Not that sweet," she managed, pushing his shirt the rest of the way off his shoulders. He bunched hers up to her waist to take in her skimpy panties. "Ah, man. First pink, now yellow—" His hands were shaky as he continued to lift her shirt up, letting out another of those sexy raw groans when he revealed her bare breasts. "Look at you," he murmured.

"Listen, I know we already rushed—Ohmigod," she choked out when he rasped a tongue over a nipple, then drew it into his mouth. "Rushed things, before, on the mountain—"

He made his way to her other breast and her eyes rolled back in her head. "Cam—Please. Oh, please—"

Her rushed, breathless words seemed to unleash him.

Them.

In less time than it took to draw in her next breath, he had the shirt off over her head, sailing across the room behind him, and his fingers hooked in her panties, tugging them down.

No slouch, she got his pants to his thighs, freeing his essentials.

And, oh God, his essentials . . . He was big and hard and hot, and her being so naked while he was still relatively clothed was a shocking turn-on. But before she could take the time to fully admire what she held in both her hands, he'd crouched down and gently spread her legs farther; then he leaned in and put his mouth on her, stroking her with his tongue.

Her bones liquefied. She dug her fingers into his shoulders for an anchor in her spinning world while he added his fingers to the mix, sliding one inside her as he flicked his tongue over the current center of her universe. Her hips pushed at him in slow, rocking circles that she couldn't control. "Cam," she gasped, on the edge, the very edge, and when he responded by sucking her gently into his mouth, she took a flying leap.

She was anchored upright by his hands on her hips, which turned out to be all that kept her from sinking to the floor. When the blood pumping through her veins dulled to a low roar, she blinked her vision clear. His eyes were blazing with male satisfaction, while his entire body practically vibrated with tension as he straightened, a condom in his fingers. Her hands bumped into his as she tried to help roll it over the length of him, but all she really accomplished was making herself hotter. Him, too, if his heavy breathing and the sheen of sweat on his brow meant anything. He lifted her up, thunked her against the door, and then with one thrust was inside her.

Filling her nearly to bursting.

God, oh God. He began to move and she moaned at the withdrawal, gasped at the delicious return as he held her trapped to the wall for his achingly slow thrusts. His hold on her hips prevented her from speeding him up, or from taking any more than he gave. He was in charge, completely, and the knowledge of that had her toes already curling. Somehow he managed to hold her off, dragging things out, stroking her with careful, purposeful thrusts that suffused her in mindless pleasure, taking her higher and higher, until she could barely stand it. "Cam—"

At the panting sound of his name on her lips, he made a rough sound, the muscle in his jaw bunching. "I know." His mouth was at her ear, his breath rough and uneven as he stroked her with those fierce thrusts that kept pushing her up and outside of herself. "God, I know."

Yeah, He was lost in her. And she was completely lost in him as well. Lost, and she tightened her arms and legs on him, holding him to her, which didn't prove to be necessary because he had her as she exploded like a supernova. He had her and wasn't letting her go; then suddenly she realized she wasn't lost at all.

But found.

Found, right there in the dark, damp aftermath, against the door, gently cradled by the strong, silent Cameron Wilder, the man who, in spite of her promise to the contrary, she'd most definitely begun to fall for.

Cam woke up suddenly in the dark. He and Katie hadn't managed to get more than a few feet from the front door, where they'd made some wild crazy love that he was still exhausted from, and were sprawled together on the couch. A tight fit, but he realized she was crying, sobbing, as if her heart had broken, which was what had woken him. "Katie?"

"No." Her voice was raw and filled with wrenching grief, writhing as if held back by something. "No, they're not dead, they're not, they're just trapped."

He pulled her in tight, stroking her damp hair back from her face. "Katie, you're dreaming."

"They're not dead." She dug her fingers into his pecs. "Please don't let them all be dead!"

"Baby, come on. Wake up."

Her eyes flew open and she went stiff in his arms, breathing like she'd been running a marathon.

"Just a dream," he repeated softly, and when she jerked out of his arms, he reached past her to turn on the lamp.

Her eyes were glassy, glazed over. Her skin was clammy and pale. She broke his heart. "Katie—"

"Water," she said, her hand on her throat. "I need some water."

"Okay." He got off the couch, went to the kitchen for a glass, and when he came back, she was burrowed under the blanket he'd tossed over them an hour ago.

She didn't move, but he didn't believe she was already asleep. He sank back to the couch and slowly pulled her against him. She went willingly, pressing her face to the crook of his neck.

He stroked his hands up and down her body to try to warm her up. "Do you do this every night?"

"It's getting better."

In other words, yes. "Katie, do you ever talk about it, because maybe that would help—"

"No." She shuddered. "It wouldn't."

She dreamed about the people who hadn't lived, was tortured by the fact that she had, even as she'd used the entire experience to try to better her life.

And what had he done with his accident? An accident that had been his own fault, an accident where no one else besides him had been injured? He'd felt sorry for himself.

Talk about humbling. Heart hurting for her, he stroked her hair, her back, waiting until he knew she'd drifted back to sleep for real.

But it was a long time before it came for him.

Chapter 17

The next morning, Annie chopped tomatoes for that night's spaghetti sauce. Knife in hand, she looked around for something else to chop dead just as Cam came in the back door. One look at him, at the sleepy-lidded eyes and the unmistakable and utter lack of tension in his body, and she knew. "Are you kidding me?"

"What?"

"Don't what me," she snapped. "It's *my* turn for sex, dammit!"

He went directly to the pot, but she lifted her knife in his direction and he backed off.

"No one eats my food until *I* get mine."

He arched a brow. "Should I tell Nick to put more men on the job?"

"You joke when I'm holding a knife on you?"

He lifted his hands in surrender, and she jerked her chin toward the door. "Stone has a group that needs a guide to take them ice picking up Tenneman Falls. You're it."

"I know. He just paged me out of bed."

"Oh, boo-hoo." She kicked him out of the kitchen, then sagged against the counter. Her life was out of control.

Her love life was out of control.

Her marriage . . .

Dammit. She'd always known this would happen, that she'd somehow muck everything up, because like the rest of the Wilders, she was always on a hell-bent mission to self-destruct her own happiness. It pissed her off. She slammed the knife into another tomato.

She could blame her mother and father, the alcoholic misfits who'd had no right having children. Or she could blame a system that let kids suffer.

But since she'd so adamantly refused to let Cam be a product of his environment, she knew she couldn't very well do it either. So she'd raised herself, so what. And so when she'd finished that, she'd raised Cam, too, and then she'd gone out and gotten herself the life she wanted.

The end.

Only she'd *still* managed to continue the cycle and destroy that life, because apparently some of her parents' genes lived deep inside her. God, that royally pissed her off. She grabbed a few green peppers and slammed her knife into those as well.

She really missed having a man in her bed to ease some of this tension. She missed having someone hold her close, someone to make her laugh, make her purr.

Warm her feet.

She missed waking up knowing she could have a quickie if she wanted. She missed cooking for someone who was *hers*, heart and soul.

She missed the skinny lug, dammit, missed everything about him. He really had some nerve taking this divorce thing so seriously.

Okay, that was her fault too. She'd pushed for it. Pushed and pushed, only wanting him to push back, even once.

She shoved the peppers aside and looked for something else, but there was nothing but his coat hanging on the hook by the back door, reminding her that he was here, within touch, and yet untouchable.

They really had stopped seeing each other, and God, that hurt. But dammit, she was turning forty, not dying. She wanted romance. She wanted to be wooed. Was that so wrong? Had she grown unattractive? Somehow lost her sex appeal? She looked down at her new clothes. No. She had it going on, and she needed him to see that, now.

Right now.

She washed her hands, grabbed Nick's spare coat, jammed on a knit hat, and headed out. It was snowing, natch, and she sank into the fresh snow as she headed around the back of the lodge to the equipment garage.

The side door was locked. She glanced at the KNOCK FIRST sign, but the compressor was on, not to mention Nick was probably wearing his iPod blasting at decibels uncharted, so knocking wouldn't do her any good. She trudged through the snow to the front of the garage, punched in the key code, and waited as the electric garage door began to lift.

Just as it did, a gust of wind blew up, knocking some branches of the trees above her. They completely unloaded, dumping snow on her head. "Perfect," she muttered, swiping her face. When she could see again, Nick stood there in the opened garage door, hands on his hips, glaring at her. He wore threadbare jeans and a Cal sweatshirt shoved up to the elbows. He looked rumpled, edgy, temperamental, and dammit, sexy. "I was painting," he grated out. "Until you open the door without so much as a knock, sending snow and gook and stuff inside, and now I'll have to start over."

She blinked more snow from her eyelashes as she mentally erased *sexy* from the list because she refused to be attracted to a complete ass. "Well, excuse me for trying to—"

"What? For trying to what? Ruin my day? You need to yell

at me some more? Ignore me? What? What was it that couldn't wait until I was done that you had to barge in here without knocking and ruin the paint job?"

Well, dammit. She was going to lose it. She recognized the tell-tale signs easily enough—burning throat, stinging eyes, tickle in her nose.

But hell if she'd cry in front of this unfeeling, unsentimental bastard. "Sign the damn papers!" And with that, she whirled away, heading back toward the lodge, where she was going to make a big batch of brownies and eat every single one in celebration of her impending divorce.

For two days, Katie pretty much smiled through her work. She couldn't think, not with all the glowing she was doing. Mostly nothing distracted her from numbers. Mostly, numbers were the only thing that had ever made sense in her world.

And then she'd come to Wilder Adventures.

Met Cam.

Fell for Cam.

Slept with Cam.

Okay, so there'd been no sleeping involved, and she knew damn well that in his mind, what they'd done had been nothing more than a relieving of the tension.

But he was wrong.

It'd been more.

Far more.

She'd been here for three weeks, three of the best weeks of her life, thanks to a certain sexy guy who'd shown up on her doorstep two nights ago and taken her to heaven and back with his body. She could use a few more nights like that, but he'd taken a trip to Tenneman Falls.

She'd hoped to spend more time with him before she left, but that time was running short. Maybe she should wish on another falling star. . . . Laughing at herself, she picked up the deposit bag and headed for the bank. Her car handled itself just fine on the clear roads, though when she got into Wishful, she couldn't park in front of the bank because of a huge mountain of pushed snow. Instead, she had to park in front of Wishful Delights, from which came the most delicious scent. She resisted, barely.

When she came out of the bank, she told herself not to inhale, but then she saw her flat tire. She crouched down to take a closer look. She'd run over a pair of pliers, which were now sticking out of the rubber. "Only me." She opened her trunk and eyed first the spare tire, then what she was wearing, a white sweater.

This was going to suck golf balls.

"Looks like someone's having a bad day."

Turning, she faced Serena. The tall, willowy brunette wore skinny black trousers and a black angora sweater that emphasized her gorgeous figure and face. It didn't escape Katie that the two of them looked like night and day. "You could say that."

"Maybe you've got bad karma. You know, from the other night when you took that moonlit snowshoe hike and almost got knocked off the cliff."

Katie blinked. "How do you know that?"

"Small town, remember?" Serena laughed, a low and husky sound that would attract any man with a pulse. "But it worked out for you. After all, you and Cam ended up alone on that mountain. I assume you slept with him."

Katie felt her brow shoot up so far it probably vanished into her hair. "What?"

"Yeah, Nick told Annie."

"And Annie told you?"

"We're friends."

"Annie told you I slept with Cam," Katie repeated, feeling more betrayed than she'd have thought possible.

"No. I said I assumed that part. Annie told me you almost fell. She was quite pissed on your behalf, actually. Annie doesn't show it much, but she's a softie for those in her circle, and you are in her circle. So I was right? The Cam thing? You and him, bumping nasties?"

Katie let out a mirthless laugh. What else could she do? "You know what assuming gets you, right?"

"Uh-huh. It makes me a bitch." Serena shrugged. "I can live with that." She looked at Katie's flat tire. "I'm pretty sure the odds of that are astronomical."

"Did you do this?"

"Hey, I'm a bitch but not a vindictive one. I can get a tire changed, though." She smiled. "If asked nicely."

"I can't ask you to help me do this."

"I offered."

"You'll get dirty."

Serena laughed and pulled a cell phone from her pocket. "Harley? Yeah, I've got a flat tire." She paused, listening while studying her manicure, which was, of course, in perfect condition. "Fantastic. Thanks." She closed her cell. "Harley's the local mechanic and tow-truck driver. How about a cookie while you wait?"

Katie's hips were already straining the top button on her pants. She'd be willing to bet big money that Serena never had to strain to fit that willowy body into anything. "No, thanks."

"Are you kidding me? You're going to turn down my cookies?"

"Okay, I have to ask."

"Why am I being so nice to you?"

"That's the one."

"It's the neighborly thing to do."

Katie didn't buy it, but she followed Serena into her bakery because her nose wouldn't let her do anything else.

Serena poured her a big mug of coffee, waiting until Katie took a sip before casually asking, "So how is he in the sack? Still amazing? Because once upon a time, he could really spin my wheels, if you know what I mean."

Katie executed a spit take.

"Oh, come on." Serena handed her a napkin. "You're not a woman to beat around the bush."

"I'm also not a woman to talk about someone behind his back." Damn, she'd gotten her sweater dirty after all. "Especially with his ex. Even if no one else around here gives the same courtesy."

"Well, Jesus, if you're going to get all sanctimonious." Serena sighed long and hard. "Annie didn't say anything negative about you. In fact, she actually only talked about Cam. She said he's smiling for the first time since his accident. He's laughing." She rolled her eyes. "He's happy."

And there it was. The first good news of Katie's day. "I think that's nice."

"Yeah, it is. Unfortunately, it has nothing to do with me and everything to do with you."

When Katie opened her mouth, Serena shook her head. "Don't. I'm a bitch, but I'm not stupid. Watching him fall for you is painful. So just drink my damn coffee and don't say anything. I'm trying to be the bigger person here by helping you out with your tire and letting him go gracefully, and I'm failing."

Katie let out a breath. "You're not failing."

"Really?"

"Really. If you hadn't come outside when you did, I'd be a muddy wreck by now. And you make great coffee."

Serena slid a plate of cookies on the counter, and Katie's nostrils twitched. "I can't. I'll get fat."

Serena smiled guilelessly. "Works for me."

Okay, not so guileless.

A big tow truck pulled up outside. Katie expected a big guy to jump down, but it was a tiny, dainty-looking, fair-skinned blonde to enter the bakery wearing Carhartt weather overalls, steel-toed boots, and a quick smile. "Who's the yo-yo who ran over a set of pliers?"

Katie raised her hand. "That would be me. Are you Harley?"

"In the flesh. You did a number on your tire. I think it's fatal. Hope your spare's in good shape." The mechanic came forward, started to offer a hand, then looked down at it and stopped, shaking her head. Her short, spiky hair danced around her face. "Sorry, I've got grease all over me."

"What's new?" Serena asked her dryly.

Harley smiled. "Had to rescue a group of kids off the highway. They'd ditched school and driven up here from the bay hoping to snowboard. Keys, city girl?"

"Oh. Here." Katie handed them over. Harley went out the door but was back in less than a minute, shaking her head. "No good."

"What do you mean no good?"

"Your spare is flat too."

"What?"

"Yeah, when's the last time you checked it?"

Oh, about never. At the look on her face, Harley sighed. "You're going to have to leave me the car. I'll tow it to my shop, but I have a test to take before I can fix you up."

"A test?"

"She's going to school to become a fancy schmancy biologist so she can go work in the forest instead of beneath trucks," Serena said.

"Yeah, I'm on the seven-year plan to a four-year degree. In any case, the test is online and shouldn't take me long."

"No problem, I can get a ride back to Wilder." Or so she hoped. "I'll just call the lodge."

Harley lifted a brow and looked at Serena. "The lodge? The Wilder Lodge?"

"Yeah, I should have mentioned. Katie here is Riley's temp at Wilder."

"Oh," Harley said, making the word about ten syllables. "So *you're* the new hire hanging out with Cam."

"Okay," Katie said. "What's it going to run me?"

Harley shrugged. "How about the cost of the new tire and a couple of those free ski passes Wilder Adventures gives out sometimes?"

"No," Katie said, "I mean what's it going to cost me to have the two of you, to have everyone, stop looking at me like I'm stealing their favorite son?"

"Well, you could leave town," Serena said helpfully.

"Play nice, Serena," Harley said mildly.

"I was just kidding. Mostly."

Uh-huh. Katie reached for the cookies, needing the sugar. "I'll take a dozen to go."

Serena picked up one of her black-and-white bags and started to fill it with a smug look on her face.

"*Two* dozen," Katie corrected, playing right into her hands and no longer caring.

Chapter 18

Cam came back to Wilder after a long two-day trip and went straight up to the offices to check in with Stone.

Okay, lie. He went straight up to the offices to catch a glimpse of Katie.

Because he'd been wrong about the whole being able to breathe after sex with her. Very wrong. He hadn't taken a good deep breath since the last time he'd seen her. He had no idea what exactly to do with that information. None. He only knew that he had to see her again.

"Looking for something?" Stone asked when he came out of his office and caught Cam staring at Katie's empty chair.

"The mail."

"Mail's on my desk. Why don't you ask me what you really want to know."

"All right." Cam searched his brain. "Where's the schedule?"

Stone just looked at him. It was the same look he'd perfected years ago, the older brother what-have-you-done-and-what's-it-going-to-cost-me-to-bail-you-out look. "Is it that hard to admit you're attached to something, someone?"

"Okay. You're right. I missed you." Cam stepped close and

hugged him, slapping him extra hard on the back. "Whew. Glad to get that off my chest."

"You didn't miss me." Stone shoved him away with a laugh. "You know who you missed. You missed the pretty temp."

"I don't know what you're talking about." Cam turned to look at Katie's desk.

"So you don't care that she left a week early."

"What? What the fuck—" He whirled back to Stone in time to see his brother's wide-ass grin. "That's just mean."

Stone just kept grinning but was wise enough to back up out of arm's length. "She's at the bank."

"If you sent her on the snowmobile by herself, I'll—"

"Car. Christ, you've got it bad. And—" he said quickly, holding up his hands when Cam growled. "There's nothing wrong with that. Nothing. Which is why, maybe, you should ask her to stay instead of leaving next week."

"Are you crazy? Why would I ask her to do that?"

"Oh gee, I don't know. Maybe because you're going nuts at the thought of her going?"

"I am not. I don't care." At Stone's long look, he turned away again. "And she wouldn't stay. She's got plans. Adventures."

"Then no one is more equipped to take her on than you."

"So, what, I should up and leave again?"

"I don't know. I don't want you to. But the alternative is to walk away from her."

"She's walking. *She's* the one walking."

"Come on, Cam."

"What?"

"You know what."

"You think *I'm* walking? Again? Quitting, again?"

"Yeah, I do."

Cam's chest hurt, like he was having a heart attack. But it was a ball of anxiety and he knew it. He *wanted* to turn around and walk. Hell, he wanted to run. And keep running, until his chest didn't hurt anymore. "You keep throwing that at me."

"And maybe one of these days it'll stick. You'll stick."

"Jesus, what do you want from me?"

Annie came up the stairs, took in the sight of them standing so close, steaming with temper, and quickly stepped between them, a hand on each of their chests. "What? What are you fighting about?"

Stone eyed Cam over Annie's head. "I'm just reminding Cam he's good at quitting."

Annie's hand was like steel against Cam's chest when he pushed at her in response. "And I was just going to remind Stone what his face would look like with my fist in it," he said through his teeth.

"Okay, back off, both of you." Annie added a shove to the directive. "You want to fight and get out all this stupid tension, fine. I'll even join you and beat the hell out of the both of you just for fun. But we do it outside. I like the furniture in here."

Stone made a sound of disgust in his throat and turned away, and Cam's chest hurt worse for it, because he knew.

Stone was right.

He strode to the stairs, needing some damn place to be alone.

"Where are you going?" Annie asked.

"He's running," Stone said.

"Shut up, Stone."

"If you're running off," Annie said to Cam, "then run into town to get my damn pies."

Cam sighed. "Tell Nick to do it."

"I'm not talking to him."

Code for Nick had been an idiot for some reason or another. "Maybe you could not talk to me either."

"No such luck for you. Two cherry, two apple, and don't eat one on your way back."

Stone snorted.

"One time," Cam said. "That happened one time." He took the stairs, grimly satisfied to see Annie smack Stone upside the head.

With frustration still fueling him, he drove into town, unable to ease any tension on the semislicked roads. By the time he drove into Wishful, he was even more tense than when he'd left the lodge.

But Katie's car was parked out front of the bakery, interestingly enough with a pair of pliers sticking out of her tire. He walked inside and caught sight of her, and then . . . *Then* all the seething, churning, shitaceous crap inside of his gut eased. Inexplicably.

Irrevocably.

She was laughing, sincerely laughing in the way only she could, with her eyes, her face, her entire body, while Serena and Harley stood one on either side of her looking at her as if maybe she had a screw loose.

Which was entirely possible, but Cam liked her exactly as she was, and if either of them had been rude to her, he'd—

What? He'd what? He staggered to a halt, stunned by the overwhelming, gut-wrenching emotion churning inside of him. Protectiveness? And even more shocking, *possessiveness*— two emotions he'd never had any use for when it came to women. Hell, he never had any use for them when it came to anything—not his home, his business, nothing.

But shockingly, he realized *she* mattered, and he stared at her, feeling like he'd been hit by a Mack truck.

She glanced over, and though she stopped laughing, her smile didn't fade. If anything, it warmed. Something came into her eyes too. Something that said, *I've held you in my hands and watched you come.*

Shit.

She pulled off her glasses and wiped them on the hem of her sweater, and he wondered if he'd fogged them again.

And was he the only man to do that to her?

Serena sighed, walked over to him, and gently tapped on his chin, reminding him to shut his mouth. "You didn't have to come rescue your little girlfriend. We're doing just fine."

"Annie wants pies. Two apple, two cherry."

"Aw, and you came to me? How sweet."

"You're the only pie in town."

She sighed again. "Okay, one of these days I'm going to get through, Cam. One of these days."

Katie was clutching a bag in one hand, with a cookie in the other, and if he wasn't mistaken, there were more than a few chocolate crumbs on the left corner of her mouth. "Saw the pliers," he said.

"Yeah. Only me, right?" She shook her head and licked the crumbs off her lips. She also took the last bite of the cookie, then stuck her thumb into her mouth and sucked the crumbs off of that, and he found himself hungrily watching the motion of her tongue. "Harley's going to fix it."

"After I take a test." Harley smiled in greeting and moved close for a hug.

They'd gone to high school together and had spent many, many, *many* days together in detention. "You getting close to that degree yet?" he asked, affectionately rubbing the spot of grease on her chin.

"Very close. So . . ." She hesitated. "How's T.J.?"

She and T.J. had spent considerable time together too. *Not* in detention. "Still in Alaska."

"Freezing his balls off, I hope," she said sweetly.

Thankful he wasn't T.J. at the moment, he reached for the pies Serena had bagged up and eyed Katie. "So you're stuck in town."

"A little bit, yes."

"Want a ride?"

"Please." She slid off the stool. "Do you have the snow-mobile?" she asked hopefully.

"Sorry, no." Up at Tenneman Falls he'd promised himself that he wouldn't take advantage of her for the week she had left. If there was a move to make, she'd have to make it, and he'd just be there for her.

Yeah.

That's what he'd promised himself. But now, with her right here in front of him, he wanted to grab her, toss her over his shoulder and into his truck, where he'd get her naked in two point zero seconds flat.

Instead, he opened the bakery door for her. Outside, she lightly kicked her tire. "Probably I should have wished for grace and poise on that falling star."

He thought she had grace and poise in abundance, just not the traditional kind.

"But actually, I'm glad about the wish I did make." Her smile went just a little bit naughty. "Very glad."

He got hard. Shaking his head at himself—that wasn't her making a move, he told himself—he opened the passenger door of his truck for her and managed to lean in for a sniff of her hair. Fucking pathetic, he told himself as he came around to the driver's side and started the engine. He pulled into the street and relaxed marginally at the silence, because maybe she wasn't going to talk. That worked for him.

"What's the matter?"

So much for that. "Nothing."

"Nothing's making you tense enough to shatter?"

He silently pleaded the Fifth.

"How about a kiss? If you don't want to talk," she said when he slid her a look. "Kind of like a hello-after-two-days thing."

"I'm driving."

"You could have kissed me before, when you first saw me."

"I promised myself you had to make the first move."

"What?"

"Never mind. Listen, I'm clearly having a problem communicating today across the board. Maybe we could not talk."

"Pull over, Cam."

"You're right. That was rude. I—"

"Pull over right now, please."

He did, then reached for her so that she couldn't escape, because that's what he figured she would do. She'd slam the door on him, then go off and pout like all the women in his life ever had. Or maybe she wanted to throw something at his head. At least she didn't have her own car, so he was fairly certain she didn't plan on trying to run him over, which was a small comfort because he didn't want her to leave his truck at all.

But apparently this woman was not done defying his expectations or surprising him, because it wasn't the door she reached for, but him. She reached for him at the same moment he reached for her. He opened his mouth to say something, anything, to make her stay, but then her mouth was on his. She bumped his nose with hers and dislodged her glasses, which she yanked off with an annoyed little sound; then she kissed him again.

At the connection of their two bodies, his went on immediate overdrive. Before he knew it, he'd dove right into the kiss as if he hadn't just been silently apologizing for all the others. He had one hand holding her head for his plunging tongue, the other inside her jacket, beneath her sweater, gliding his thumb over her breast, thrilling to the low, desperately hungry noises she made in the back of her throat. God. Her hands were just as busy, in his hair, on his chest, heading south, playing with the button fly of his jeans—

"How was that for a first move?" she murmured, pulling back.

He let out a breath. "I thought you were trying to get away from me."

"Did that feel like I was trying to get away from you? Really?"

He looked into her glossy eyes, at her cheeks that were bright with color, at the mouth he could never get enough of, the one still wet from his, and felt boggled.

"If you can't remember," she murmured. "Maybe I'd better kiss you again."

"Maybe you'd better."

But she was looking around them, staring at the windows, which were completely steamed up, cocooning them in their own world. "How long were we at it?"

"I have no idea." But he was going to need a minute before going back to the lodge.

Maybe two. He had to laugh at himself. At her. And then she was laughing too. Their eyes met, the laughter faded, and in the next beat they dove at each other again, hands fighting to get inside clothing—

At the knock on his window, Cam nearly bashed his head on the roof. *"Jesus."*

"Who—"

"No idea—" Through the fogged windows he caught the tall outline of Stone.

Katie was working frantically in the opposite direction now, trying to straighten her clothes instead of getting out of them. Cam waited until she gave a nod, then turned the key and hit the button for the window, and met Stone's cynical expression.

"You don't care, huh?" Stone's steady gaze flicked to Katie. Cam turned to look at her too. She hadn't gotten her jacket zipped back up, revealing the fact that she'd misbuttoned her sweater. She looked like he'd cared all over her.

Stone chewed on his tongue a moment. "I got the call about your tire, Katie. I went to go check on you, to give you a ride back."

"Thanks, but, uh, Cam found me."

Stone's gaze once again slid toward Cam, whose hair was probably as messy as Katie's. His shirt was rumpled, and let's not forget the boner he was sporting.

He looked like someone who cared a whole helluva lot.

Stone merely patted the door, gave Cam one last long look, then walked back to his truck.

"What did he mean?" Katie asked him.

"Did I ever tell you Stone's got a drug problem? I keep telling him crack kills but . . ."

She laughed. "Cam."

"Okay, he's got early signs of Alzheimer's."

"Or . . ." she said, smile fading. "Shut up, Katie. Is that right?"

Or that.

"So this is like all the other times then?" she asked quietly. "Where I get too close and you need your distance?"

"I—" Christ, he felt like he was spinning. "Maybe. Look, honestly? I'm an ass."

"I appreciate you realizing that." She sighed. "But actually, this is my fault. I need to remember we're just . . . What are we exactly?"

At the look that crossed his face, she put up a hand. "You know what? Never mind."

Kicking his own ass, he started the truck and drove them back to the lodge. Katie started to get out, then turned to him, and he braced himself.

"I've made it pretty clear how I feel," she told him. "I've told you I'm attracted to you. I've *showed* you I'm attracted to you. I've assured you that I'm not looking for a white picket fence and a diamond ring. At least not this winter, and not from you."

He met her gaze, which was steely and determined and filled with frustrated affection.

Affection for him.

"I've told you all that," she said with that inner strength he admired so much shining there. "And yet still you hold back. Why is that, Cam?"

He wished he knew.

And when he didn't answer, couldn't answer, she sighed softly, shut the door, and walked away. Wanting him but not needing him.

And the hell of it was, the stupid crux . . . it was *him* who needed *her*.

Katie kept herself busy. She rented out the snowmobiles when a group came by. She helped Nick get another group ready for a snowshoe hike. She arranged for a family reunion to take place up on Alpine Ridge. She worked on the books. And after all that, she was *still* stirred up, both sexually and temperamentally.

Cam had wanted her to make the first move. Well, she'd made *all* the first moves.

But she was done. If there was another move to be made before she left, he'd have to make it.

"Mail." Annie tossed it down to her desk. She was back in her baggy clothes. Today's apron read: IF YOU DON'T LIKE MY COOKING, LOWER YOUR STANDARDS.

Katie sighed. "What happened?"

"Nothing. Nothing happened. Which is my point. Why shave my damn legs and wear uncomfortable clothes if nothing is going to happen?"

Exactly. "He didn't notice you?"

"He yelled at me because he said I ruined his painting."

"Did you?"

"Sort of." She grimaced. "I ignored the KNOCK FIRST sign and brought in a whole bunch of snow with me. I ruined whatever he was working on. He got all pissed off before he even looked at me."

"And let me guess," Katie said. "In return, you were sweet and kind and understanding."

"Yes!" Annie sagged. "Okay, no. I snapped. I snapped and yelled and stalked off."

Yeah, She could relate. She'd snapped and stalked off on Cam as well. "Before he got a look at you?"

"Before I even took off my coat."

"Well, then, it doesn't count," she said firmly. "Look, *some-one* should get things right today. You have to try again."

"No." Annie shook her head. "No way. He had one shot at me, and that was it."

"Are you saying then that *you* only deserve one shot too? Because what if that was yours, Annie? Wouldn't you want another chance?"

She sure as hell did.

And yet it wasn't up to her and she knew it. It was up to a man who had no positive experiences with relationships, a man who may not ever *want* a positive experience, a more stubborn man than she'd ever met.

Chapter 19

At five o'clock, Katie left the lodge and stepped into the lightly falling snow. Her car was parked out front with no note and no sign of how it'd gotten there.

Cam?

Given how she'd left things with him, she sort of doubted that. Stone? Maybe. Unfortunately, she had no one to ask because both brothers were out on a cross-country ski trip to Stone Creek.

And Annie was nowhere to be found either.

Hoping that meant the chef was busy seducing Nick, Katie got into her car and drove back to Wishful to thank Harley, and also to pay her. She took the lightly covered roads slowly and carefully, letting out a breath of relief when she made it to town with no problem. Driving down the main street, she realized she had no idea where Harley's garage or shop was, so she pulled up to Wishful Delights. Serena was just turning the CLOSED sign around on her front door, and she didn't look overly thrilled to see Katie.

"I'm only going to let you in if you buy something," she said. "Something big."

Katie hadn't come for anything to eat, but at the scent of

the place, she decided that her mind could be changed. "I wouldn't turn down some more cookies."

"There's a three dozen minimum."

"Since when?"

"Since you came to town."

"Serena," Harley said mildly from a barstool at the counter, "that shade of bitch doesn't go with your Prada."

Serena rolled her eyes and moved aside for Katie to come in. Harley waved at her and Katie smiled back, her gaze locked in on the fresh delicious cookies in the glass displays.

Serena moved back behind the counter. "You know, typically women having great sex don't need as many cookies as you do."

Katie left that statement alone and looked at Harley. "What do I owe you for fixing and delivering my car?"

"I've already been paid, and I didn't deliver it."

"What? Who paid you?"

"Oh, for God's sake." Serena bent behind the counter and came up with a bottle of vodka and three shot glasses. "I'm going to need reinforcements for this."

"Me too." Harley nodded in appreciation. "I smashed my finger with my own hammer and I got a C-minus on my test. In fact, make mine a double."

"You and me both, babe." Serena doubled each of theirs, and then on second thought, tipped more into Katie's as well.

Katie had never had a shot of vodka in her life, much less a double. She wasn't a big drinker. In fact, on the few rare occasions she imbibed, she'd gone with a pansy-ass wine cooler.

But today she figured she could use a little heat.

"Cheers." Harley lifted her glass.

Serena clicked hers to Harley's. "Cheers," she said, waiting for Katie to lift her glass.

Katie then watched as both women tossed back their drinks

in one swallow. While in Rome . . . She tossed hers back as well, and nearly choked to death when the fire burned its way down her throat.

Harley slapped her on the back a few times. "You okay?"

When she could breathe, Katie nodded, eyes streaming. "Yikes."

"Don't worry." Serena poured them all another. "The second goes down easier."

Katie wrapped her fingers around her glass. "Who paid you?" she asked Harley.

"Oh, please," Serena said. "We all know it was your knight in shining armor."

"Cam?"

Serena lifted her second shot. "What, you have more than one boyfriend in town?"

"He's not my boyfriend."

"So you're not sleeping with him?"

"You didn't ask that." The vodka seemed to be making thinking a slower process. "You asked if he's my boyfriend."

"True," Harley told Serena. "You did."

Serena rolled her eyes. "Fine. Are you sleeping with him?"

Katie paused. "Isn't it over between you two? Which technically makes it none of your business."

Harley grinned at her. "You are way tougher than you look. I like that."

Serena lifted a shoulder. "So you know the story of Cam and I."

"Like you said, small town."

"And you catch on quick." Serena pointed to Katie's still-full glass. "You drinking with us tonight or not?"

Katie tossed back the shot. Serena was right, it didn't burn nearly as bad this time.

Serena poured again and turned up the radio. Harley began

singing along with it at the top of her lungs, until Serena lifted a brow. "Who sings this song?"

"Alicia Keys."

"Yeah? Well, let her sing it."

Harley laughed and kept right on singing. In fact, she stood up to add an ass-shaking boogie to go with it.

"Don't quit your day job, Harl."

Katie wanted to sing too. And her toes were tapping, though she managed to stay seated. Then she remembered that she no longer held back, that she lived every single second, so she got up and joined Harley. But even though she knew the words, she couldn't quite get in sync, with either the song or her own vision. "Wow." She straightened her glasses, but that didn't help.

"It's the vodka," Harley told her helpfully.

Serena raised her glass again. "To letting go. Dammit."

Katie stopped dancing to grab her glass. "I'm sorry it didn't work out the way you wanted."

"Not your fault." Harley nudged Serena meaningfully. "Is it?"

Serena sighed, then tossed back her third shot. "She's right. It's my fault. And as long as we're sharing, you should know. I loved the idea of Cam much more than I loved the reality of him. So don't worry, I'm done being a bitch." She lifted a shoulder. "Mostly."

"There you are." Harley hugged Serena. "Good girl. You did your best with him before it was over. You told him what you were feeling. You couldn't have done more."

"Let's be honest. I could have done more."

"Okay, well, except maybe you could have dumped him *before* you slept with someone else."

Serena winced. "Yeah. That." She covered her eyes. "I know, dammit. But when you're right, you're right. It just wasn't meant to be."

Katie drank her last shot. Didn't burn at all, and actually, it went down like smooth silk. However, she was having some trouble balancing on her barstool and grabbed on to the counter for balance. "I told Cam some of my feelings, but not what I *should* have told him."

"Yeah?" Serena looked at her speculatively. "Like what?"

"I should have told him that—" She hiccupped, then covered her mouth. " 'Xuse me. That he's hiding behind all those muscles and cool eyes. That he's really just a scared little boy, scared of one woman." She sighed. "So dumb."

"You could tell him now." Katie's cell phone was sitting on the counter next to her empty shot glass. Serena put a finger on it and pushed it toward her.

A small voice inside Katie said drunk dialing was never a good idea, but there was a louder voice saying, *Do it. Have your say.* And the next thing she knew, she was punching in Cam's number.

He answered with that low, raspy, sexy voice, and she tried to find her tongue.

"Hello?" he repeated.

Oh God. She'd lost it. She'd lost her tongue.

"Katie?"

She blinked. "How did you know?"

"Caller ID."

Right.

"Tell him," Serena whispered.

Katie held up a finger to Serena. She was getting up to the telling part. "Cam."

"Still me."

Was he amused? Dammit, she had a way of cracking him up at her own expense. "I want you to know, chickens aren't sexy. Not to me."

This was met with silence.

"Are you there?" She was slurring her words now, which

was embarrassing, so she took a deep breath. "Cam? Can you hear me?"

"Yes, chickens aren't sexy. Uh . . . I don't think they're meant to be."

"I was referring to you. You're the chicken. And . . ." And she was losing her train of thought.

"He's just a little boy," Harley reminded her helpfully. "Scared of one woman."

"Yes. That!" She pointed at Harley and smiled. "Thank you. You, Cam Wilder," she said into her cell phone, "are acting like a little boy. I'm only one woman; you can't possibly be scared of one woman, and . . . and . . ." Dammit. "And I want someone who isn't going to let me walk away. I want someone who sees my faults, all of them, and there are many. Many, *many* . . ." Wait. Not a good idea to point that out. "Scratch that. Okay? Forget my faults, this is about you and *your* faults."

"Katie—"

"I see them, Cam. I see all of them, and you know what? I want you anyway. I want you *because* of them. Because you're human. Because . . . Because you represent someone who's lived his life balls out—" She broke off at Harley's choked laugh. "Oh. Am I not supposed to say balls to someone who has balls?"

"Where are you?" he asked her tightly.

She hiccupped. "Eating cookies."

"And drinking," he guessed.

"A little. And pretending that you weren't relieved when I walked away from you this afternoon."

"*Katie.*"

She could hear the regret in his voice now, and also the utter assurance that he'd done the right thing in letting her walk away. Which was stupid because though she'd done the physical walking, *he'd* been the one to go. Frustrated at her own jumbled thoughts and at Cam himself, she shook her head. "That's all I can string together, but you get the gist."

"Yeah, I get the gist. Katie—"

"Good-bye, Cam." When she shut her phone, there was a moment of silence.

"That was impressive," Harley finally said.

Katie dropped her forehead to the counter. "I wasn't that impressive."

"I think you were perfect," Serena told her. "And brave. I like that you tell it how it is. I'm not charging you for the cookies. In fact, maybe we could work out a trade. I keep you in desserts, and you . . . you can help me out with my books. They're a mess."

"I'm leaving in a week."

"Where to?"

"I'm going to go back to LA first, visit my parents, pay my rent, and then drive wherever the car takes me."

"Bummer for both of us then."

Katie sighed and lifted her head, looking at her new friends, both as drunk as she. Well, maybe not quite as drunk as she. "I should have wished for *two* nights of great sex on that falling star."

"Huh?" Serena asked.

"I wished and it came true. I think I need another falling star."

Serena and Harley craned their necks and looked outside, where the brief storm had moved on. Night had fallen in its place, complete with a sky full of stars.

"I want to wish for great sex," Harley said to Serena.

"Me too," Serena said, and the three of them grabbed their coats and staggered outside, unsteady on their feet.

"It's cold." Harley announced the obvious as they sat down

on the curb in front of Katie's car. Shivering, they leaned back and waited for a falling star, their breath crystallizing in front of their faces.

"The vodka is warming me up," Katie said.

"Lightweight," Serena said.

That was true enough, so she didn't respond.

They all watched and waited, and when it happened, when a star twinkled bright and fell, all three of them gasped in unison at the beauty of it, and fell backward so that they were flat on the sidewalk.

"Wow," Serena whispered, staring upward. "Oh, wow, that's amazing."

"Shh." Katie couldn't take her eyes off the sky, where the last of the bursting light was fading. "Quick, wish. Wish hard and mean it."

Serena scrunched up her eyes and wished.

Harley followed suit.

And Katie made another wish: That when she was done with her adventures, she could find a place like this, a place where she belonged, with people in it to care about her. And maybe with a Cam of her own to keep . . .

They were still lying like that, flat on the sidewalk, faces upturned to the sky, when a truck drove up. Katie heard the door open, heard the crunch of footsteps stop at their feet.

"What the hell?"

Wow, he'd driven quick. But then again, he wasn't a weenie on the roads like she was.

"Why are you lying in the snow?" His voice was low and even, with a hint of incredulous disbelief, the voice of a man with the strapping physique and physical prowess that pretty much flatlined Katie's heart whenever she listened to him, not to mention all that quiet, sexy charm that went with. Embarrassed, she jerked upright at the same time that Harley and Serena did the same, and—

And bonked their heads together.

"Ow."

"Ow."

"*Ow.*"

"Great, it's the three stooges," Cam said over their comingling groans. "Or I should say the three *drunk* stooges."

Chapter 20

Holding her head, seeing stars, Katie fell back to the sidewalk again.

Cam's face appeared in her view as he leaned over her.

It was a gorgeous face, really, with those mesmerizing green eyes, and that scar above the left one. And then there was his crooked smile that had snagged her heart, but he wasn't smiling now. Nope, he was frowning, but she still wanted to kiss that mouth.

"What are you doing?" he asked.

"Making friends. Friends who won't walk away when I'm still talking."

"I didn't walk away. *You* did."

"Semantics." Or that's what she tried to say, but her tongue tripped all over itself.

Serena laughed and staggered to her feet, smacking Cam in the chest. "You're driving her plowed butt home, right?"

"I'm driving all of your plowed butts home." He held out his fingers. "Keys."

"Harley and I are good." Serena pulled on Harley's sleeve, helping her upright, where they leaned on each other. "We're going to hang out here and consume massive quantities of the best dessert in town."

"Psst," Harley said in a stage whisper. "You're the *only* dessert in town."

Serena shushed her and looked at Katie. "You could join us. Your choice."

"I could?"

"She could?" Cam said, just as surprised.

"Yes, but vaginas only. No dicks." Serena grinned and pointed at Cam. "And you, Cam Wilder, are a d—"

"Whoops," Harley said, covering Serena's mouth, pulling her toward the door. "I think that's enough vodka-induced insults."

Katie stared after them, feeling a warmth that had nothing to do with the vodka and everything to do with . . . belonging.

"Are you grinning at anything in particular?" Cam asked.

She focused in on him. He was irritated. Wait. Not just irritated, but actually holding her upright. When had *that* happened? "They like me. They really like me."

"Okay, Sally Fields, let's go."

"They really do."

"Look, don't take this wrong, but it might have more to do with Serena wanting to hurt me than her liking you."

Well, hell, if that didn't cut through the nice buzz she had going. "Did you ever think that maybe not everything is about you?"

"She's my ex, Katie."

"And now she's my friend." She pulled free of Cam and went to straighten her glasses but managed only to poke herself in the eye. *"Ouch."*

Cam tried to take a hold of her again, but she shook her head, which then swam. "Whoa." She winced at both that and her increasingly slurred voice. Apparently, she really was quite tanked. "Listen, I might be your employee, and I might have a crush on you, and I might want to have some more . . ." She lowered her voice, *"Sex."*

He blinked, and she poked him in the chest. "But that doesn't mean you can tell me who to be friends with."

He lifted his hands. "All I'm trying to do is take your drunk ass home."

"I'm not—"

"Please, you're ripped one hundred ways to next week."

"You know what? *Fine.*"

"Fine." He gestured ahead of him to his truck. She lifted her chin and took two steps toward it, then tripped over her own feet, hitting the sidewalk on all fours.

"Goddammit." She was scooped up into a set of hard, warm arms. Which really was just where she wanted to be. So she sighed and snuggled in, pressing her face to his throat, exposed since she still had his scarf.

And then, because she couldn't help herself, she kissed the warm flesh. And then, because she *really* couldn't help herself, she gently sucked a patch of his skin into her mouth.

"Okay," he said shakily. "None of that."

"You're no fun."

"I'm no fun?"

"No, you're not. In fact, you're the opposite of fun. You, Cam Wilder, are a fun sucker."

He opened his passenger door and deposited her inside, then came around and got in the driver's side. "I'm the definition of fun."

"If that were true, you'd have had me naked by now."

"You're drunk."

"Not that drunk."

He swore beneath his breath again and started the truck.

"Huh."

He slid her a look. "Huh what?"

"I can't tell what you're thinking."

He said a big load of his famed nothing to that.

"You're hard to read. I mean, sometimes I can tell. Like when you have your tongue down my throat, I know what you're thinking then."

This tore a laugh from him.

"I came here for adventure, Cam. To risk. To live."

He stopped laughing. "I know."

"And I got all that. Especially the adventure—which turned out to be you. You're my adventure, Cam, all dark and dangerously alluring."

He slid her another long look, but he still didn't enlighten her on his thoughts. And he didn't take her to Wilder Adventures either, but instead pulled into a driveway in front of a house near the end of town.

The two-story Victorian had a sign out front that read: Dr. Sinclair, Urgent Care. Closed. "You're sick?" she asked.

"No, Annie asked me to pick up some supplies. She likes to get stuff from old Dr. Sinclair rather than drive into South Shore."

"I thought she gets her diabetes supplies from the UPS guy."

"This is for our first-aid kits." He paused. "Dangerously alluring?"

"It's all in your eyes. Well, and your butt. You have a great butt. Doc's closed, Cam."

"He's recently had a heart attack and hasn't yet found someone to take the place over for him." He turned off the truck and opened the door. "I'll be right back." He pointed at her. "Don't go on any joy rides without me."

"I've never been on a joy ride in my life."

"Well then, don't start now."

When she was alone, she let out a long breath and watched him walk up the path. Both of him. Good God, she really was quite drunk.

Something rang, startling her; then she laughed. It was her cell phone. She patted down her pockets before she realized it was in her purse on the floor. She reached for it and ended up on the floor boards. Odd how being drunk really did affect one's motor skills. . . .

Cam gave up knocking on Doc's door and went back to his truck. He opened the door, then paused at the sight of Katie on her knees.

Her hair had slipped out of its restraints. Her eyes were glassy but full of the life that was like a punch to his gut every single time he looked at her. Her cheeks were red, her mouth curved in the smile that never failed to cause a chain reaction on his.

"My purse was ringing," she explained.

He nodded and resisted the temptation to say, "While you're down there . . ."

Because he wasn't going there.

Not.

Going.

There.

Yeah. And maybe if he kept repeating it to himself, his body would get the message. But God, look at her. Adorably trashed. Sexy as hell.

And utterly and completely unaware of the hold she had on him. Without meaning to, he was finding his heart cracking, tentatively opening in spite of himself, and God knew, hell *everyone* knew, he wasn't fond of the sensation.

Oblivious to his inner turmoil, she laughed at herself, then crawled back up into her seat and shoved her hair out of her face to grin at him. "Hey."

"Hey right back atchya."

She stared into his eyes. "You're so pretty, Cam."

"And you're hammered. Seriously. Your vision is impaired."

"Come on. You have a mirror. You know you're pretty." She waved a hand, managing to avoid hitting herself in the face this time. "But actually, I meant that you're pretty on the inside, even if your heart's been hurt."

"That was a long time ago."

"Still matters."

"Only if you let it." He went to start the truck, but she put a hand over his. He shook his head even as he turned his hand over, entwining his fingers in hers. "I don't like to look back."

"I know that. You don't look to the future either. You live in the moment to avoid more hurt. I can understand that. I think." She fisted her hands in his jacket and tugged him close enough to give him a big, smacking kiss on the lips that tasted of vodka and sweet, warm woman. "I'm living in the moment while I'm here in Wishful." She batted her eyes. "I'm in the moment right now. How about you?"

Oh yeah. Unable to resist, he kissed her, then firmly pulled back.

"I almost did donuts in the lot while you were gone," she admitted, recovering from the kiss much more quickly than he.

"*Donuts?*"

"In the snow," she explained, twirling her finger in a circle in the air to demonstrate. "Fast."

He had to smile. "What, are we twelve?"

"You say that because you probably *did* donuts in the snow when you were twelve."

True. He'd stolen Annie's car to do it too. She'd nearly killed him, but even that hadn't taken away the joy of that night, driving a forbidden car, going fast beneath the stars, laughing his ass off. . . . With a sigh, he put the truck in reverse, took them to the middle of the parking lot, and stomped on the gas while cranking the wheel hard to the left.

Katie screamed and laughed and screamed some more, and

when he stopped the truck, she collapsed against the back of the seat and sighed in utter bliss.

For two seconds.

Then she suddenly went ashen, then a spectacular green. She slapped a hand over her mouth and said "uh-oh," signs he recognized all too well. Leaning in front of her, he shoved open her door just in time for her to lose her lunch, dinner, dessert, and vodka right there in Doc's parking lot.

He held her from falling out of the truck on her face and scooped back her hair, while silently congratulating himself for being stupid enough to take her for a spin while drunk. "You okay?"

"Kill me," she murmured, accepting the bottle of water he'd grabbed and handed to her. She rinsed out her mouth and leaned back. "Just kill me and spare me the agony of embarrassment."

"For throwing up?" He shook his head. "Hell, Katie, I've had evenings end far worse than this."

Eyes still closed, she smiled weakly. "You're such a nice liar."

"Seriously."

"Seriously." She let out a low, miserable laugh. "I'd be willing to bet that every single time you've had a woman in this truck, you've gotten your hands on her, and not to hold back her hair while she puked."

"Actually, believe it or not, I'm out of the habit of seducing cute drunk women."

She cracked open one eye and laid it on him. "Because of your accident. I can't believe you stopped having sex."

"Yeah, well, until you."

She managed a weak smile. "I'm glad you broke your dry spell with me. I guess I'm irresistible."

"I guess you are." He started the truck again and got them on the road. She was surprisingly quiet all the way back to the lodge. Or maybe not so surprisingly, considering when he stopped in front of her cabin, he realized she was out cold, and snoring while she was at it.

He shook his head, turned off the truck, and carried her to the front door, which she'd locked. Without any guilt whatsoever, he frisked her for her keys.

She didn't so much as budge.

She was still snoring when he set her on her neatly made bed, though she stirred when he tossed a blanket over her.

"Cheese," she muttered as he pulled off her glasses for her and set them on the nightstand.

"What's that, Goldilocks?"

"Have to put out cheese for Chuck."

"You'll get something other than Chuck if you do that."

"Please?"

He caved. Of course he caved. One look into those vodka-reddened eyes and he'd do whatever she asked of him. So he got some cheese out of her small refrigerator and placed it on her front step. When he moved back into her bedroom, she was up on her knees, attempting to strip out of her clothes. She got her sweater off but looked stymied by the fact that she was still wearing two more layers. She tried to tug the two undershirts off as well, which took a while because she got them stuck on her head for one brief second during which her breasts threatened to have a serious wardrobe malfunction and fall out of her bra.

Ah, hell. She looked adorably flushed, and adorably sexy, but he was not going to seduce her when she was drunk, no matter how much he wanted her. "Get in bed."

Instead, she fell to her back and went to work on the zipper of her pants.

And he began to sweat. "Come on, Katie, just get under the covers."

Nope, and there went her pants, which promptly got

snagged on her boots because she'd failed to remove them first.

"Not again." She flung herself to the bed, flat on her back in nothing but royal blue bra and panties, with her pants around her ankles, caught on her boots. "Oh boy. I'm dizzy."

So was he, because she made quite the picture lying there.

Drunk, he reminded himself.

Hands off.

"De cha vu," she said, and laughed.

Closing his eyes, he inhaled deeply, which didn't help. He reluctantly moved in to assist, removing first her boots, then her pants.

"I'm really quite drunk," she informed him in surprise, sliding her fingers into his hair, tugging his face to hers. "Very, very drunk."

He looked into her eyes, saw the light and joy that she'd represented since he'd first laid eyes on her. "Yes, you are."

And sweet.

And sexy.

And mind-bogglingly beautiful.

"Cam?"

"Yeah?"

"You're hot."

He let out a low laugh and backed up. Way up. "Okay, that's enough out of you. Go to sleep."

" 'Kay," she said agreeably. "But you are." And with that, she resumed her snoring.

An hour later, she dreamed. She was in her car, stuck in traffic on the bridge, frustrated and angry at the damn truck that had trapped her behind it.

And then the shudder.

She'd no idea at the time what it meant, but she knew now and whimpered as the bridge gave way beneath her, as all the cars around her vanished, as she slid off the side, rolling, rolling, slamming to a stop.

Upside down.

Panicked, she tried to see, tried to figure out what had just happened, but then there were flames, and the heat. The horrifying heat, and then the worst part—discovering she was the only one who'd made it. She, who didn't really have a life, she'd lived while others hadn't. She could probably run her entire life looking for things to distract her from that and never forget it—

"I've got you."

His voice, low and easy and as soothing as the snow outside, surrounded her. So did his arms, pulling her out of the nightmare and firmly into the present. Without looking back, she crawled into that delicious strength he was offering, burrowing in like she planned to hibernate for the rest of winter, and sank into a deep, dreamless sleep.

Chapter 21

Annie tightened the tie of her jacket around her waist. It was a full-length stadium jacket, made of down, which was helpful since it was just dawn and the temperature hovered right at freeze-her-ass-off cold.

But she was doing this. She'd thought of nothing else all night, which was when it'd come to her.

Katie had been right. She was giving up too fast, without giving Nick a real chance.

Without giving *them* a real chance.

She thought she had a handle on that now. She'd been too vague. She'd been vague because she'd wanted *Nick* to figure out what was wrong all on his own, but guys didn't appear to be equipped for that level of thinking.

Plus, how could she expect him to know what exactly had gone wrong, when she herself didn't know?

Maybe together they could figure it out.

God, she hoped.

So to that end, she stepped into her boots, and still clutching the jacket to her, left the cabin that once upon a time she'd shared with Nick. She walked along the path to the cabin he used now. Knowing he never locked his front door, she simply let herself in.

There were dishes in the sink and clothes on the floor. Typical. She moved through the living room toward the bedroom, unable to hold back her anticipatory grin, because what the man lacked in house skills, he more than made up for in bedroom skills.

And she was so ready to get back to that portion of the program of their marriage. *Needed* to get back to that. They'd had some fairly major communication problems of late, but she figured there was no better way to force communication than while getting a little.

With that very goal in mind, she unbelted her coat and let it drop as she stepped into the doorway to his bedroom, naked. "Wake up, big guy."

The bed was empty.

He was already gone. *Dammit!* She covered herself back up with the jacket and stomped outside again. The equipment garage's lights were on. Shivering, she headed over there with rising frustration and purposely, *carefully*, knocked on the side door.

She was not going to screw this one up, not this time.

Nick didn't answer, so she pounded on the door, and finally, it opened. The drone of the compressor and generator engines blasted out around Nick. He wore a pair of beloved Levi's, faded nearly white, with a hole over one knee and the other thigh. He had on a thick, padded plaid shirt over long underwear and a ski cap on his head. He hadn't shaved yet today, and probably not yesterday either. He looked a little tired and a whole lot disheveled.

And sexy as hell.

"What's wrong?" he yelled over the machines.

Nothing, except he was still dressed.

"Annie? You okay?"

Yeah, she was getting there. Getting warm, too, despite the frigid temps. Nodding, she pushed her way in, once again unbuttoning her jacket as she kept her eyes on his, turning her back to the room to keep him in her sights. They were going to do this, right here, right now. "Close the door, you're letting out all the bought air."

"What are you doing here?" he yelled as he shut the door. "We're—"

That was all he got out before she let the jacket fall.

His eyes bugged out first. Yelling *"What the hell!"* he leaped for her, yanking off his plaid overshirt to throw around her. "Jesus, Stone's here!"

Clutching Nick's shirt to her body, she whipped around and for the first time surveyed the garage.

Stone indeed stood there by the compressor, mouth agape in shock before he slapped his hands to his face. "My eyes!"

Nick shot him a look of fury, then whirled on Annie. "What the hell was *that*?"

She grabbed her jacket from the floor before shoving Nick out of her way to get to the door. "That was me trying to seduce you, you ass. And trust me, it was the last time. So I hope you got a good look, because it won't be happening again!" And with that, she maturely slammed the door behind her.

She managed to wait until she was in her beloved kitchen, surrounded by a few leftover brownies, before she burst into tears and then consumed every last crumb.

Damn idiot man! How many ways were there to screw this up? And had she found them all yet? Miserable, she stood up to make herself another batch of brownies.

Katie opened her eyes. The bright sunlight pierced her eyeballs, making her moan miserably and burrow into her pillow.

"Yeah, vodka's only fun for a few hours. They should probably put that on the bottle."

Crap. Risking losing her sight, she squinted her eyes open again. She was in her bed. With the shades up, sunlight streaming in.

And the sexiest, most ridiculously good-looking man she'd ever seen in her life was in bed with her. "Hey," she whispered.

"Hey, yourself, Goldilocks. Any more bad dreams?"

"No." And that was the good news. "What are you doing in my bed?"

"You don't remember?"

She remembered the trip into town to thank Harley.

She remembered the vodka shots.

The wishing on the falling star.

And then Cam, finding her, Serena, and Harley lying on the snow on the sidewalk staring up at those stars.

And . . .

And nothing.

Try as she might, she couldn't remember anything past that. Narrowing her eyes at him, she lifted the covers to see if she was still dressed.

She wore her bra and panties. Okaaaaay . . .

Cam was looking pretty damn amused, so she lifted the covers higher to see *his* body, but found him fully dressed. "Why am I half naked and you're not?"

"Are you asking me to get half naked?"

"That would be great, except—" She sat up, then groaned and held her head, because otherwise it might fall off.

"Yeah," he said at her groan of misery. "I wouldn't recommend any fast movements after six shots of vodka."

"Three. I only had three."

"Serena pours doubles."

"*Crap.*"

Still looking amused, he rolled over and out of bed, stretching that long, leanly muscled body before running his hand over his hair to tame it. Not fair. He looked great. It would take her an hour minimum to get even halfway to great.

"Back to what was our first argument," he said, his morning voice husky and sounding like sin. "You snore *way* louder than I do."

"I do not!"

His eyes were lit, his mouth full of laughter. "Oh yeah, you do."

"Wait a minute. We didn't . . . ?" She waggled a finger back and forth between them. "Did we?"

He looked more curious than guilty. "You really don't remember?"

"Nothing past you showing up at Wishful Delights."

"Ah," he answered sagely.

Dammit! "How did I get in my underwear, Cam?"

He rocked back on his heels. "Keep thinking."

Ohmigod. "Please fill in the blanks."

"I put you in my truck and drove you home, but we made a stop first. Well, two. One at the doc's for supplies for Annie, and one to do donuts in the snow because you begged me to."

"I did not beg—" Oh God. "I did. I remember that part now, and then I remember—*Oh no*."

"Yeah," he said with a nod.

She groaned through her fingers. "You saw me puke."

"I held back your hair. I believe I get brownie points for that."

She sighed miserably. "And then . . . ?"

"I brought you home."

"Where you took off my clothes?"

"You don't remember your little striptease?"

She stared at him as the rest of it all came slamming back into her. Pulling off her shirt. Getting it stuck on her own head. Shucking out of her pants without taking off her boots first—

"Oh God," she moaned.

"Yeah, there it is."

"Oh no. No, no, no . . . Tell me it didn't happen."

"I'm afraid it did."

She covered her face. "I don't know what's worse, puking in front of you, or the striptease, or being so bad at it."

"Definitely the puking." He shrugged at her expression. "Okay, so that was a rhetorical question, sorry."

"Oh my God."

"You've said that."

She wasn't ever going to be able to look at him again. "So we really didn't . . ."

His lips quirked. "Nah, I prefer my women conscious." He opened the second set of shades and she cringed, diving under the covers. "Sorry, Goldilocks. You have work. End of the month stuff, and you know how Stone loves his reports. So does T.J., who's going to be home tomorrow."

Oh, God. Another Wilder. She couldn't handle the two she had. "What time is it?"

He tugged the covers off her head. Looking way too cheerful, he said, "Past time for you to get your cute little ass out of bed."

She sat up and moaned at the quick movement.

He was watching her, both sympathetic and annoyingly *not* hungover. "You going to live?"

"Yes," she lied. Because with a bottle of aspirin, maybe she'd have a shot, but it was not going to be pretty. "I'm good. You can consider yourself relieved of baby-sitting duty."

She'd have figured he couldn't wait to run out of here, but he took the time to lean in and kiss her. "Try some pain reliever."

"Oh, I'm all over that, trust me."

"Good." He paused, smile fading. "Katie, about your dream."

"What about it?"

"I know you say you're doing great and everything is all just peachy, but can that be true if you're still dreaming like that?"

She felt herself close up just a little. "It was a fairly big trauma. I think it's understandable."

"It is. It absolutely is. It shook you up, left you grieving and guilty, and—"

"Guilty?"

His gaze, stark and green and unfathomable, met hers, and something inside her tightened uncomfortably. "You know," she said. "You had a trauma too. I'd think you'd get it."

"I do. But mine didn't involve survivor's guilt. Mine was my own stupidity, and my own fault, so I have no one to blame but myself. I think that's why I sleep at night, because I know it, I accept it."

"You accept it? Is that why you roamed the planet for a year?"

"Okay, so it took me a while," he said quietly, not rising to the bait. "I fully admit that. I let it fuck with my head, but I'm working that out now. You—"

"Are fine." Dammit, her heart hurt, and she didn't know why. "I'm fine. You're right, my situation is different from yours. I wasn't living my life, I was just breathing through it. Now I'm doing things differently. Taking chances—"

"You went looking for something else in your life, something to soothe the ache. I get that. I believe in that. But I'm beginning to believe something else too. Yes, you took a chance leaving LA, but don't mistake it for what it is. Maybe you've risked a new lifestyle, you've certainly risked life and limb on certain adventures out here, but as for the biggie, your heart, you haven't put that on the line at all. Instead, you ran away from your world to escape the memories."

She couldn't scarcely breathe. "Don't even try to tell me you know what it's like to put your heart on the line."

"I realize I haven't mastered that particular skill. Haven't even tried. But at least I know the difference between being a little reckless and truly taking chances. And you, Katie Kramer, aren't truly taking chances. You're hiding."

"That's ridiculous."

"Is it? Then tell me about the accident. All of it."

"Now's not a good time."

"When would a good time be?"

"Never. Does never work for you?"

He was quiet a moment. Then he let out a very quiet, very final sounding "fine," and walked to the door.

She didn't stop him, and when he was gone, she let out a breath. Her throat was burning, but she was not going to cry. Instead, she stood up. Bolstered by the fact that she didn't die, she headed to the shower, stopping short at the sight of herself in the mirror. It took her a whole five seconds to form another "Ohmigod." Her hair was . . . well, wild was too kind a word. Rioted came far closer to the truth. Her mascara had run in attractive rivulets beneath her eyes, and she was pale as a ghost. Actually, she looked like death warmed over.

And she'd blown it with Cam. Irrevocably, irreversibly blown it. Not able to go there without wanting to lose it, she got into the steaming shower and then rushed through her morning routine because she was already late.

She ran, while holding her head, up the stairs of the lodge, skidding to a painful halt in front of her desk, behind which sat Stone. The last time she'd seen him, she'd been in his brother's truck, where they'd clearly been attempting to jump each other's bones. She had no idea how he felt about that, but she had a feeling she was going to find out.

Stone was wearing snow gear, signaling that he had imminent plans to go outside. He was frowning, signaling irritation, which just might be her fault. And he was rifling through her files, managing with his sheer size to make her chair and desk seem very small.

"Hey," he said without looking up. "I need to see the printout of receivables from last month. T.J. wanted to know about—"

"I'm sorry I'm late."

"Yeah, no problem. I probably could have found it in the computer, but mine isn't booted up yet."

"Stone, I'm really sorry."

He looked at his watch. "It's only five after eight."

"That's not what I mean." Guilt and remorse tightened her throat. "I'm sorry about the other thing."

"Which?"

"Yesterday. When you found me in Cam's truck and we were—"

He winced. "Listen, we—"

"You don't have to worry about anything. I'm leaving soon, and—"

"Katie."

She took a breath. "Yeah?"

"The thing with you and Cam? If he's happy, I'm good. And you should know, he seems happier now than I can remember him being. I think that's because of you."

"That might have just recently changed. Big time."

Stone looked into her eyes. "What did he do?"

"Actually, I did it."

"Ah." He just looked at her a moment, his eyes so like Cam's. "He's pretty tough. I imagine if you told him your feelings and he retreated, he just needs to think. He's a thinker, our Cam, and—"

"My feelings?"

"You know. How you feel about him."

"I don't know how I feel—" But she did. She so did. "You

don't understand," she whispered, her throat thick. "I've hammered him and hammered him to open up, to share, and then when it came right down to it, when he asked me for the same, I backed off."

"Well, welcome to the Wilder House, where we all screw up, and often. Luckily, we're hardheaded but pretty forgiving. You'll figure it out, and so will he." Standing up, he gave her a shoulder squeeze, then took the file he needed and left her alone.

She leaned back against her desk. She'd figure it out? When? And how? She was leaving in less than a week.

Being at Wilder had truly been one of the most amazing experiences of her life, and she knew for many reasons, on so many levels, she'd never forget it. Never forget him—

The entire lodge suddenly shook with a loud, thundering *boom*. In blind panic, she whirled, and plowed right into Cam's hard chest.

"Hey." He pulled her in close. "Hey, it's okay, it's just Nick closing one of the steel doors on the Dumpster outside."

She lifted her head. Her ears were ringing. "What?"

"I know, it's loud as hell, but it's not gunshots if that's what you were thinking."

"No, I—" She'd been thinking of the shuddering boom sound the bridge had made right before it'd collapsed, but she swallowed hard and fought for composure, which meant relaxing the fingers that had fisted tight in his shirt. "Just caught me off guard that's all!"

"It's more than that." He backed up. "You want to be mad at me for earlier, for what I said, fine, but at least admit it. You dwell on the past as much as I have."

"I have nothing to admit," she said coolly, her heart still hammering. "And less than nothing to be dwelling over. I didn't lose a career. A life. A loved one. In fact, I've lost nothing, so I feel obligated to do the opposite of dwell." *All in the name of those who hadn't lived*.

"Katie." His hands were on her arms, still steadying her, when Stone poked his head out of the office. He took one look at her and frowned in concern.

"What's the matter?" he asked.

"Nothing."

"She's lying," Cam said.

"You be quiet." She moved past him to the filing cabinet. He'd showered and smelled like heaven, of course. He'd also changed into a pair of threadbare jeans that were so loose they'd sunk low on his hips, and a long-sleeved Henley that smelled so good she wanted to bury her nose in it again.

Or maybe that was the man himself.

Stone had said she had feelings for him, and Stone had been right. She loved him. She loved him and had no idea what to do with that.

Annie came up the stairs and as she did every day, tossed the day's mail onto Katie's desk. She wasn't smiling and was back in her baggy clothes. Her apron said: EAT ME. "Don't start," she said, then turned to Cam and Stone. The three of them stared at each other awkwardly.

"Stone told you," Annie said to Cam.

"I'm trying to forget it if that helps."

"Stone told Cam what?" Katie asked.

"Nothing," Annie said.

They all stared at each other some more.

"Okay, seriously," Katie said. "What's going on?"

The silence got even heavier. "Okay, here's an idea. Maybe each of us should just spit out our problem and move on."

"We already talk plenty." Annie sent the guys a scathing look. "We *see* plenty. I'm going on record as not needing to be seen again."

"Why don't you go first?" Cam said to Katie, arching a brow.

"Fine. I was stupid enough to get drunk last night, okay? I needed a ride home, and then I puked. I puked in front of Cam, which means now I can't even look him directly in the eyes. There." She let out a breath and tossed up her hands. "I feel so much better. Now who's next?"

"That's not what I meant," Cam said quietly.

"Hey, I get brownie points for going first. One thing at a time. Who's next?"

They all just looked at her. Not a single one of them was free with their feelings, and who was she to judge? At least they loved each other, through thick and thin, to hell and back. Sure, their love was in the form of yelling and shoving and bullying, but it was there, it was real, and she . . . and she wanted to be a part of it. Damn. Damn, that was really unexpected. "Anyone?"

Cam kept his mouth firmly shut.

So did Stone.

Annie crossed her arms over her chest. "Well, my husband is an idiot. There. You're right. I do feel better."

"You're giving him a complex," Stone told her. "And now he's trying too hard."

"*He's* trying too hard? Are you kidding me? *I'm* the one trying too hard!"

"All you do is yell at him." Cam put his hands up when she whirled on him. "Hey, I'm just saying that you could try something else."

"Really? Should I try something else, Cam? Like maybe try to seduce him, only first ruin his painting, and then strip naked in front of Stone?"

"Well, Jesus Christ, Annie." Stone was already cringing. "You're supposed to scope out the room first. I was standing right there." He rubbed his eyes, like the sight of her was still burned on them and he needed to get rid of it.

"Well, there won't be any need to scope out anything,"

Annie informed him. "Because he doesn't get a third shot at me. No way, no how."

And with that, she stormed off.

Stone looked at Katie. "Yeah, now see, that's why we don't do much talking."

"No, that was good. She'll feel better for having vented."

"Maybe some of us should try that," Cam said, and sent her a long look.

She pretended not to look at him.

"We'll all be eating our boots for dinner," Stone said a little glumly.

"Or," Katie said. "One of you could just go to Nick and have him reverse the damage. Tell him how badly Annie wants to reconnect, that she's trying to get him back, and if he could just meet her halfway, that would be great."

"She broke his heart," Cam said.

"So you think he has no interest in getting back together with her? Are you kidding me? It's all over his face how much he loves her."

Cam was already shaking his head. "It's not that easy, Katie. It's never that easy."

"Maybe when it comes to matters of the heart, it *is* that easy. You just follow its lead."

"Down Fuck-You-Up Road maybe."

"Pretty damn cynical."

"Hello, Ms. Pot, meet Mr. Kettle."

Stone headed toward the stairs. "Tell you what. You two keep snapping at each other. I'm sure that will fix everything."

Cam sighed and headed toward the stairs as well.

"Cam."

He turned back. "I'm not sorry about what I said to you," he said.

"I know you're not. And I'm not sorry about what we've had."

"Okay, that makes two of us." He was looking at her with frustration and heat and affection and temper. "So where does that leave us?"

She held her breath. "With a few nights left that we could spend together?"

"Not talking," he guessed.

"Not talking. Will you come?"

He blew out a breath as that heat in his gaze flamed to life. "Yeah, I'll come. And so will you."

Chapter 22

L ater that day, Cam walked into Stone's office and found his brother sprawled back in his chair, booted feet up on his desk, hands folded over his belly as he spoke to the speaker phone. "And Cam just walked in, so you can tell him yourself, Teej."

"I'm held up by a bitch of a storm in Seattle," T.J. said, his voice tinny and faraway sounding. "But I should still be there by tomorrow."

"Just in time." Cam headed for Stone's computer. "Annie might kill Stone." He opened the browser thinking as he typed "Santa Monica bridge collapse" into Google that he should have done this weeks ago.

Nick opened the door. "Holy crap, it's icy today. What's going on?"

Stone set his feet down. "What are you talking about? There's no ice out there."

"I meant Annie. She's icy."

"Yeah, that's because you're a little slow on the uptake."

"Huh?"

"Your wife's trying to patch things up, and you're not paying attention," Stone told him.

"I'm paying attention all right. She's trying to drive me crazy. Giving out signals one minute and yelling the next."

Through the speaker, T.J. said, "That's what women do. Deal with it."

"Says the guy who slept his way through every woman in town," Stone interjected. "Several times."

"Hey, not every woman."

"No? Name one."

"Harley."

"Yes, because she was the only woman who ever turned you down, remember?"

T.J. sighed heartily. "I remember."

Cam's gaze was glued to the news reports and pictures of the bridge collapse. Horrifying, devastating pictures of cars smashed into sheets of steel. The fiery fire of the brush on either side of the collapsed bridge. People lined up on the streets trying to find out about their loved ones.

Thirty dead.

One survivor.

Katie.

Jesus. Cam rubbed a hand over his mouth and thought so much about her made more sense every day. Her needing out of Los Angeles. Heading north to snow country, where everything would be new and different, where nothing could remind her of what she'd faced.

But things *had* reminded her, that couldn't be helped. And whereas he'd slowly come to accept that, she'd not gotten there yet. Ironic, since all along he'd thought she was the one of the two of them to have their shit together.

If anyone had asked him even a minute ago who'd gotten more out of this past month of knowing each other, him or Katie, he'd have laid down his very last dollar that it had been him.

And yet now he could see, that maybe, just maybe, he'd given her something too. That he had more to give still. Lots more. He turned to face Stone and Nick. "I slept with Katie."

"Shock," Stone said.

"I'm going to sleep with her again."

"More shock," Nick said.

"I'm sleeping with Katie, and you're all okay with it?"

"Yeah," Nick said. "But I'd have figured getting laid would relax you a helluva lot more than it has. You doing it right? Or do you need some pointers?"

All of them laughed except Cam, "You guys are a riot." He looked at Stone. "Explain this to me. When you slept with the cleaning crew, T.J tried to beat the shit out of you."

"Because he was an ass," T.J. pointed out.

"Yeah, it's not the same," Stone agreed.

"Why the fuck not?"

"Because I wasn't halfway in love with either of those women."

Staggered, Cam stared at Stone. "What?"

"He said you're halfway in love with Katie," T.J. repeated.

Falling in love, his ass. Stone had no idea what he was talking about, none. He grabbed the phone from its cradle and put it to his ear. "And what the hell do *you* know about this?"

"I know love," T.J. reminded him very quietly. "And I've talked to you often enough over the past month to hear it happening to you."

"Jesus." Cam slammed the phone back down, ignoring Nick, who leaned over the desk and hit Talk again before T.J. was disconnected.

"Classic sign of being a goner," Nick said with a *tsk*. "A quick temper."

"Shut up." Cam shoved his hands through his hair and

glared at them. "And thank you all for being no help at all." With that, he walked out and slammed the door, leaving no mistake as to how frustrated he felt.

In the office, silence reigned for a full moment.

"Well, that went well," T.J. said. "Great idea, Stone. 'Nudge him in the right direction,' you said. 'Let him know we're behind him,' you said. Now he's a flight risk again."

Stone looked at the door and let out a breath. "Nah, he's just being bullheaded, like any good Wilder. He's sticking."

"How do you know?"

"Because Katie's still here."

"Yeah, well, I'd stay out of his way just the same if I were you, at least until I get there to referee."

Nick snorted in amusement until Stone gave him a droll look. "Like you have it all together?"

"Hey, I have it more together than you."

"Really? Think Annie would agree?"

Nick just let out a long breath. "How did we all get so fucked up?"

"Practice, man. Lots of practice."

Katie wasn't behind her desk, and Cam's heart did an odd little lurch. Dammit. He strode down the stairs and found her outside organizing a cross-country trek to Gold Cove, which he was to lead.

"It's not on my schedule," he told her.

She looked down at her clipboard. "No, it's on T.J.'s, but he got held up by that storm." She looked up into his eyes, her own shuttered for the first time since he'd known her. "Should I cancel?"

"It takes two guides," he lied without compuncture.

"What?"

"I need an assistant." He smiled grimly. "Suit up, you're it."

"I don't—"

"You want adventures. You want risk, then take one. Change." He took the clipboard. "We'll wait."

She took less than five minutes, which he appreciated. She didn't speak much to him, which once upon a time he would have appreciated even more, but things were different now. He didn't know how exactly, or why, only that they were, and that he missed listening to her talk.

Halfway out to Gold Cove, he slowed. "It's three miles straight out," he told the group. "First one there gets the championship title and a framed picture of the group."

They all took off. Katie, too, but he snagged the back of her coat and pulled her to his side.

She planted her poles and looked at him warily. "What?"

"I thought we could—"

"Here?" She eyed the trees speculatively. "What if one of them comes back?"

"Not that." But he eyed the trees, too, suddenly liking her idea a whole lot better than what he'd planned on doing. There was a nice thick group of trees just ahead, he could have her in there, wrapped around him like a pretzel in like thirty seconds—

"Oh, if not that, then what? I could have had that championship title."

"Yes, you could have. For holding back. I know, Katie."

"Know what?"

"About the bridge collapse."

"Yes, because I told you."

"I know the details. How your car was flung out from between the two cement blocks like a piece of toast. How you hung upside down off that cliff for an hour after they got the flames out before they could get to you."

Staring at him wide-eyed, she tried to take a step back, but the skis tripped her up. He slipped an arm around her waist while hitting the release on her skis with his pole so that she was released from the bindings.

Freed, she staggered away from him. "The details don't matter. Not to me."

"Then why are you still dreaming about them?"

The truth of that flickered across her face. "Fine. I didn't tell you because this is a temp job, and I'm a temp, and—"

"Bullshit. That's all such bullshit. You didn't tell me because despite the fact that I'm supposed to trust you, you don't have to trust me."

"No," she whispered, "that's not it."

"Then what? What is it? You're the only one in the whole world who's ever been in a life-altering situation and wondered what to do with themselves now?"

Her face closed up, and even while the apology was already forming on his tongue, she shook her head and pointed at him. "You, Cameron Wilder, you can go to hell." She stomped back into her bindings and skied off, leaving him staring after her.

One consolation in this whole mess: She'd learned to ski like a damn pro.

That night Cam was slumped on his couch staring at the game while thinking about Katie. Katie smiling at him and making him smile back. Katie laughing with her whole face, that contagious laugh that made him let out a helpless one of his own.

Katie accepting him for who he was, and making him want to be the best man he could be.

When the knock came at his door, he figured it was Stone. Hoping like hell he'd pick a fight so Cam could cut loose of this tension, he got up and pulled open the door.

Not Stone.

It was Katie, with one of those smiles he'd just been daydreaming about, though it was a nervous one.

"You busy?" she asked

"Nope, I'm just watching a game. You know, before I go to hell."

"Yeah." She grimaced. "About that whole going to hell thing. Can I come in?"

"Sure." He backed up so she could pass by him, and he all but buried his nose in her hair, that's how desperate he was for the scent of her. She didn't disappoint, smelling like some complicated, deliciously sexy mix of flowers and woman. "If you plan on yelling at me some more," he said, "maybe you could wait until the commercial. The Patriots are down but at the ten-yard line."

"I once accused you of being an ass and you apologized for it." She turned to face him. "Today, I was the ass. Yesterday too. You didn't mention it in so many words, but I'm still going to say I'm sorry."

He looked into her eyes and wanted . . . wanted to hold her, touch her, be with her.

That terrifying.

That simple.

"You asked me earlier why I didn't trust you," she said softly. "The truth is, I didn't trust *me*. I'm working on that. I'm working on a lot of things. But for now, between us, maybe we should just go back to doing what we do best."

Well, he knew what *he* thought they did best . . . "You mean . . ."

"Yes."

It couldn't be that easy. Could it? "Look, I've been wrong, a lot, so I want to be clear. We're talking about . . . *sex*."

"Well, it is a documented stress reliever."

There, he thought. There was the light coming into her

gaze, the one he'd missed. "My very favorite stress reliever," he said. "And as a bonus, it scratches all itches, solves the universe's problems, and—"

And Nick walked right into the cabin as if he owned it. He headed past Cam and Katie and straight for the refrigerator, helping himself to a beer.

"Nick?" Cam gestured with his chin toward Katie. "A little busy here."

"No problem, I can wait." He plopped down on the couch, sprawled his legs out, head back, eyes closed. "Take your time."

Cam opened his mouth to say "Get the hell out," but then he caught a good look at Nick's face and the utter misery on it. Hell. He turned to Katie, who shook her head worriedly. With a squeeze of his hand, she let herself out.

Double hell.

Oblivious, Nick took a pull on his beer. "She's fucking with my head."

"Annie?"

"The UPS guy asked her out and I think she's going to go. She's waiting for me to sign the damn papers."

Cam sighed and went for his own beer, but Nick had taken the last one. Perfect.

"You Wilders are crazy. All of you."

"Yeah, sorry about that." Cam sat on the coffee table facing Nick and nudged his knee with his own. "Look, you have two choices here, just two, and you know what they are."

Nick set the beer down and nodded. "Actually, there's only one. One choice." He stood up and headed for the door.

"So that's it?" Cam asked Nick's back. "You chase the girl out of here and don't even stay?"

Nick opened the front door. "You have two choices, Cam, and you know what they are."

Yeah, hell if he wasn't right. Cam followed Nick out, then

turned in the opposite direction, heading in the falling darkness to Katie's cabin. He knocked on her door and then stood there waiting, his blood pounding, his body on high alert.

"Who's there?"

"The scratcher of your itch," he said.

She opened the door a crack and stuck her nose out. "Was that supposed to be romantic?"

"Okay, how about this. I came bearing all the answers to the universe's problems."

She lifted a shoulder, distinctly unimpressed.

Huh. This wasn't going quite as planned. He decided to try her favorite thing—words. "Okay, here's the thing. I've never been much of a romantic. Honestly, I've never had to be."

"Because women always throw themselves at you."

Well, yeah. In the past, that was definitely true, not that he was stupid enough to say so. "Does it count that there's no one, *no one* I'd rather be with right now?"

She opened the door a few more inches, standing there all whiskey-eyed, her lips shiny with lip gloss that smelled like . . . watermelon.

He loved watermelon.

"Right now," she repeated. "As in you might change your mind a minute from now? To what did you call it? Scratch the itch?"

Okay, he was beginning to sense an attitude. "I'm sorry. I'm . . . really sorry. But it's been a helluva long day, and I'm dead-ass tired, and to be completely honest, I'm out of practice at seduction. You are sweet and beautiful, and you have a way of being positive no matter what the hell is going on. It's sexy as hell, *you're* sexy as hell, and I just want to be with you."

"Well, there you go," she murmured. "The magic password." And she opened the door all the way.

He smiled in relief. "Yeah?"

"Yeah. Look, I know I'm leaving, and this is just fun, but I didn't want to be like all the other women who've been in your life. In and out. Gone and forgotten."

"You aren't. You won't be."

She stepped aside for him to come in. She wore jeans and a long black sweater, with bunny slippers. Her hair was loose and shiny. Everything about her stirred him up, but he had to ask, "You like that I'm out of practice at seduction?"

"Uh-huh." She stepped close, smelling like heaven. "Our first time, on the rocks, it wasn't practiced or old hat. It was real. And so was afterward, when you came to my cabin when you thought you'd get me out of your system."

He let out a long, shaky breath when she pressed up against him. "Apparently it didn't take."

"Which is unusual for you," she said.

"Yeah." When she locked her arms around his neck, he ran his hands down her back and did his best to inhale her in, deep inside, where she always, always made him feel good.

"I told myself whatever happened here with you, I just wanted it to be real." She looked at him, really looked at him, the way only she seemed to do, and he knew she saw things that he couldn't hold back, things he didn't show to anyone else. "And it was," she whispered. *"Real."*

She was sweet and hot, and more than a little crazy, and she completely slayed him. "I thought you wanted it to be great."

"Oh, I think we've got that part covered as well." Pressing her face to his throat, she breathed him in, too, as if she needed that as much as he did; then she sighed in pleasure. "Cam . . ." Her mouth was near his, her hands sliding beneath his shirt, her fingers—frozen solid, thank you very much—running over his flesh. "Maybe we should do what you came here for."

Yeah, maybe they should. Bending his head, he rubbed his jaw to hers. Everything about her felt new for him. New and wild and just a little bit out of his control. Yet somehow she was also slow and steady, more than any presence in his life. Her hair was all around him like a soft, silky cloud, and he closed his eyes and just kept breathing her in like she was his lifeline. "I wanted you all damn day. For *days*. I wanted you all hot and sweaty and panting my name."

"Tell me no one's going to need you for the next few minutes," she said breathlessly.

A few minutes. That's the best she thought he had. He had to laugh; then he kissed her, filling himself up with the scent of her shampoo, her warm skin, loving having her soft curves pressed up against him. "This is going to take longer than a few minutes."

Her glasses fogged, and he pulled them off, getting his mouth on hers again. She opened for him, but he didn't deepen the kiss, not yet, because the high of the anticipation was flowing through him now, and for the first time in his life, he was enjoying it instead of trying to race it, because it all made some sort of crazy sense.

Being with her was making crazy sense.

He'd been so careful with himself, holding back, not giving anything of himself away. Building defenses one layer at a time.

But she'd stripped those layers away, one at a time, painstakingly, leaving him totally and completely bare.

And still he stood there, holding her. Wanting her. "I plan to take my time with you, Katie."

Her breath shuddered out. "I don't think—"

"Perfect, go with that," he murmured against her mouth, picking her up.

"Your knee—"

"Is fine, now *shh*. No thinking. Nothing but this. Hope you're not tired."

Her breath caught. "It's going to take that long?"

Not if she kept looking at him like that. So he leaned in, murmured "all night," and then kissed her, waiting until her eyes fell closed before closing his.

Chapter 23

Katie's heart executed a slow rollover in her chest as it exposed its underbelly.

All night . . .

All night worked for her. Yes, it did.

"Your room," Cam murmured huskily in her ear, his arms tightening around her as he carried her across the cabin.

One of her bunny slippers fell off, but he just bent his head and kissed her, a deep, wild kiss, their tongues doing the same glide and dance that her body so desperately wanted. He was a force, she thought dazedly, a force of destruction as it pertained to her heart, one of passion when it came to her soul, and unbearable pleasure for her physical being—

"Oh!" she gasped as she hit the mattress. Before she'd bounced once, Cam had followed her down, his big body sprawled over hers, eyes glittering as he held her tight. "Caught you," he murmured.

Yeah, he had. She had the feeling he always would, no matter how far she fell.

He was pulling off her clothes, his clothes, and she joined the fray, helping him shove off his outer shell and T-shirt to latch her mouth to his chest. She ran her hands up his smooth, sleek back, touching the tattoo around his biceps, touching everything she could reach. "We made it to a bed," she murmured. "Finally."

"Mmm-hmm." He spread hot kisses along her jaw. "Now let's make it on the bed . . ."

With a laugh, she met his mouth with her own, straining to get the rest of his clothes off. She tugged at his pants and he met her halfway, surging up to unbutton them; then she was once again distracted by the sight of that rugged chest. His six-pack abs made her mouth water, but even more amazing was the way the muscles quivered when she ogled him. She realized she finally had the space and the time to explore, and her own body humming at the thought, she pushed him down to the bed.

"Katie—"

"Shh." She touched her tongue to his hips, traced it over his belly.

"Katie." His voice sounded a little strangled as she made her way lower. "Don't—"

She wrapped her fingers around his impressive erection and licked him like a lollipop. "Don't . . . ?"

"I mean don't—I don't want this to be over before I get inside you."

"We can always start again . . ." Another lick.

And another deep, rumbling groan from the man sprawled beneath her, breathing hard, a light sheen of sweat coming out on his chest as he slipped his fingers into her hair. "This was supposed to be about you—God—" he choked out when her tongue swirled over the top of him.

"We'll get to me." She kissed him again, then gently, slowly sucked him into her mouth.

He jerked, his hips arching up to meet her. His fingers were still tangled in her hair, the tendons in his neck stretched taut, his expression such sheer, hot pleasure that she felt herself go damp just watching him react to her. And then suddenly she was flipped to her back, held there by over six feet of long, lean muscle.

Skin-to-skin, her bare breasts were mashed up to his chest as one of his powerful thighs slid between hers, pressing the heated core of her, ripping a needy little sigh from her. "So damned soft . . ." Holding her wrists in his hands, he shifted lower, then lower still, his shoulders urging her legs open. He kissed an inner thigh, then the other.

Then in between.

While she lost her mind, he ran his tongue over her, finding what he sought with feather-light strokes, then a little harder, until she twisted against him, her fingers caught in his, as she arched up into his mouth. "Cam—"

"You taste as good as you feel," he murmured against her. At the next unerring stroke of his tongue, she cried out and her toes curled. At the next stroke, she bucked, but he had her, held her through it as she exploded in a kaleidoscope of sensations. When she opened her eyes, he was kissing her thigh, moving his way up to her belly, a breast . . . He lifted his head, and then his hand, which had a condom dangling from his fingers, which had her heart taking off again. Together, they struggled to get it on, a process that left him damp and trembling, and her ready to jump him.

When he sank into her with one thrust, she cried out in pleasure, and then again when he cupped the back of her thigh and tugged, opening her up to him even further.

"God, you feel good." His voice was a thick whisper against her ear. "So goddamn good."

She thought he felt pretty damn good, too, but she didn't have the words, not then, and certainly not when he began to move within her. In and out, again, and then again, the fire licking down her body, settling between her legs. "Cam . . ."

Love me.

Lifting his head, he stared into her eyes, his own open to her, open in a way he didn't usually allow, showing her all he felt.

Helpless against the pull of that, her throat tightened as she strained against him so that they were plastered together, hot, damp skin to hot, damp skin.

She could feel how big he was, how wet she was, and he pushed even deeper within her. "Cam," she whispered again.

He made a sound, a low, raw, rough sound, and slid a hand between their bodies, gently stroking her where he'd just had his tongue.

When she came again, it was with his body so deeply embedded in hers she didn't know where she ended and he began, and it didn't matter. He kissed her through it, his tongue gliding against hers as her body contracted around his, as with one last hard thrust, he followed her over, her name tumbling from his lips.

Cam woke up the next morning wrapped up in a warm, naked woman. Now *that's* what he'd been talking about. The first time hadn't taken, but this time. . . . This time he'd be able to breathe again. He'd be able to go about his day without feeling as if he had a fist around his heart, tightening, squeezing.

Choking him.

And maybe now he'd be able to think about something other than Katie twenty-four/seven. Yeah, he probably wouldn't even think about last night, how hot it'd been, *she'd* been, or the sound of her panting out his name, how she gripped him tight when he'd nudged her over the edge . . . how sexy she'd sounded in the throes.

No, he probably wouldn't think about that much at all . . .

He let out a breath, extremely aware of the fact that his body was already there, thinking, hoping, yearning.

Damn.

Maybe one more time . . .

She opened her eyes and smiled softly, and he rolled her beneath him. Yeah, one more time should do the trick, really nail it home. "God, you feel good."

"You make me feel good." She cupped his face, her entire heart in her voice, and when he met her gaze, he was slammed by the look in hers.

Soft.

Dreamy.

Emotional. Oh, Christ, she was looking so damn emotional over him.

"What is it?" she murmured.

It was almost incomprehensible, but his brothers, the knuckle-heads, had been right.

This wasn't lust.

Not even close.

No, it was something much, much deeper. Horrifyingly deep. Confused, he rolled away from her and slid out of the bed.

"Cam?"

"Yeah, would you look at the time?"

"It's only seven. I didn't look at the schedule. You have a trip?"

"I . . ." He couldn't remember. He just needed to think this thing through. God, he needed to think, which he'd proved over and over again that he couldn't manage in her presence.

Out. Get the hell out. He wasn't proud of it, but that's all that he could think.

Get out.

He whipped around, looking for his clothes, having never felt more naked in his entire life. He found his snow pants and yanked them on.

No shirt.

No shoes.

He'd probably have hypothermia before he got to his own cabin, and was weighing the odds against it when he felt her hand on his back. Nearly leaping out of his skin, he turned and found her standing in front of him.

Naked.

Beautifully, gloriously naked, except for her glasses, and he had the most ridiculous urge to grab her close and hold on, like he'd never held on to anything in his entire life.

"So," she said very softly, still standing there, "you're looking a little panicked."

"I can't find my shirt or my shoes."

She walked over to the foot of the bed and picked up his T-shirt and his outer shell, still entangled since he'd ripped them off together last night. "No comment on the panicked thing?" she asked.

No. Again, he was going with the Fifth. And since she appeared in no hurry to give him his shirt, and also if he didn't get out of here right this very second he was going to suffocate, he turned and headed to the door without it.

"Cam."

"Yeah, I'm late. Very late."

"I see." Some of the softness went out of her voice, and he was quite certain, with a sudden sick dread, that if he looked into her eyes now, he'd see that the light usually in them, the precious light in those shimmering whiskey depths, would be gone.

"Late for what?" she asked. "The rest of your life?"

Yeah, something like that. Christ, he really was an ass. But knowing it didn't alleviate one ounce of his sudden, irrational, undeniable panic.

Or the need to run. "I'm sorry," he said with utter inadequacy.

She didn't answer. Hating himself, he opened the door;

then because he couldn't stand it, glanced back at her over his shoulder as he did.

His two shirts hit him in the face. Pulling them down, he mumbled "sorry" again and turned to the very bright, sun-shiny morning, which hurt his eyes and hurt his gut. Hurt every damn thing as behind him the door slammed, nearly knocking him down the steps.

"Hey, genius."

Annie stood on the path. She wasn't alone. Of course she wasn't alone, because hey, why should he face this moment of The-Biggest-Most-Stupid-Move-He'd-Ever-Made in private, when he rarely did any of his spectacularly stupid stunts in private?

Nick stood next to Annie, and there was Stone, and oh, per-fect, T.J.

And . . . *Riley*, their office manager? "You're back?"

"Not officially," Riley said. "Just wanted to come by now that we're back in town and see how your temp was faring, see if she needed anything for these last few days of her time here. But it seems as if you have it—and her . . ." he said wryly, "handled."

Cam ignored that and moved down the walk to greet his brother, bracing himself to be questioned and grilled on his year-long absence, maybe hounded about his lack of responsi-bility during that time, because being the oldest, T.J. had al-ways drilled that home.

But T.J. didn't do any of that, or even say a word. He simply grabbed Cam and pulled him in.

It had always driven Cam crazy when people so easily and casually touched each other, and yet he found himself wrap-ping his arms around his brother and holding on.

With a low sound of relief, T.J. hugged him hard, then shoved him away to get a good look at him, his eyes suspi-ciously bright. "Damn, you're a sight for sore eyes."

"Yeah." Cam's throat was tight, too tight, and he shifted on his feet, uncomfortable with the audience *and* the emotion. "Same goes."

Annie's hands were on her hips as she regarded his appearance, reminding him he stood there in only his unfastened pants, still holding his T-shirt and outer shell, his feet freezing.

"Where're your boots?" Nick asked. "Man, you're not supposed to let a woman keep your boots."

"Oh, for God's sake." Annie turned to Nick. "Are you kidding me, you're still mad I took your damn boots?"

"Hell, yeah. Those were my favorite boots, and you threw them away. I found them in the trash."

"They were a hundred years old and smelled like rotten eggs."

"My favorite," he repeated. "My dad gave them to me."

"He did?" The temper drained from Annie's face. "Oh, Nick. I didn't know."

Nick lifted a shoulder. "It's okay."

"No," she said softly, "it's not. I was wrong."

"Wait." Nick lifted a hand and cupped it around his ear. "What?"

"I was wrong, dammit."

Nick smiled. "Yeah, I heard you. I just wanted to hear it again."

T.J. stepped in front of Nick so Annie couldn't kill him, though he hadn't taken his eyes off Cam. Neither had Stone. Nope, they both stood there looking at him freezing his balls off. With a shiver, he worked to turn his shirt right side out. "What the hell are you all doing out here?"

"Besides watching you take your walk of shame?" Stone asked. "Coming to tell you T.J.'s back. Didn't realize you were busy getting dumped."

"Yeah." Cam pulled on his T-shirt. "Thanks."

"So how did you fuck things up in one night?" T.J. asked.

Cam yanked on the outer shell next, wishing for his boots. Or socks. Or a hammer to hit himself over the head. He wanted to say something scathing, but his teeth were knocking together.

"Men are so stupid," Annie muttered, just as Katie opened her front door. Everyone turned and looked at her.

She tossed out Cam's boots, then shut the door with a rather loud finality.

Annie shot Cam a *see* look.

Yes, men were stupid. And he was their king.

Then the door opened again, and one more time everyone looked at Katie.

She had her gaze locked on T.J. and Riley.

"Hi," Riley said. "I'm your counterpart Riley. Nice to meet you."

"Nice to meet you too," Katie said slowly, clearly surprised. "Did I mark your return date wrong on my calendar? I thought I wasn't leaving until Sunday."

Sunday, Cam thought. Four days from now.

How had that happened?

"Just visiting," Riley assured her. "Unless you want out of here early."

She hesitated, and Cam's knees actually went weak. All he'd wanted was a moment to think, to breathe, to . . . process his feelings for her. The thought of her going early killed him.

Her gaze touched his for a long, torturous beat, during which time he held his breath. "No," she finally said, "I don't need out of here early." She turned to T.J.

"Hi. I'm the smart brother."

Him she offered a genuine smile. "Nice to finally meet you in person."

Cam shoved his freezing feet into his boots and then turned to look at her, but she waved at everyone except him and then went back inside her cabin.

The click of the bolt sliding home echoed in the morning air. Yeah. That sounds *final*. He followed Annie and the others up to the lodge and into the kitchen for breakfast, which he happened to desperately need.

Fucking up his life made him hungry.

Annie had already made the fixings for breakfast burritos. Cam threw one together for himself, took a big bite, then paused when Katie walked into the room, headed directly for the pot of coffee to pour herself a mug.

"Morning," Annie said to her.

"Morning," she said back, nodding to Stone and T.J. while completely ignoring Cam. Which seemed about right. He'd ignore his sorry ass if he were her too.

Annie looked at him like *say something*, but Cam didn't know what he could possibly say in front of everyone: *Sorry I don't know how to think and look at you at the same time. Are you sorry you kicked me out of your place in the subfreezing morning without all my clothes?*

She didn't look sorry as he drank in the sight of her, and when she met his gaze defiantly, the room fell quiet.

Not to mention the temperature dropped by ten degrees.

Nick sipped his coffee with a *slurp*.

Stone rocked his head to whatever beat he had going on his iPod.

T.J. cleared his throat.

And Annie sighed, then shoved Riley, T.J., and Stone toward the door. "Go." Then she turned back to Cam with a look that said "fix this now" before vanishing herself.

Katie grabbed a tortilla, slapped some eggs and sausage into it, her irritation level high enough that even Cam, reigning King of the Stupid Males, could read loud and clear. "Katie—"

"I've got work."

He managed to catch her at the door, barely, and she frowned down at his hand on her arm. "Sorry," she said, "I don't need my itch scratched right now."

"Katie—"

"In fact, I don't need anything from you; but if that changes, I'll be sure to let you know."

With that, she tugged free, and with her nose so far in the air that she was in danger of getting a nose bleed, she took off.

Cam looked at the empty kitchen, feeling just as empty. It wasn't a new feeling. In fact, the emptiness had become an old friend, even before his accident. In the past, he'd combat it by getting on the mountain, or finding someone to keep his feet warm for a few hours.

But his old habits didn't appeal. Oddly enough, for a guy who'd spent his entire life avoiding conflicts, the only thing he wanted to do was go after Katie and have it out with her.

Katie didn't go upstairs. She was going to be late, and for once, she didn't care. She needed a moment alone, away from Stone's knowing eyes, Annie's prying ones, and now there would be T.J.'s as well.

Good Lord, he looked just like the rest of them, all big, bad, sexy, and wild.

The Wilders were made of some pretty fine genes.

Damn them anyway.

Still gripping her burrito, she went out the front door and was promptly blasted by the icy air. No problem, it could cool off her temper. Nibbling on her breakfast, she walked around the back of the lodge, past a set of picnic tables. She didn't feel like sitting. It looked as if it might snow any minute, but that didn't stop her. Even given how she'd spent her night, she had an excess of energy that she needed to get rid of. So she hit the trail that led past the storage sheds and cabins, the one they'd snowshoed all those nights ago, which wound along the bluff high above the valley. She needed the gorgeous view with no one talking, no one charming, no one looking at her from a set of green eyes that tended to melt brain cells, heart, and panties with equal aplomb.

The trail had been gone over with the snowmobiles many times since their last storm, so she was able to walk it in her boots without sinking in, but it was still tough going. One thing about hiking with a spiked temper, the chill vanished. The crunch of the snow beneath her boots soothed her, as did the whistle of the pines in the light wind.

Someone was following her. She knew it was Cam, but he kept his distance, so she continued to hike and finish off her burrito while she was at it. She was going to see her pretty view, and when she was no longer steaming, she'd go back to work.

But Cam's booted footsteps began to catch up with her. "Go away," she said.

"I'm sorry, okay? Come on, Katie. Stop. We should talk."

Ha! "That's pretty funny, coming from you." She sped up.

"Katie, seriously, wait up. You need to slow down—"

"Why, so you can charm my panties off again? No thank you." She craned her neck to look at him while picking her pace up to a full-blown run now, which turned out to be a bad plan because in her brilliance, she ran right off the trail.

And slipped down the hill.

Chapter 24

"Katie." Heart going off like a jackhammer, Cam ran to the edge of the drop-off where she'd vanished. "Katie!"

"Not good. So not good."

At the sound of her voice, he took a deep, steadying breath, because holy shit. She'd slid off at a sharp incline, which during summer would have been a nasty fall, but now, in the dead of winter, the snow had softened the angle and the landing. She was about twenty feet down, way too still, which had his relief short-lived. "Are you okay?"

When she didn't answer, his gut tightened because he knew it was her worst nightmare coming true all over again. "Hang on, okay? I'm coming."

He eyed the best way to get to her without falling and possibly smacking into her and then knocking her farther. He could take the trail another hundred feet where there was a more gentle slope, than traverse back to her. Which, without snowshoes, was going to be tricky. "I'll be right there."

"Breathe," he heard her say to herself as she set her forehead to her knees. "Oh, God. Just keep breathing."

"I like the sound of that." He said this lightly, while feeling anything but light. "Don't move."

"Brilliant idea."

Okay, she was joking. Joking was good too. He ran up the trail, then left it to climb down to her, which was every bit as challenging as he'd known it would be. It had begun to snow now. Covered in it by the time he reached her, he crouched in front of her, gently cupping her face to lift it to his. She was shaking like a leaf and breathing hard, halfway to hyperventilating, alternately clenching and unclenching balls of snow at her sides. She had a little cut over her eyebrow, which wasn't so much a concern as the egg-sized bump behind it. "Okay, slow it down a little," he said, taking slow, deep breaths of his own so that she could mimic him and hopefully not pass out.

But she only squinted at him, making him realize she'd lost her glasses. "I'm trying not to freak," she panted. "There's no fire."

"No fire, baby, I promise." He looked up above her, saw the rock exposed from this angle, and his stomach knotted. That's what she'd hit her head on.

"I really, really want off this cliff." She looked over his shoulder at the valley far below and went a little green. "Oh, God. Goddammit."

"We're going to get off in just a minute." He probed at the cut over her eyes. "What's your name?"

"Stupid city girl."

He let out a low, relieved laugh and ran his hands down her trembling legs and arms.

"Effing pathetic." She was completely out of breath. "I'm going to freak now, just so you know. After the fact."

"Nothing wrong with a little panic now and again."

"Says the man who knows."

Yeah, he knew. When he got to her shoulder, she hissed out another breath. Dammit. "Squeeze my fingers."

Shivering wildly now, she did.

"P-pretty impressive, you managing to c-cop a feel during a r-rescue."

He pulled her into his lap and tugged her close, trying to give her his warmth. "If you didn't want to be rescued, you could have stood up and met me at any point during my climb down."

"It l-looked like hard work."

"Admit it. You didn't because—"

"It's not because of the b-bridge," she said tightly, shuddering. "I wasn't that hurt then, I was just stuck. Literally stuck. If I c-could have gotten out, I would have—" Her voice broke a little, and so did his heart. "I w-would have tried to h-help the others—"

"You couldn't have." He hugged her resisting body as close as he could. "You were too far down the hill, and you know now that even if you weren't, there was no one alive to save."

She sniffed, her face buried against his chest. "I didn't know that then."

"It's not your fault that you lived. Tell me you know that."

"I'm getting there." She sniffed again. "And on a bright note, I've met another cliff and lived. I think the universe is trying to tell me something."

"You're the bravest woman I know."

"I'm a little dizzy, Cam. And you sound funny."

He felt funny. And weak-kneed with what might have happened to her. "Your head needs looking at."

"No kidding. I need to have it examined for getting myself into this situation."

Pulling free enough to lift up his sweatshirt, he tore a strip of material off his T-shirt.

Katie let out a sound, and he looked at her. "What?"

"I hate that I'm pitifully attracted to you ripping your shirt like a he-man, especially after your escape this morning." She winced and held her head. "How bad is it?"

He pressed the material of his shirt to her wound, applying a little pressure to stop the bleeding. "Not bad." He pulled out his phone and called the lodge. "We're going to need a snowmobile about a quarter of a mile past the trailhead," he told T.J.

"A quarter of a mile?" Katie asked. "That's all I went?"

"What happened?" T.J. asked.

"Katie slipped off the edge, fell twenty feet. Slight head injury and shoulder."

"Slight," Katie muttered. "And that doesn't count the damage *you* did to it, of course."

Cam closed his eyes. "Hurry," he told T.J.

"Stone's already out the door and heading for you. I'll be right behind him."

"Put a call into Doc Sinclair first. Tell him we're bringing him a patient."

"I'm fine," Katie said. "Relatively speaking."

Yeah, she was fine. But she'd be even more so after an x-ray and a once-over by a professional. He slipped the phone back into his pocket and lifted her up against him.

"What are you doing?"

"Carrying you back up."

"I can walk." When he didn't set her down, she sighed and slipped her arms around his neck, setting her head down at the crook of his shoulder as he carried her up to the top. "You feel like a superhero."

"Because I carried you?"

She made a noise that said she thought that assessment fairly ridiculous. "My heroes aren't cocky, ex-world champs who have lots of muscle."

"Well, ouch."

"Yeah, and they don't wear capes or have superpowers either, in case you were wondering. They . . . *feel*. They hurt." She cupped his face until he looked down at her. "They can love and be loved. They know they're worthy, and that they deserve it."

He stared down into her face, his blood pounding. She knew how he'd felt. She'd sensed it, or he'd given himself away, and he didn't know what to do with that.

From the direction of the lodge came the whine of a snow-mobile engine.

"The cavalry," she said.

I think I've got it together now, he wanted to tell her. He wanted to say that and more, but then Stone was there, reaching out for her. Left with little choice, Cam handed her over, watching Stone settle her in front of him before taking off for the lodge.

The snow had continued to come down now, lightly, and the trail was icy, hampering his speed. He wasn't as quick on the ice, not these days, but oddly enough, that thought didn't come with the usual gut twist.

T.J. met him halfway on a second snowmobile. When they got back to the lodge, Cam leaped off and turned toward his truck, intending to start it so he could drive Katie into town, but there was a Jeep in the driveway, blocking him in.

Changing direction, swearing at whatever idiot had parked right behind him, he yanked the lodge door. Stone stood in the foyer doorway, looking disconcerted.

"Katie," Cam said.

Stone stepped aside.

Katie was wrapped in a blanket on the couch with a woman leaning over her holding a stethoscope.

"The doctor was already nearly here, as it turned out," Stone said, "bringing Annie some supplies."

Cam looked at the young, stacked beauty. She was dressed more for a cover shoot than a patient run. "That's not good old Doc Sinclair."

"Good eyes, bro. It's his daughter. Emma." Stone, a guy

who'd never met a woman he didn't want to get to know better, was frowning. "Apparently he coaxed her to Wishful with the promise she could run his place, but we get injuries out here all the time, and with the ER thirty miles away, we need a competent doctor, not Dress-Up Doctor Barbie."

As Cam was usually the one requiring the emergency services, he knew this all too well. "How do you know she's not competent?"

"Look at her."

"I am. She's easy enough on the eyes, if that's what you mean."

Stone shot him a shocked look. "She's like *twelve*."

"Actually, I'm more than twice that." The auburn-haired "twelve-year-old" lifted the stethoscope from Katie's chest and set it around her own neck, reaching for Katie's wrist to check her pulse. "I'll be thirty next week. And are you pouting because I turned you down the other night at Moody's, or because I beat you down Wilder's Run?"

Cam lifted a brow in Stone's direction.

"I didn't ask you out," Stone said. "I asked if you wanted a drink. That was me being polite. You weren't the same in return."

"Because I said no?"

Stone appeared to grind his back teeth together. "And you didn't beat me down Wilder. My binding broke."

"Ah." Emma was probing the wound on Katie's head. "Well, then."

At that, Stone made a noise as if his head had gotten a flat tire.

Cam had no idea what had crawled up his brother's ass, but he didn't care. "How is she?" he asked Emma.

"Not concussed." Emma dug through a black bag and pulled out Steri-Strips, which she used on the gash on Katie's eyebrow.

"The shoulder?" Cam asked.

"Strained. Icing it will help. Oh, and before I forget"—she tossed a brown bag at Stone—"for your aunt."

If Cam hadn't been so concerned about Katie, he might have been amused at the look on his brother's face. Stone, the middle child, the people person, the peacemaker, didn't soften or offer his usually charming smile, didn't work the magic that he usually had in spades when it came to women. Instead, he ignored Emma and came around the couch. "You better?" he asked Katie.

"Yes." She offered a weak smile. "I'm sorry to be such a PITA."

"Nah. Now Cam? *He's* the pain in the ass around here." He said this gently, with all his usual charm firmly back in place for her. "But maybe you should stay away from cliffs until you go home on Sunday, what do you think?"

She laughed softly, but Cam didn't. Because, Jesus Christ, Sunday was almost here. "That's a really bad day to travel," he said.

"Why?" Katie asked.

"Because . . ." Why? "Because there's always traffic on Sundays."

Stone gave Cam a shit-for-brains look that said, "Really? That's the best you got?" before shaking his head in disgust. With one last gentle squeeze of Katie's hand, Stone straightened and headed for the door.

Emma followed him out.

Which left Cam alone with the patient.

"You know," she said quietly, staring at the flames rip-roaring in the fireplace. "It's funny. I should have felt so out of place here." She turned to him. Her eyes were filled with things that made him swallow hard and feel torn between running like hell and grabbing her tight.

"But it fit," she said. "Being here fit. I feel so good about that. So damn good. I hope I get as lucky next time."

Struggling for words, he came closer and sat next to her. "Having you here fit."

"I'm glad." She went to stand up, but he held her still.

"I'm sorry, Katie."

"I'm a big girl. And this was a job. It's got some nice perks, I'll admit." She flashed him a small, tight smile as she pulled free. "But all of that is nearly over now. And I'm ready to move on."

"Where to?"

"LA first, to visit my parents. Then . . ." She lifted her shoulder, then winced in pain. "You know, maybe I *should* let Riley come back early."

"No, don't." *He'd* done this. He'd pushed and pushed, and she'd given up on him. "Don't leave early because of me." He looked into her eyes. "My life's not ever going to be the same, Katie. I want you to know that. You've changed me."

"How?"

"Well, for one thing, you turned me into this person who tells people how he feels."

"And how do you feel?"

He tugged at his sweatshirt, sticking to him from the snow. He'd rushed out after her without grabbing his jacket. "A little cold and wet at the moment."

She didn't look impressed, and in fact, turned away, but he caught her hand and met her frustrated gaze. "Okay, listen." He struggled to find the right words. "I feel bad about this morning."

"Are you referring to when you ran out of my place like a bat out of hell because we had great sex?"

"It *was* great sex." He let out a breath. "And, yes, okay, it unnerved me because it was also more." He paused, thinking she'd be pleased at that admission.

But she wasn't. In fact, she looked just about the polar opposite of pleased. And something else unusual, she didn't say a word. That was *not* a good sign. "Yeah, see, now I sort of thought you'd have something to say about that."

"Maybe if you'd expanded on that thought, I would."

He let out a breath. "Expand?" Okay, he was going to run into trouble now. He wasn't much of an expander. "I just poured out my soul and you want me to go on?"

"Pouring out your soul, Cam, would be telling me a lot more than that you're *unnerved*. It would be telling me why, and what that more is."

"Yeah, I guess I know that." He managed a smile, then reached for her hand and brought it up to his mouth. When he kissed her fingers, she shifted, turning her hand so that she could press her palm to his jaw. Then with a sigh, she leaned in and kissed him. "Let me make this easy for both of us. You made my time here more special than I could have hoped, and I'm grateful. We have a connection, and I'm grateful for that too. You're smart and sexy and funny, and I enjoyed being with you."

Past tense, he couldn't help but notice. "Except for when I was stupid."

"True. Except for that." Her smile faded. "I promise you, I really understand that this thing between us is as temp as my job was. I knew it going in, and no matter what happens, or how much I fall for you, I will know it going out."

Her eyes were soft and sweet now, and so deep it almost hurt to look at her. Quite simply, she staggered him. "Katie."

"I swear to God, if your next sentence has anything to do with you regretting what we've had, or that you're still worried about me falling for you, I'm going to—"

He kissed her. He just leaned in and kissed her, soft and deep and hot, the way all their kisses ended up being, and when she pulled back, she smiled. "Yeah, now see *that's* how we should communicate from now on out. It's clearly what we're best at."

He let out a half laugh half groan and hauled her close, burying his face in her hair, still smiling, even as he wondered . . .

How was he ever going to let her go?

Chapter 25

Annie stood at the counter in the lodge kitchen, listening to the radio tell her that a huge storm was coming, which fitted her mood just fine, as she beat her dough into submission.

She was making bread. Because bread was the salt of the earth, and the owner of her heart. Dammit.

She was going to eat warm, buttered bread and feel better.

Until her jeans got too tight.

Which, given what Katie had her wearing, wouldn't be too long. She had no idea why she'd stuffed herself into one of her new pairs this morning. It wasn't as if Nick would notice, the big, clueless lug. She'd also put on a snug sweater that showed off the boobs she'd spent most of her life hiding. Her hair was down, which men supposedly loved, not that she'd ever heard a word either way from Nick. She punched the dough.

All she'd ever wanted from the man was words. *You're pretty today, Annie. You're my life, Annie. I love being married to you, Annie.*

You're hot, Annie.

Ha! The man had no words. He was the strong silent type, and she'd known that going in, but criminy. Once in a while, a woman needed more. And now her more was food.

Damn him anyway.

The door opened behind her, and without turning around, she rolled her eyes. "Cameron Wilder, you just ate my entire refrigerator. I'll call you when I have more food for you to shovel into your mouth."

"It's not food I need."

Nick. She went still, eyes glued to the dough in her hands. She had flour across the front of her, in her hair, and probably, given that she'd just scratched her cheek, all over her face. The man had a knack for seeing her at her worst. "I'm far too busy to deal with you right now."

"Really?" He wandered into her sight, looking tall and lanky and rangy, and so damned sexy she wanted to chuck the dough at his head.

How unfair was it that when she was working, she looked like shit, and when he worked, he got dirty and rumpled and all the hotter for it?

"Looks like you're making bread."

"So?"

"So . . ." He leaned a hip on the counter and studied her. "You used to like my company when you made bread."

"I used to like a lot of things."

"Like me?"

Her heart stopped. She still liked him. She loved him.

"Annie."

Ah, hell. His voice was low and gruff and terrifyingly gentle. And that's when she realized he was holding a filc.

The divorce papers.

He was going to tell her that he'd finally done what she'd asked and signed them, that the divorce was a good thing. That he wanted it too. Well, fine. She lifted her chin and faced him, flour and all.

His gaze swept down her, definitely noticing, then stopped short on her apron, and suddenly, he burst out laughing.

Having forgotten what this one said, she looked down at herself: I'VE GOT YOUR LOW-CARB DIET RIGHT HERE, PAL. . . .

Below that, there was a black arrow pointing downward, ending right about crotch height. It was inappropriate but pretty much summed up her mood. "If you're looking for another good laugh, you should know I have no plans to strip naked for your amusement."

"Annie—"

"And I certainly don't plan on trying to seduce a man who's too self-absorbed and stupid to notice a naked woman when he has one right in front of him."

"*Annie.*"

God, that voice. "You have the papers," she whispered.

"Yes." He tossed the file to the counter and stepped closer.

"I'm covered in flour here, Nick."

"I know." He put his hands on her arms and dipped his head a little to look directly into her eyes. "I know because I'm seeing you."

Her breath caught and she wanted to turn from him rather than give herself away, rather than let him see how much those words meant, because that file on the counter told her it was all too late. "Nick—"

"No, let me get this out, before I can't." He took a gulp of air. "I've missed you."

"I've been right here. All along, I've been right here."

"I know. And it was my shame that I didn't get that. That what you wanted wasn't your freedom from me, but something else entirely. The opposite, really."

"Yes," she whispered, feeling her throat tighten. Oh God, he did get it. Now that it was too late. "The papers—"

"I missed you, Annie," he said again, his voice gruff and thick with emotion. "I miss you in my bed, and in my life. What happened to us?"

"I don't know. We stopped communicating."

"Stopped seeing each other," he said softly, her words.

"Yeah." She tried to smile. "It got so . . . out of control."

"I don't know how, but yeah." He cupped her jaw, then smiled at the flour now on his fingers. "And I know you've been trying. I was afraid you'd stomp on my heart. But forget the fears, I want another shot. I can make you happy again, Annie, I know it."

Her heart squeezed hard. She swiped her hands on her apron, but they were still messy and sticky, and she made a sound of frustration when he came in for a hug. "No, don't. You shouldn't. Look at me. I'm a mess."

"I see it. I'm seeing you, Annie. And I don't care about the mess."

"Well, you should." She ran her gaze down him. "You're actually wearing a clean shirt."

He smiled at her, his self-deprecatory, crooked smile. "I'm sorry I've been so slow and self-absorbed and . . ."

"Stupid," she supplied helpfully, trying to control the wild, crazy seed of hope that had taken root within her belly.

"Stupid," he agreed.

"Yes, well, we've both been that."

"Maybe. I've been locked in my own self-misery at the fact that you wanted a divorce. And then you started in on that whole 'seeing you' thing, and I didn't get it. But then you started paying attention to me."

"I started seeing you," she whispered.

"Yeah, it took me a while. At first, I didn't even notice that you were trying to fix things all on your own. But you're not on your own, Annie. You never were." He picked up the file and opened it, showing her the signature line, where he *hadn't* signed. Then he took her by the hand and led her to the huge great room, where he tossed the entire file into the fireplace. It went up in flames with a little *whoosh*, and as it did, he pulled her close, touching her face, his thumb grazing over her cheek. "I see you. You're covered in flour and you've never looked more beautiful to me, not even when you were sixteen and smoking hot."

"Don't." Embarrassed, she pushed his hand away. "It's at least twenty years and twenty pounds. I know I don't look anywhere close to that cute young thing you seduced in the back of your truck."

"Is that what this is all about? Your looks?"

"No, of course not." She shifted uncomfortably under his direct, patient gaze. "Okay, maybe some. It's ridiculous, I know."

"Annie, I don't want you to look the same. We've laughed and loved and lived, and how we look reflects that. Every single line on our faces."

"Yes, but *your* lines make you look better. You look just as good as you did when you were seventeen and coaxing me into the back of that damn truck."

He flashed a grin.

"It's a little annoying, actually."

"Yeah?" He put his hands on her hips, then bent so that his mouth could nuzzle near her ear. "Well, then, let me try to unannoy you . . ."

He was doing a damn good job already. Her nipples hardened and her thighs quivered.

"You look good enough to eat," he whispered against her ear. "Especially with that flour and sugar all over you. I think I'll start at the top and nibble my way down . . ."

Her knees wobbled some more. Nearly forty years old and her knees were wobbling. "I thought we were going to . . . communicate."

"Uh-huh." His voice was husky. Like a man completely confident in the knowledge that he was about to get lucky.

And he was. He so was . . .

"Can you think of a better way to start communicating than with our bodies?" he murmured, his mouth already quite busy.

No. No, she couldn't. "But it's the middle of the day."

"Yeah." He lifted his head and flashed a wicked smile, the same one that always had her naked in under two minutes.

He reached behind him to latch the kitchen door, eyes flashing with all sorts of erotic ideas. The lock tumbled into place and so did her heart. "Here?" she whispered. "*Now?*"

"Here." He lifted her to the counter, putting his hands on her thighs, pushing them open so that he could step between them. "Now."

When Katie woke up the next morning, her shoulder was stiff and sore from her fall, her heart hurt like a mother, and the storm had moved in.

By four o'clock that afternoon, it was pitch-dark outside. The winds were whipping up a good howl at over sixty miles an hour and climbing, and the snow was coming down thick and fast.

When the lights flickered a few times and the subsequent power surge made her computer act all wonky, she gave up. She shut down for the night and headed to the kitchen, which was uncustomarily empty.

She had no idea where Annie was. Or where anyone was for that matter. She knew that a group of skiers had arrived an hour before the storm had hit, so she figured everyone was settling them in for what would surely be an epic powder day tomorrow.

She made it back to her cabin for the night; then a few minutes later, she heard an odd scraping noise at her door. Curious, she opened it to . . . *"Chuck."*

He was scrawny and miserable, fur soaked to his skin in spots, sticking straight up in others, covered in white frost, huddling close to the doorjamb to escape the wind. "Mew."

"Oh, baby," she whispered, staggering back at the sharp, icy wind that sliced right through her, slapping snow into her face. She couldn't even see outside; it was nothing but slashing lines of white as the snow was driven sideways by the winds. "It's okay, come in . . ."

But he only shrank back.

Apparently, she *still* didn't have quite the right touch with the skittish men in her life, but at least he didn't run off. She hunkered down, making herself smaller, and once she did, the cat stuck his tail straight up in the air and walked past her, and right into her cabin.

He went straight to the kitchen and sat, eyeing her with very cautious care.

"So." She looked him over just as cautiously, her heart melting at his skinny frame, at the fur that needed some serious care. She wanted to wrap him up in a blanket and warm him up, but he'd never let her get that close. So she moved to the refrigerator, got out the milk, and poured a little into a sauce pan.

Chuck didn't move. Neither did she. And when the milk was warm, she dumped it into a bowl and set it on the floor. "Try it," she said softly. "You might like it."

When he just looked at her warily, she rolled her eyes at herself. When would she learn to give up? She bent to lift the bowl away, but at the last minute, he lunged forward and stuck his head in it.

And started lapping.

Katie stood stock-still, her heart feeling too full for her chest. The only sound in the room was Chuck's tongue lapping at the milk. And then suddenly a rough rumble sounded, then stopped, then started again, like an old diesel engine cranking over for the first time in years.

He was purring.

Swallowing past the lump in her throat, she stayed still so as not to spook him. "So I finally won you over." She sighed. "And I'm leaving in a few days."

Chuck kept lapping up the milk.

Yeah. Her throat burned now, but fact was fact. She might have got Chuck to trust her, and even to some degree, Cam, but not enough to claim either of them as her own.

The job had been temporary. She'd gone in singing the praises of that, promising Cam just how temporary she saw it. But just between her and Chuck, she'd fallen for this place. For Wishful. For the people in it. For the character and charm, and so much more.

Chuck finished the milk. Still purring, he lifted a paw and began to clean his face.

"It's not all bad, my leaving," she told him. "After all, I got over myself here. I had adventure."

Chuck switched paws and went to work behind his ears. Either this whole cleaning himself thing was new for him, or he was completely ineffective, because he didn't look any cleaner.

"I had really, really great sex too," she told him. "Do you think that's odd? It took leaving my comfort zone to get the best sex of my life?"

Chuck lifted a leg and went to work on his private parts.

Katie nodded. "Yeah, you're right. It's odd. But most of all, I really did fit in. Or at least I think I did."

"You did."

She turned and faced Cam, standing in her doorway with the wild storm all around him, which matched the sudden wild storm in her gut. He wore a thick jacket with the hood up. He shoved it back now and unzipped the jacket, revealing a dark fisherman's cable sweater and jeans.

"You left your door unlocked." He shut it while she attempted to control the fierce leap of her pulse. "That's not like you, Goldilocks."

Yeah. Apparently on top of everything else, she felt safe

here. She'd faced her demons and had gotten comfortable. Hell of an attractive combination. And a small part of her wished she never had to leave, because this world with scrawny cats and gorgeous men, with new friends and wide-open spaces, no traffic, and some pretty amazing adventures left to be had, felt good.

Too good.

"Chuck's in here," Cam said in some surprise. His gaze met hers, his soft and questing. "You conquered him."

Her throat tightened. "It took a while. At first he didn't feel like he could be friends with me. He didn't think that he deserved it, what with being a wanderlust renegade and all."

Cam's eyes never left hers. "I suppose even wanderlust renegades deserve a bowl of milk and a sweet woman every once in a while."

"Even wanderlust renegades who've gone their whole life thinking that maybe love isn't for them because it's never worked out. But Chuck understands now, he gets that there's always a first time."

Cam let out a low breath and finally looked away, the only response to what she'd just said being a muscle ticking in his jaw.

"Still, it's not a complete success," she said. "He hasn't let me touch him."

He slid his hands into his pockets. "He might never let you."

"I don't believe that."

"Ever the optimist."

"Apparently even the mountains can't beat that out of me."

"Speaking of that. How are you feeling? Your head—"

"Still on."

"Your shoulder—"

"I'm fine, Cam."

He nodded, looking through the living room to her bedroom. Her suitcase was on the bed. She'd been thinking about getting some things packed.

"There's a big storm coming in," he said, still looking at her suitcase.

"It's already here."

"No, a bigger one's going to hit the morning. It's going to hit hard and heavy, maybe sock us in for a few days."

That wouldn't be so bad, getting to see one last storm. It could match the one in her heart.

"I wanted to make sure you're stocked with candles and batteries and everything."

She looked at him. "So you're . . ."

"Leaving in the morning, before the big one hits. Nick and I are flying a group of six hardcore snow hikers out to Desolation Wilderness. From there we're snow hiking to the peak. It's a four-day trek round-trip."

"In the storm?"

"They want it that way. They want to sleep in the blizzard inside a snow cave under the Sierra stars."

She managed a laugh. "Sometimes I'm very glad I don't have your job." She watched the amusement transform his face, turning it from pensive and edgy to open and so attractive he took her breath. "It's not racing, but you're into it," she murmured, happy for him.

"I didn't think I would be, but yeah. If I can't be going balls out down a mountain, then this fits too." His smile faded. "I just wanted to check on you."

"I'll be fine while you're gone."

"And when I'm back, you'll be gone."

She stared at him as the truth sank in. He appeared relaxed enough, but just beneath the surface she took in his tension. It was there in his eyes, his mouth. "You came to say good-bye," she realized. "Tonight. Now."

He let out a breath. "I want you to know that I get that I

tend to keep myself emotionally distanced from everything and everyone. But you . . ." He shook his head as if a little overwhelmed. "I'm not emotionally distanced from you, Katie. I never was."

Her throat tightened. She moved around the counter to come to stand before him. "The day the bridge collapsed, I was tired."

"Katie." He reached for her hand, his eyes soft. "You don't have to—"

"I want to. I want to tell you what I wouldn't before. I was really tired of my life. My boss was cheating on his wife with the copy clerk and expected me to keep his secret. My last date didn't call for a second one. Things felt . . . sucky. I looked at the bridge and thought—" She shook her head. "I thought if I drove right off the edge, no one would even notice."

His gaze held a raw compassion. "Oh, Katie."

"It was just a fleeting thought. Stupid and pathetic, and gone before I could blink. I looked around in the traffic and saw all the other people around me." She drew a shaky breath. "Living their lives, talking, singing to the radio . . . and I thought, you know what? Life is what you make of it. I needed to make more of mine. And then in the next minute, it happened. A truck cut me off, I got mad, and then I was skidding toward the edge. Only one thing went through my mind." She looked into his warm, grieving eyes. "I *didn't* want to die."

He closed his eyes briefly and let out a breath. "I can't tell you how grateful I am that you didn't."

"Everyone else did," she whispered.

"I know." He hugged her in close, hard. "I know."

"That's why I dreamed. You were right. It's what I was running from." She looked up into his face. "I had planned to keep running until I knew the answer to that."

His smile faded, his eyes filled with all sorts of things that, frankly, took her breath. "I want you to know I'm okay with it all now," she told him. "I think I finally have my head on straight. I lived. And now it's up to me to do something with the second chance. Something more than what I was doing before, which was nothing."

"I feel the same, Katie. Because of you."

She smiled. "I guess there's only one thing to do then." She lifted a hand and touched him, sinking her fingers into his hair, tugging his head down so that their lips were only a breath away. "Have our good-bye."

"Katie," he murmured, his lips brushing hers. "I don't think—"

"Perfect," she whispered, mirroring his long-ago words back at him, backing him to the throw rug in front of the fireplace where she pulled off her sweater, shucked out of her jeans. "Don't think . . ."

And she tugged him down to the floor.

"*God.* Be sure." From flat on his back, he cupped her face and pierced her with those green eyes, gently stroking a finger over the bandage on her brow. "I don't want you to regret—"

"No regrets, remember?" She straddled him then, her knees digging into the thick throw rug. "No looking back. . . ." She reached for her bra, which he immediately lent a helping hand to, skimming it off her as she wriggled out of her panties, which had him letting out a heartfelt groan of approval.

"Nothing but us," she whispered. "This." Getting his jeans down wasn't a problem, they were baggy and already so low on his hips as to be almost indecent. "Just good-bye . . ."

His hands were as rough as her own, and the second he was freed, she wrapped her fingers around him and guided him home, wrenching another low groan from him.

"Wait." His voice sounded like gravel. "I'm not—You're not—"

Caring only that this was it, the end, the big finale, the last chance she would ever have to feel him inside her, she began to move, and letting her set the pace, he rocked upward to meet her. She bent over him, pressing her mouth to his shoulder as they moved, more wild than the storm raging outside. She needed to get there, to the big bang, to the explosion, to the mindless place where there was only sensation, glorious sensation—

"Katie . . ." He dug his fingers into her hips, slowing her down, skimming a hand down her belly, his fingers taking her there, as always, taking his time, taking her right where she needed to go.

Shuddering, she fell over him as he caught her in quaking arms, in the throes of his release. Still trembling, she pressed her face to his throat and pretended that he didn't completely shatter her world, her heart, her soul. Pretended that she was okay with this good-bye, as okay as he was. And when she realized that maybe he didn't need her smothering him, that maybe he didn't crave this last moment of togetherness and tried to pull away, he tightened his arms around her as if maybe, just maybe, he wanted it every bit as much as she did.

Chapter 26

The next morning, Cam was spared from too much thinking by having to gear up mentally for a tough few days on the mountain. He was stuffing supplies into his pack, but his mind kept wandering from the trip to the tight smile Katie had given him when he'd left her.

He hated knowing he'd hurt her. The worst part was that he hurt, too, more than he'd imagined possible.

Annie came into the kitchen and he glanced over, then did a double take at the unmistakable look of bliss on her face. Nick was right on her heels, practically in her back pocket. "Coffee, baby?" she purred to her husband.

Purred.

Nick grinned dopily and nodded.

Cam shook his head. "Aw man. Why don't you two just wear a sign?"

"Because I've got an apron." Annie slipped one on and turned to face him: I'M MAGICALLY DELICIOUS.

Cam winced and closed his eyes. "Overshare."

Nick kept grinning.

Annie patted Cam on the shoulder as she pushed him aside

to start her coffee. "Hey, you're not the only Wilder who likes hot sex, big guy."

"Seriously." He put his hands over his ears. "Stop it."

Annie laughed.

Laughed.

And then leaned in and kissed Nick.

Nick, not a stupid man, grabbed her close, wrapped her in his arms, and kissed her back.

"Hey, hey, hey . . ." Now Cam had to slam his eyes shut too. "Get a room!" But they kept going at it. "I've stepped into the Twilight Zone, right? I'm on some alternate plane, the disgustingly happy plane."

"It's a new era." Annie disengaged her lips from Nick's to say, "You ought to try it, you might like it."

"Try what, exactly?"

Annie reached for Cam's hand, her eyes shining with love— for Nick, but also for Cam. "Being happy. Falling in love." She paused. "Letting yourself be loved back." She squeezed his hand gently. "It's okay to let yourself be loved, Cam."

She was speaking softly, earnestly, with an utter lack of sarcasm, and her words unexpectedly sneaked in past his defenses and leveled him flat. He'd heard these words before, from Katie. "Stop it," he said again.

Instead, she wrapped her arms around his waist and hugged him. "You deserve it, Cam. So much."

"Okay, look." He pulled free and picked up his gear. "I'm happy for you, happy for both of you, but Nick and I have to go."

Nick grabbed his own pack, gave Annie one more disgustingly long kiss, and then they were off for their four-day trek directly into the storm from hell. Which pretty much matched the one in Cam's heart.

* * *

For two days, Cam climbed mountains and slept in snow caves, his mind way too far from what he was doing, which was a bad, bad idea with his life and other lives on the line. Still, he managed to get them all safely to Desolation Peak by late afternoon on the second day, and ten minutes later, the storm that was still raging doubled in intensity, complete with 120-mile-an-hour winds, sideways snow, and utter whiteout conditions.

"We aren't going anywhere until this baby is over," Nick grumbled.

Cam looked out into the growing night, and for the first time ever on a trek, felt claustrophobic. Katie had one day left, and he was here, on a mountain, miles away.

Snowed in.

Helluva time to realize he wanted to do what Annie had said, and let himself be loved by the sweet, brave, amazing Katie Kramer.

She didn't need him, she straight up didn't need him. She wanted him just fine, but she didn't need him, and Christ if he didn't totally understand now—that's what had always been missing for him. "No," he agreed with Nick on a tight breath, disgusted with himself for not seeing it sooner. "We're not going anywhere."

Nick sighed, looking like maybe he was thinking of Annie.

And Cam got it. He really got what it was like to miss someone with all his heart, with his soul, with a yearning that defied description.

Katie woke up on the day she was supposed to leave, knowing that since she'd already had her good-bye with Cam, there was nothing good about the day at all.

Not one single redeeming quality.

Getting out of bed, she realized she had no power in her

cabin, which was far too cold for a pansy ass like her, so she dressed to go to the lodge. "And if there's a God," she told Chuck, who'd slept in front of her fireplace for three nights running, "Annie will be there with hot coffee and possibly, hopefully, food."

She opened her door and found four feet of fresh powder on the ground, and it was still coming down like Mother Nature on a tirade. Big, thick, dinner-plate-sized flakes floated through the air with an almost eerie silence, layering on top of each other as they hit the trees, the ground, coating everything.

White.

Okay, so maybe she wasn't going home after all, at least not yet. T.J. was at the end of the path with a snowblower, clearing her a walkway to the lodge.

She stood on the step with Chuck sitting at her feet, both of them staring out into the winter wonderland with matching dazed expressions on their faces. Holy crap . . .

T.J. shut off the snowblower, and though he looked tense, he nodded up at her. Like Stone, he was bigger than Cam, broader, tougher, but that edgy expression and sharp green eyes were all Wilder. "You're made of some stern stuff if you've survived out here all month."

"I am," she agreed. "Though I've never seen anything like this."

"It's a good one," he admitted, still not smiling. "Power's out up at the lodge, too, but maybe you could keep Annie company. She's losing it."

Some of his seriousness began to sink in. "Why? What's the matter?"

T.J. looked down at the snowblower, then back into her face, and somehow she knew. "Oh, God. Is Nick hurt?" she breathed. They'd been gone two days. They'd left the heli at the base of Desolation, at the ranger station there, and when she'd closed up yesterday afternoon, walking away from her desk for the last time, they'd been only a few miles below the peak.

"No, not hurt," T.J. said. "Not that we know of. We lost radio contact."

She turned toward the direction of Desolation Wilderness, but the storm had visibility at zero and she couldn't even see the mountains. "What does that mean exactly, you lost radio contact? They lost their radio?"

"Or they're out of range."

"Has that ever happened?"

"No."

She'd thought her days of panic were over. She'd thought wrong.

"It's okay," he said, reading her mind. "We're going out after them as soon as the storm lets up."

She whirled back inside to grab her boots and jacket and Cam's scarf, and then went running up to the lodge, where she found Annie pacing the kitchen with her cell phone in one hand, a Nextel radio in the other. "Damn fool idiot men," she was muttering, whipping around when Katie walked in the door, a look of such hope on her face that it hurt to look at her.

"Just me," Katie said in apology.

Annie nodded curtly. "Coffee?"

"You don't have to be polite, Annie. Not today."

"Thank God." She sagged. "Because I blew my wad with that one question. I don't have any more polite in me, I really don't. Not this morning. T.J. told you?"

"Yes. Any news?"

She shook her head and sank to a chair. "Nothing."

"When did you last hear from them?"

"Yesterday afternoon, when you were here. They were closing in on where they planned to camp for the night and then . . . nothing."

"And you expected to hear from them again last night?"

"Yeah." Annie rubbed her temples. "I think. I'd think Nick would have checked in . . ." She shook her head. "But even if he didn't, Cam would have, at least with Stone or T.J. Stone didn't worry until this morning, when neither Cam nor Nick could be reached by radio or cell."

Katie looked out the window. The snow was coming down even harder, if that was possible. Visibility was nil. She couldn't imagine being out in it. Surviving in it.

"Stone rode into Wishful to put Search and Rescue on alert, and also the new doc," Annie said.

"They'll all go out?"

"Not until the storm clears. Stone and T.J. would go out right now with Search and Rescue if they could, but the weather is deteriorating and the heli's grounded." She rubbed her face. "Dammit. I don't know whether to contact the families of the clients or not."

Katie sat next to her and put her hand on her arm. "Isn't it possible that they just don't have reception?"

"Yes." Annie stared at the cell phone and radio. "Yes, it is. In which case, I'll kill kick their asses for all my new gray hair."

Without power there was little to do. Katie made her way outside, where the wind almost blew her away. T.J. was still trying to keep the snow from taking over the front of the lodge. She grabbed a shovel and tried to help, but it was a losing battle, and T.J. motioned her back inside.

"I want to help," she yelled over the roar of the storm.

"There's nothing that can be done."

So she huddled near the fire with Annie. They had sandwiches, and as the last of the dubious daylight faded into early evening, lit candles.

And stared at their cell phones.

At eight o'clock, the Nextel radio squawked.

All three of them lunged for it, but T.J.'s arms were the longest.

"We're socked in," came Nick's voice over the radio. "We started back down. We're in a cell hole halfway up Desolation. We have a big problem—"

His voice broke up.

"Repeat that," T.J. said. "Nick, repeat."

Nick tried, but whatever he said was unintelligible.

T.J. let out a breath, then pushed the Talk button again. "*Nick.*"

Nothing but static.

T.J. looked at Annie. "You know where halfway up Desolation leaves them."

"Forty-five miles from here," Annie said grimly. "What do you suppose the 'big problem' is?"

Katie prayed it wasn't Cam. Annie gripped her hand tight, but before she could say anything more, Nick was suddenly back.

"T.J., can you hear me?"

T.J. grabbed the Nextel again. "Yes, go ahead. Your problem?"

"We have a missing guest. Two went out for a leak and only one came back. I think he slid down the west side. Cam went after him, but neither have come back."

Katie's heart jerked to a painful stop.

"Fuck." T.J. pushed the Talk button again. "Stone and I are coming. We'll get S and R—"

"No one will fly you here until morning," Nick responded. He said other things, too, but he faded out and never came back into range.

T.J. stood up and headed to the door. Annie leaped up and just barely caught him. "No, T.J. *No.*"

"I'm going to find a pilot who will fly me there."

Annie was shaking her head, her eyes wet. "You can't even

get Stone back from town. You'd never make it there in this."
She gripped him tight. "I'm not risking two more of you. No
way, no how. You're not going anywhere until the morning, at
least." She threw her arms around him. "Promise me."

T.J. hugged her back, then moved to the window alone, his
back to them, stiff and tense as he stared helplessly out at the
storm. "I should have gone instead. He didn't need this."

"Cam is stronger than you think," Katie told him quietly.

T.J. turned and looked at her.

"He is. He's strong enough for this." Her voice broke, but
she nodded with resolve. "He really is."

"Because of you."

"No, I—"

"It's true," Annie said. "You gave him something we couldn't.
You gave him himself back."

Maybe. But as far as Katie was concerned, she'd gotten a
whole hell of a lot more than she'd given.

She slept with Annie in front of the big fireplace in the living room, and when dawn came, the sky was clear as a bell,
making it hard to believe that a storm had been raging for
days.

Except for the eight feet of snow blanketing absolutely
everything. T.J. took the Sno-Cat into town, met up with Stone
and Search and Rescue, and took off for Desolation. They arrived at the base of the peak by mid-afternoon and literally ran
smack into Cam just as he climbed back up from where he'd
slid down the night before. Uninjured but frustrated, he was
happy to have the additional help because there was still no
sign of Scott Winston, their missing client.

At the news about Cam, Annie and Katie hugged and cried
in relief and went into the kitchen to eat an entire batch of
fudge. Then Annie went to check on the fire in the living
room and the radio squawked. Katie jumped on it. "Go
ahead," she said, heart in her throat.

"Where's Annie?" came Cam's unbearably familiar voice.

Emotion flooded her. She wanted to say how very glad she was that he was okay, that she hoped he was warm and dry. That she'd discovered one last thing—he was right about her being willing to take risks on adventures but not with her heart.

Never with her heart.

She wanted to tell him all that, and she wanted to hand her heart over to him and risk it all.

Right now.

But most of all, she wanted to tell him that she loved him. "She'll be right back. Cam—"

"I don't know how long you'll be able to hear me. Tell Annie to call the clients' families. The contact info is in the files."

Nothing else. Nothing personal. No "Hey, you're still there," or "I miss you." Much as that hurt, she understood. A man was still missing, his life in jeopardy. A life Cam was responsible for. He couldn't let down his guard or be weak, not now. Probably not ever again, at least with her. It broke her heart, but she got it. She was gone, or would have been except for the storm.

And in truth, this had all been a fluke, a fantasy. A really great fantasy, but a fantasy none the less.

And it was time to move on.

Word came in at ten o'clock that night that Scott Winston had been found. He'd slipped down a snowy ravine on the opposite side of where Cam had done the same thing. Unable to climb back up, and equally unable to make himself heard over the wind, he'd decided to walk around and try to climb up another way.

And then had gotten himself lost.

He'd been picked up three quarters of a mile from where Cam had ended his search. He had frostbitten toes and fingers, but other than that was uninjured.

In her cabin, Katie was alone with Chuck, who'd shown up for the last of the cheese in her refrigerator. They sat together looking out the window at the stars.

And then, one fell. Katie looked at Chuck. "Did you see that?"

He blinked.

"A falling star." She slammed her eyes shut, but she didn't have to think, she knew what her wish was—Cam's safe trip home. She also knew something else, that she wasn't quite finished here. "I have one last thing to do, Chuck."

"Mew."

She reached out to scratch him behind the ears, certain he'd hiss, but he went very still and let her touch him. "I have to do this," she whispered. "I have to try with him too." She threw on her jacket and boots, and raced back up to the lodge, to the kitchen where she found Annie making more fudge. The Nextel was on the table.

"Hey there," Annie said in surprise. "What are you—"

"I need to tell Cam something." She picked up the radio. "Who has the radio out there?"

"Cam. But—"

Katie pushed the Talk button. "Cameron Wilder, are you there?"

She got a return squawk but couldn't hear anything but static. But somehow, she knew he could hear her. It was in her gut, in her heart. And so was a bunch of other stuff she had to get out. She took a deep breath and pressed the Talk button again. "Cam? Goldilocks here. I know, I'm gone, or almost, but I have to tell you this first."

"Katie," Annie said. "I don't think—"

"It's okay. I know what I'm doing." Or so she hoped. She pressed the Talk button again. "You once accused me of holding back. Not risking my heart. You were right."

"Katie—"

She held up a hand to Annie to hold her off a minute. "As you pointed out to me, I risked everything *but* my heart, and I can't leave here until I fix that. So here I am, risking it all." She paused, breathed, and let it out. "I love you, Cameron Wilder."

There.

She'd done it. She set the radio down on the table and sent a shaky smile in Annie's direction. "Sorry. I had to do that before I left. Besides, you already knew anyway."

"I knew," Annie agreed. "But I'm not sure the rest of the guys knew. Or the entire Search and Rescue crew. Or the clients."

Katie stared at her. "I thought you said Cam had the radio."

"Uh-huh, but they're all together in the snow cave."

"So I just told everyone in the free world that I love Cam?"

"No, just everyone within sixty miles or so."

Chapter 27

Cam stared at the radio in his hands, ignoring the whistles and "woo-hoos" all around him.

She loved him.

"Aren't you going to answer her?" Stone asked.

"He can't." This from T.J. "You know he can't. They can't hear us worth shit. Besides, look at him. He's all wigged out."

"Am not." Cam rubbed his chest. His heart felt too big, too full. And he couldn't breathe. Simply couldn't draw air. Having no idea what he was going to say, or if there was any way at all that she could possibly hear him, he pushed the Talk button. "Katie."

Nothing but static.

"Katie?"

More static.

He bowed his head and pressed the radio to his forehead. "Shit."

"Probably you should have told her first," Nick said.

"Told her what?" Scott, their rescuee, wanted to know. He was wrapped in a blanket, fully recovered, the stupid ass.

"That he loves her," Nick said.

"Jesus." Cam tossed down the radio. "We need to get back."

"Agreed," Nick said.

But saying so and doing so were two different things.

As if karma and fate had joined forces to shit on him, the climb out was ladened with technical difficulties. It was late afternoon the next day by the time they got back.

And Katie was long gone.

The drive back to Los Angeles was completely uneventful, at least once Katie got out of the wild Sierras that she'd never forget. Exhausted, she stopped halfway down Highway 5 in the middle of farmland country and stayed the night before getting back on the road.

She didn't have a nightmare, but she did dream. She dreamed that she'd stayed at Wilder.

To be with Cam.

And in her dream, they made it work.

She made it into LA just in time to hit traffic, choke on the smog, and then drive into the carport of her apartment building.

Back to her world.

At least until she visited with her parents, bought a new map, and headed out again to her next adventure, where this time she'd risk all.

From here on out . . .

Her apartment was warm and stuffy. Wanting only to pass out for a few hours, maybe have one last pity party, she headed through the living room, pulling off her sweater. Already she missed the weather in Wishful. She missed Annie and the others. She missed Chuck, who was probably right this minute waiting for a handout from Annie.

No regrets. She'd promised Cam no regrets.

She came to her bedroom and stopped short at the sight of the black duffel bag on the floor that wasn't hers. She might have panicked except for one fact. She recognized that duffel bag. Her head whipped toward the bed.

Someone had beaten her to it.

Cam.

He rolled over and opened his eyes. "Goldilocks."

"Actually," she said, nerves making her voice weak as she came into the room and kicked off her shoes, "that appears to be your name now."

With a small smile, he sat up, fluffed her pillows, and leaned back against the headboard.

He wasn't wearing a shirt.

She wondered what else he wasn't wearing.

He looked as exhausted as she felt, but he held out a hand, which she took, allowing him to pull her closer until she was sitting on the edge of the mattress looking at him, running her fingers over the tattoo on his biceps, helplessly smiling at him. "What are you doing here? How did you get here?"

"Scott Winston owed me. His brother's a pilot and flew me down here in his Lear."

"Wish you would have picked me up on my way down." Her heart was pounding, pounding so hard she was surprised he couldn't hear it.

"I'd have picked you up on the moon if you'd answered any of my calls."

"My cell ran out of battery, and I left my cord at the cabin somewhere, I think."

"Ah." Eyes never leaving her, he nodded. "That explains that. I want to tell you something."

"Okay."

"I have this habit of quitting."

"Cam—"

"No, listen. Boarding was never tough, it was easy, so damn easy. Until it wasn't. And then I just walked away. Relationships got tough, and I walked away. Mentally, physically, whichever. The truth is, I walked away from Serena long before she cheated."

"I . . ." She shook her head. "I don't know what to say."

"I know. Believe me, I wouldn't know either." He looked a little worse for wear. He hadn't shaved, there were dark circles under his eyes, and his mouth, that beautiful mouth, was grim. "But I met this woman. She'd been through hell but didn't let that stop her. Nothing could make her quit." He drew a deep breath, looking into her eyes, his so clear and green. "It made me want to be a better man. I don't want to quit you, Katie." He scooted over in the bed, tugging her under the covers with him. He was naked, and went to work making her the same. "You came looking for an adventure, but you turned out to be mine. The boarding, the skiing, the whatever . . ." He was unbuttoning her shirt. "They're all things that I loved to do, so it was easy to hide behind the wild, free-spirit label. And yet, I never put myself out there, not once. Not like you did." He smiled at her, a heartbreakingly real smile, and nudged her shirt off her shoulders, his hands slipping down her fluttering belly to her jeans. "You, Katie, are the bravest spirit I ever met. You gave me something to dream about again, you made me whole. Lift up." When she arched her hips, he tugged her jeans off.

Her heart felt full to bursting as he pulled her in close against that glorious, warm, hard body. He nuzzled at her throat and unhooked her bra, tossing it aside. Her panties went next, and then, finally, she was naked too. "And without you," he said, "it all means nothing." His hands slid down her back, pressing the core of her up against a most impressive erection. "Nothing at all."

When she opened her mouth, he put his finger on her lips. "I hurt you." He looked tortured at the thought. "When you would never, ever hurt me. I hurt you, and I'd do anything to change that, but I can't. That's one thing I learned the hard way, you can't change the past." He drew a breath. "But I can change myself, and I can learn from my mistakes. My biggest mistake was letting you go home without telling you how I feel about you. I love you, Katie."

"Oh, Cam." Her heart felt like it was going to burst. "I love you, too. But what do we do with that?"

"I know you want to head out on your next adventure. But I also know you fell for Wishful. Riley asked Stone if he could cut his hours in half so he could stay home and be a full-time dad. Oh, and Serena looks like she has it together, but she keeps her accounting in a shoebox beneath her counter. And Harley? She keeps her books in an office that looks like a cyclone hit it."

She could scarcely breathe. "What are you saying?"

"I'm saying that Wishful needs you, Katie."

"You mean . . . run my own business?"

"I mean whatever you want. Run a business, work for us . . . keep traveling if that's what you choose. I'm a good guide in case you haven't heard."

"You'd really come with me?"

"Anywhere. Whatever's in your heart. Which hopefully includes me."

In answer, she let out a sound that might have been a laugh or a sob, she wasn't quite sure. Oh, God. He was real, this was real, and she knew. Her next adventure wasn't a place but a person. "What I want is you."

"Yeah?"

"Yeah."

"Can't tell you how glad I am to hear it." Cam rolled her to her back and cupped her face, giving her one of his no longer quite-so-rare smiles, the one that warmed her from the inside out. He made himself at home between her thighs; then he slid inside her, making her gasp and clutch at him. "God, I love you." He kissed her as he began to move within her. "Love me back."

If she'd been standing, his vulnerable smile would have brought her to her knees. But she wasn't standing. She was surrounded by him, and there was nothing better. "I do." She slid her fingers into his hair. "I always will."

With a groan, he rocked his hips, thrusting deep.

"Is your client's plane still available?" she managed to ask.

"I think so." He rocked again, and they both gasped. "Why?"

"Because I want you to take me home figuratively." Her eyes drifted shut with his next achingly perfect thrust. She was so full to bursting she could hardly stand it. "After you take me home in the literal sense, of course . . ."

Don't miss Diane Whiteside's latest book,
KISSES LIKE A DEVIL,
available now from Brava. . . .

Doors slammed below and the train's first passengers began to spill into the square, gaily bargaining for a ride to the town's more upscale districts.

Morro woofed deep in his throat and rose, wending his way between the two humans to look over the balcony.

A single man stepped out of the station, isolated by a swirl of travelers. He was tall and broad-shouldered, clad entirely in black. His broad-brimmed hat readily identified him as an American, a rarity here in Eisengau despite its famous summer music festival and military maneuvers. His clothes were well-made yet neither dandified nor a uniform. Straight black hair brushed his collar, and his skin was tanned golden brown from the sun, something seldom seen amid these stone walls. His blade-sharp nose, high cheekbones, and stubborn jaw could have been carved by a master sculptor.

He paused on the top of the steps to look around, graceful as a hawk scanning a meadow, yet utterly un-self-conscious. His brilliant blue eyes flashed over the crowd like light passing through the finest stained glass—and lingered briefly on the old pension, where Meredith stood.

Her breath caught in her throat. How many newspaper articles about American adventurers had she devoured? How many cheap novels about men like him had she bartered for? And to finally see one in the flesh . . .

Morro thrust his muzzle between the banisters and took a long, considering sniff.

Despite any claim to logic, Meredith opened her mouth to hail the American.

A British officer, shorter, stockier, and using a cane, rushed up to him. The healthier man slapped him warmly on the shoulder, his face lighting up in welcome—and broke the thread holding her attention.

She closed her eyes for a moment and jerked herself back to the relentless present.

And keep an eye out for
THE EDUCATION OF MADELINE,
by Beth Williamson, coming next month!

"**D**o you play any games, Teague?" Maddie asked as they left the dining room after supper.

He didn't answer, so she turned to look at him. A mischievous grin played around those beautiful lips, and one eyebrow arched over humor-filled eyes.

"What kind of games?"

Madeline felt a bit flustered and she hoped it didn't reflect in her cheeks. She didn't want him to know that her self-control was melting like an icicle in July.

"Checkers, chess, backgammon. Those kinds of games."

When his grin turned into a full-blown smile, Madeline gripped the doorjamb to stay upright. She thought she was prepared. She was so very wrong. That smile was devastating. It lit up his whole face, made his eyes crinkle at the corners, and turned her into a puddle of unrequited passion.

"No, but I play a mean game of poker. Do you play?"

Madeline shook her head, disappointed. That cancelled her distraction idea.

"Would you like to learn?"

She felt an urge to blurt "No!" but grabbed it before it could be let loose. The proper lady wasn't going to make the decisions this time. Proper ladies may not play poker, but Maddie Brewster was going to learn.

After searching for thirty minutes, they found a deck of cards in her father's old desk. Teague suggested they play in the kitchen since it was in the back of the house and relatively private.

When they settled at the table, the lamplight threw a cozy glow over the room. Madeline watched Teague's hands, fascinated by how quickly he shuffled the cards. His fingers were lithe and strong at the same time. She wondered how those fingers would feel on her skin, making her temperature rise degree by degree.

Teague explained a game called five-card stud. The rules were a bit complex, but Madeline understood most of them. He let her play a couple of practice hands, and then they started to play in earnest.

Madeline lost five hands in a row before she started to really enjoy playing the game. She won the next hand. Teague actually looked surprised. "Very good, Maddie. You're getting the hang of it."

Madeline smiled. "I think I understand why gamblers like to play this so much. Can we gamble too?"

Teague threw back his head and laughed. It was the first time she'd heard him laugh, and the rough, raspy sound of it did something strange to her equilibrium. "Don't you think gambling is the root of all evil?"

"No, I don't. I've seen the root of evil, and it's definitely not poker."

He looked like he wanted to respond, but he didn't. He shrugged. "I don't have money to play for."

Madeline watched his hands as he shuffled the cards again.

"How about we play for truths?" he said without looking up.

"Truths?"

"Yes, each time one of us wins a hand, we get to ask the other a question, and the loser must tell the truth."

His hands shuffled faster. By the time the cards started flying off the deck, his fingers were a blur of motion. In a few seconds, five cards lay in front of her.

"I'll play for truths. There isn't much I've got to hide, anyway."

Madeline lost the first truth hand.

"Are you ready for the first question?" he asked with a small grin.

"Yes, I'm ready."

"Why did you paint your house blue?"

It was her turn to laugh. "I thought you were going to ask me what color my bloomers are."

His eyebrows rose. "Now you've spoiled it. That was my next question."

"I painted it blue because it is my favorite color, and I wasn't allowed to wear anything that bright. After my father died, I indulged myself."

He nodded. "That answers why it's so damn bright."

She laughed and waved her hands at the cards. "Deal again, Teague. I'm itching to ask you a truth question."

This time, Madeline won. She pondered her question for several minutes, earning a sigh and rolling eyes from the sore loser.

"Why didn't you say yes to my proposition to bed me?"

He clearly hadn't been expecting a personal question like that. The cards he'd been shuffling fell out of his hand like an explosion, raining down all over the table and floor. "I had to stop myself from saying yes too quickly."

Heat pooled low and insistent in her belly, and a throbbing began between her legs. "Does this mean you're saying yes to my . . . proposal?" she asked. Her mouth felt as dry as cotton. "I mean, it sounds as if you're going to say yes."

He stood abruptly, and she could see the outline of his penis clearly in his pants. My, oh my! That certainly was a large-looking organ. Much larger than ones in the drawings in the book.

Teague let the rest of the cards fall from his hands and he came around the side of the table. The primal way he walked was enough to make her nipples pucker. He clearly wanted her. *Her.* Madeline Brewster!

When he reached her side, he knelt down on the floor next to her and cupped her face in his big hands. "Why me?"

She shrugged, somehow. "I need a big man. I'm not . . . petite or feminine like most women. I didn't want my teacher to feel embarrassed by the size difference if I was bigger. You . . . you're bigger than me. And . . ."

"And?"

"Just looking at you makes my body hum."

His pupils widened, and he licked his lips.

He's going to kiss me!